DEVIL'S GUARD

BLOOD & IRON

ERIC MEYER

First published in the United Kingdom in 2011
by Swordworks Books.

ISBN 978-1-911092-50-6

Typeset by Swordworks Books
Printed and bound in the UK & US
A catalogue record of this book is available
from the British Library

Cover design by Swordworks Books
www.swordworks.co.uk

DEVIL'S GUARD

BLOOD & IRON

ERIC MEYER

FOREWORD

After the bloody battles that took place around Kharkov, the Germans eventually retook the city. Under the control of Field Marshall Erich von Manstein's Army Group South, Hitler felt that once again he was in such a position of strength that his offensives into the Soviet Union could begin again. To the north and east of von Manstein's forces lay the Kursk salient, a tempting bulge into the German lines in the centre of which lay the city of Kursk. Despite evidence that the Soviets had constructed massive defences in depth, it was too much for Hitler to resist.

The Battle of Kursk began in July 1943. It became the largest armoured clash in history and at its climax, the Battle of Prokhorovka, thousands of armoured vehicles were deployed throughout the salient. That battle was also to be the costliest single day of aerial warfare. It was the last strategic offensive the Germans were able to mount on the Eastern Front. The result was neither a convincing victory nor a defeat for either side, but the German losses were irreplaceable and the Red Army took the initiative for the rest of the war.

Like most battles in most wars, there were colossal errors or judgement, as well as epic feats of bravery. Hitler's insistence on waiting for the new Panzer V heavy tanks was to prove disastrous, the delay allowed the Soviets to reinforce their positions even further and when they did arrive the new Panzer Vs proved to be unreliable and virtually useless in the battle.

Arguments still rage over a number of issues related to the battle. Perhaps chief among these would be the role of the intelligence services of both sides. The Lucy spy ring certainly did exist and was a thorn in the side of the Germans and they never truly uncovered the traitors who were passing their secrets to the Russians. The role of Martin Bormann was never fully understood either, whether he was a Russian spy or not, as unlikely as it seems. Other leading Nazis were suspected of treachery too, not least of which was Admiral Canaris, head of the Abwehr, Military Intelligence, who was executed in 1945 for complicity in the plot to kill Hitler.

After the battle, von Manstein insisted to Hitler that his forces should be allowed to continue and he maintained his view that victory was possible. Nonetheless, the high tide of Hitler's war on the Soviet Union had passed. The Italians had surrendered in Africa, the Allies had landed in Sicily and his armoured divisions were needed to plug the holes in his defences.

Afterwards, Hitler was asked, "Was it really necessary to attack Kursk, and indeed in the east that year at all? Do you think anyone even knows where Kursk is? The entire world doesn't care if we capture Kursk or not. What is the reason that is forcing us to attack this year on Kursk, or even more, on the Eastern Front?"

Hitler replied:

"I know. The thought of it turns my stomach."

There are indications that The Fuhrer may have realised even then that his forces were unlikely to ever recover .

INTRODUCTION

After his experiences in Devil's Guard – Blood and Snow, the young SS officer Jurgen Hoffman leads his men into the maelstrom of the Battle of Kursk. Before the main battle has even begun there are opportunities for Obersturmfuhrer Hoffman to lead his men into action. The pressing need is for intelligence and he leads his men on a dangerous mission behind the lines to uncover the secrets of the Soviet defences.

Once more, the enemy is not always recognisable by the uniform he is wearing. There are traitors sending the German military secrets directly to Moscow. Known as the 'Lucy' spy ring, the Gestapo, Sicherheitsdienst and Abwehr hunt the traitors who are leaking information, yet it seems that not every senior German officer is anxious that the traitors are found. Even Martin Bormann, Hitler's secretary and the second most powerful man in the Nazi hierarchy behaves in a way that suggests his motives are far from clear.

Under attack from the Red Army, Cossacks, Soviet partisans and German traitors, Jurgen finds that this time he is up against almost insurmountable odds. Escorting the Sicherheitsdienst is no guarantee that they will treat him fairly and he finds that they are as brutal with his friends and allies as they are with the enemy.

When General Hoth's Fourth Panzer Army moves to attack the southern part of the Kursk salient, Jurgen finds himself pitted against a storm of fire from the Russian defences that have been built into an impregnable wall of tanks, guns and mines. It is a battle of attrition and victory will be decided by who is left standing on the battlefield when all else had fallen.

CHAPTER ONE

'Whenever in future wars the battle is fought, armoured troops will play the decisive role.'

Heinz Guderian

We were on an island called Kharkov, an island of shattered, broken apartment blocks, houses and factories. An island surrounded by a sea of mud and line after line of parked, mighty but impotent Panzers, the armoured might of the Third Reich, waiting for the chance to strike again into the Russian heartland. The rasputitza had arrived, the twice-yearly season when unpaved roads become difficult or impossible to traverse in Belarus, Russia and the Ukraine. Immediately outside the city the paved roads ended and the mud started, in some cases it was a metre deep, possibly more. The mud stopped all movement in the countryside.

We could at least content ourselves that the enemy suffered similar difficulties, so the risk of counterattack was low. I remembered reading an information leaflet written by General von Greiffenberg, 'the effect of climate in Russia is to make things impassable in the mud of spring and autumn, unbearable in the heat of summer and impossible in the depths of winter'. He finished with the dramatic statement, 'climate in Russia is a series of natural disasters'. Was I the only military officer that had listened to his warning? We'd suffered the counter-offensive outside Moscow in December 1941 when our armies had reeled back from the Russian ability to fight in sub-zero conditions when we were all but immobilised. We'd retreated and attempted to fight back through the clinging mud of the rasputitza in 1942 and then seen the Sixth Army literally freeze to death in Stalingrad before the weakened survivors were forced to surrender. Yet the Red Army still seemed able to constantly catch us on the back foot. From knocking on the door to Moscow eighteen months previously, we had been thrown back into the Ukraine and now we were facing the battle of our lives around the Kursk salient. It was a battle that many of us suspected would decide the victor and the loser in this war. We were certainly all agreed on one factor, a German victory was by no means a foregone conclusion. As soon as the mud began to dry we had to hit the Russians hard and fast before they could use the drier conditions to put in place the formidable defences that we had encountered in the past. And yet there was no obvious sign that we were ready to attack any time soon, we were still very understrength, deficient in men, materiel, food, fuel and even aircraft. Armour was the most serious shortage, the open steppe inside the salient was tank country and yet we had barely two hundred tanks operational within our Army Group South to combat the massed Soviet armour that we knew we would have to face when the battle started.

My platoon was quartered in a house on the edge of the city, sharing it with a surly Ukrainian family who showed their bitter resentment every time a German soldier came through the door of their miserable concrete dwelling. There was only one opening that served as a window but it was normally covered with a piece of tarpaulin, there was no glass. Neither was there any electric light, a huge luxury in the Soviet Union, this dwelling had an old oil lamp to light up the room and even that was a luxury for most. The walls were papered with old newspapers with prominent pictures of Stalin, Communist Party newspapers, probably all that was available in the workers' paradise. The family slept outside with the animals, a cow and two pigs that were kept in a straw lined shed at the back, and only came inside during the day. Despite the primitive conditions, the lice that caused us to scratch incessantly, the stink of unwashed bodies, rancid cooking fats and animal dung, we were relaxing around the warmth of the stove of the single room that comprised as the whole house. Voss had cooked up a meal using our pooled rations. He'd become quite a good chef and sometimes talked of his ambition to open a restaurant after the war. Another soldier's dream, none of us expected to survive the Eastern Front but we had to keep our dreams alive, otherwise we would collapse into a welter of despair. Scharfuhrer Mundt was as good a thief as Voss was a cook and he spent part of each day foraging for supplies, fresh meat and vegetables, often in the Division's stores.

When the meal was prepared we offered part of our food to the Ukrainian family, it wasn't their fault that enemy soldiers were billeted on them. They looked half-starved, as did most of the citizens in Stalin's benighted empire. The children looked especially malnourished, with the extended bellies of the starving, and yet we were in the Ukraine, supposedly the breadbasket of the Soviet Union. It seemed to us more like a basket case than a breadbasket. Mundt passed around a flask of Ukrainian vodka and we lit up cigarettes. Mundt lit his pipe and we settled down to spend a rare, peaceful afternoon, warm, well fed and lubricated with alcohol. Even the occasional hit and run raid by Soviet fighter-bombers was no more than a nuisance, except for the mysterious U-2 night bombers, the almost silent, black biplanes that flew over, dropped their bombs and disappeared. They were invisible to our fighters and anti-aircraft guns in the dark sky. Here in Kharkov we were outside of enemy artillery range and our main worry was the local snipers, partisans who popped up, shot a couple of soldiers and vanished. The Gestapo were doing their best to track them down, aided by an Einsatzgruppe company, but their tactics were too heavy handed. Most of us thought they did more harm than good, often they captured ordinary citizens and then tortured them for information they didn't possess. As far as we could see, all they achieved was to create hostility against us that served to recruit even more partisans. Why couldn't their senior officers see what damage they were doing?

"How long do you think we'll be stuck here?" Schutze Bauer asked me. "Some of the lads from Der Fuhrer Regiment reckoned that we'll be moving on down to Sebastopol soon, what do you think, Sir?"

I looked up. They were all watching me, waiting on my reply. "As soon as they let me know, I'll tell you, but until we're told to move, Bauer, you may consider that we're stuck here for the duration. Where's Wagner, he's overdue?"

He'd been sent to collect our mail from Division and was due back almost an hour ago. They shook their heads, but just then we heard a shout outside, "It's me, Wagner, I'm coming in, I had to use a longer route because of the snipers."

Mundt stood up and moved the tarpaulin to one side

to look out. "Yeah, it's him, he's carrying our mail packet."

I saw him wave to Wagner, and then sit down. We all heard the shot, the loud 'crack' of a rifle bullet fired from somewhere close.

"Sniper!" several voices shouted at once, we dived to the floor, out of sight of the window, grabbing for our weapons.

"Mundt, see if Wagner is ok," I called out to my Scharfuhrer.

He crawled over and peered over the window ledge. "He's down, Sir, the sniper got him, a head shot."

"Damn. Voss, Bauer, set up the MG34 to cover us, the rest of you, let's go out through the front and work our way around. We need to finish this bastard, he's making our life a misery!"

The day before the Second Platoon, billeted three houses along the same street, had lost two of their men to a sniper, probably the same man. He'd never been caught. We picked up our MP38s, put on our steel helmets and stuffed stick grenades into our webbing, all done on the run. One of the men opened the door carefully, shouted, "Clear!" and we swept out into the street.

"Mundt, take Voss and Bauer and work around to the south side, I'll take the rest of the men to the north. Trottman, Beidenberg, Wesserman, come with me and keep your heads down!"

We sprinted around the side of the building and I

skidded to a stop. The sniper's stand was obvious, a tall warehouse less than a hundred and fifty metres away, an unshuttered window was on the top floor. While the men waited I looked through my binoculars, there was no sign of a rifle barrel poking through. We had to move fast, he had already moved away.

"Follow me, we'll run across to the alley between the next two buildings."

One was a house, the other some kind of a small workshop, with a narrow alley in between, strewn with rubbish. I ran across the open space, jumped over a heap of rusting ironwork dodging into the alley, out of direct sight of any windows. We kept running and came to the end where we could see the warehouse, but there was no sign of the sniper. As we watched, a person wearing a long black coat and clutching a rifle darted out of a side door and walked diagonally away from us across a patch of open ground. I heard Beidenberg catch his breath, "The fucking bastard, he thinks that he doesn't even need to run."

"Probably because it would attract more attention if he ran, Josef. Let's disabuse him of that notion, we'll get him before he vanishes."

We ran out, there was little need for caution now that we could see him. We got halfway across when he heard the clatter of our boots and looked around in alarm. Then he jerked up his rifle as if to shoot, decided that he was vastly outgunned and turned and walked quickly away. We ran at full speed, I looked around as I heard a grunt and a clatter as one of my men tripped and fell, when I looked again the sniper was disappearing into an apartment block, thirty seconds later we reached the door. I looked around. Josef Beidenberg and Gerd Wesserman were still with me. Roland Trottman was walking towards us, nursing an obviously sprained ankle.

"Trottman," I shouted, "hurry up and get under cover, the sniper is still around her somewhere!"

He waved cheerily to us. "It's my fucking ankle, I tripped on something. An old pipe I think. Don't worry about me."

"Get down, man, you're in full view!" I shouted again.

I saw him smile, heard the crack of another rifle bullet, then he flung his arms up and spun around, dropping his machine pistol with a clatter.

"Roland!" Wesserman shouted to his friend.

I took hold of his arm. "He's finished, Wesserman. All we can do for him now is get this sniper."

The partisan was incredibly brazen, knowing that heavily armed Waffen SS soldiers pursued him he'd stopped to find a target and kill another of my men. I determined to finish him no matter what it took. Until he was killed we'd be hamstrung in the city, unable to move in the open without fear of being shot. "You'd better stay here and watch our backs, Gerd. Leave Trottman, he's finished, we'll try and flush out the sniper."

"I want to come with you and kill the bastard!" he shouted.

"You'll stay here, Wesserman, I've lost two men already, and I don't want to lose another one because you're too hot-headed to obey orders."

I was about to enter the apartment block when Mundt came running around the corner with Bauer.

"I've left Voss to guard the back door of the building, Sir, we've got him sealed in."

"Very well, Scharfuhrer, let's go and find this gentleman. Be careful, he knows we're coming."

Glass crunched underfoot as we crept through the lobby. I heard a noise, we swung our machine pistols around but it was a woman descending the stairs, shapeless in a long, black dress, apron and headscarf. The babushka, without a doubt the building's concierge. She would also be the resident NKVD spy. The People's Commissariat for Internal Affairs, the NKVD, was the public and secret police organisation of the Soviet Union that directly executed Soviet control for Joseph Stalin. The NKVD controlled the police force as well as the Gulags and State Security. It conducted mass executions, ran the Gulag system of forced labour camps, suppressed underground resistance, conducted mass deportations of entire nationalities and Kulaks to unpopulated regions of the country. It also guarded state borders and possessed a network of informers, including the concierges who reported to them from almost every apartment block in the Soviet Union. She would need to be watched carefully, I beckoned her over to us.

"Did you see a man up there with a rifle?"

She shook her head in incomprehension.

"Josef, try her with Russian."

He asked the question and this time she pointed up the stairs. I nodded to thank her and we started moving, but something was wrong, something jarred with the way she'd given up the information so readily. In the police state of the Soviet Union no one ever gave away information that easily. I whirled around, she had a gun in her hand that she'd been hiding under her apron, a pistol, and her face was now contorted with hate. In one continuous motion I swept up my MP38 and fired off the whole clip in a single burst, the 9mm bullets hit her and threw her body to the ground where it lay in a shapeless, bleeding mass. Her pistol skidded across the floor and stopped at the feet of Wesserman who had just run in when he heard the firing.

They all gaped in astonishment. "How did you know it was the woman, Sir?" Mundt asked.

"She was too helpful, Willy. People are not helpful in the Soviet Union, not to anyone. Take a look for her rifle, it will be upstairs somewhere close. We need to find it, we don't want to leave it here for someone else to use against us. "

Mundt found the rifle leaning against the wall at the top of the first flight of stairs. We left the body where it was, burying partisans who'd slaughtered our comrades was not a task we were interested in doing. We picked up the body of Trottman and carried him back to our quarters. We laid him out carefully in the woodshed and put the body of Schutze Wagner, the first casualty of the sniper, next to him. Then I walked the five hundred metres to Regimental Headquarters to tell them about my losses. Obersturmbannfuhrer Muller, the acting CO, saw me approaching.

"Hoffman, you're the very man I want to see. What's the problem?"

I told him about the sniper. He nodded. "It's good news that you got the bastard. I'm not surprised that they used a woman, they use a lot of them, soldiers, pilots, partisans, maybe they think we won't be so quick to shoot them as men."

"They're quite correct, Sir, she almost got past us."

He grunted. "I'll make sure that the rest of the Regiment is warned. I've got a reconnaissance mission for you, come into my office and I'll show you what I need."

The room was festooned with maps pinned on the walls, orders, organisational charts and unit rosters. There was a large-scale map of our part of the front, a wavy line that pushed a bulge, or salient, into the German lines. In the middle of the salient was a city marked in bold letters, Kursk, and the bulge surrounded by German armies. To the south Erich von Manstein's Army Group South that included Hoth's Fourth Panzer Army, of which our regiment was a part. To the north was von Kluge's Army Group Centre, stalled in their drive on Moscow and desperately trying to win back the offensive. In the centre were the unknown hordes of the Red Army. Most of the Russian area was blank with no information. He saw the direction of my gaze.

"Exactly, Hoffman. We know they're there, but we don't know who they are and how many of them. How many Soviet armies, artillery, infantry, anti-tank guns, minefields, we need to know what they have."

"So we are going to try and take Kursk, Sir?"

"As you can see, we can bring the weight of Army Group Centre and Army Group South crashing down onto the Soviets, one group from either side of the salient. It's the classic encirclement manoeuvre, one that we've succeeded with many times before. The Fuhrer is anxious to restart the offensive and Kursk is our best opportunity."

"Kursk must be two hundred kilometres from here, Sir."

"There's no need to go that far, other units will carry out their own reconnaissance. We'll get you to the nearest front line and from there you can cross over and observe our assigned sector. It is also very important that you capture a couple of Soviet officers that you can bring back here for interrogation."

"And the mud?"

"What do you mean the mud?"

"It prevents all movement, Sir. How can we move around the salient when the whole of the country is one huge swamp?"

He dismissed my question with a wave. "Use your initiative, man. You're an officer in the SS, not a boy scout. Besides, the muddy season is ending. There will be routes that are passable, you'll just have to find them."

I had a picture in my mind of my platoon staggering through mud like in a Flanders battlefield.

"When do we leave, Sir? My platoon is under-strength. I was hoping to get replacements. We're even worse off now since the sniper killed two more of my people."

Muller looked tired, even worse than usual. "I want you to jump off tomorrow evening. There aren't any replacements, I'm afraid we all have to make do with what we have. Since the surrender of the Sixth Army, the Waffen SS has been called on more and more to fill the gap. Our manning levels are critically low, we have the volunteer units, the SS-Freiwilligen from the Greater Reich, but they're not of the calibre we're used to. Not the same commitment as our own men."

I nodded. "I understand, Sir."

"Look, I'll see if I can find someone to help out with the manual tasks when you get back, there are thousands of Hiwis serving with our Fourth Panzer Army. That'll take the pressure off you, allow you to get some rest."

The Hiwis, or Hilfswilligen, were enlisted volunteers from the occupied territories and worked as drivers, cooks, hospital attendants, ammunition carriers and messengers, some even fought alongside our front line troops and were known as Cossack Sections.

"I'll ask intelligence too, they may know of someone who has local knowledge. If there is anyone suitable, they will report to you before you leave. I've arranged for a half-track to transport you to the front, you leave at six o'clock tomorrow evening. Just make sure you bring back some prisoners to interrogate. I'll send the maps over to you in the morning, everything we have that may be useful."

"Yes, Sir."

"One more thing before you go, Hoffman, we have a new CO taking over the Regiment shortly."

I stared at him, surprised. "I thought that they'd given it to you after the death of the previous CO, Sir."

A sniper had killed Standartenfuhrer Brandt during the fighting around Kharkov and Muller had taken charge. He was an honest man, perhaps not the most imaginative senior SS officer, but he always did his utmost to ensure the security and welfare of his men.

"Yes, I had hoped to keep command, but our superiors decided otherwise."

"Who is he, this new officer, Sir?"

"His name is Standartenfuhrer Ritter von Meusebach, he transferred only recently to the Waffen-SS."

Muller's tone was slightly derisory, he obviously thought that this new man might be a problem.

"Was he an infantry officer before he joined the SS?" I persisted, wondering what fighting skills he could bring to our Regiment. We needed every advantage in the battles to come.

"Not exactly, no. Standartenfuhrer von Meusebach served in the Hauptamt SS-Gericht in Berlin, he has only recently transferred to the Waffen-SS."

The Hauptamt SS-Gericht was the legal department of the SS. It was responsible for formulating the laws and codes that the SS and the secret police, as well as the Wehrmacht, had to adhere to. In fact, our new commanding officer was a lawyer. He saw my crestfallen expression.

"He made a brave decision volunteering to take over a fighting regiment on the Eastern Front, Hoffman, I'm sure that he'll do his best."

I didn't believe it, and neither did he.

"Christ, a bloody lawyer, it's not just me, Sir, even the Fuhrer despises lawyers."

"We'll just have to do our best to help him then, we have no choice. Give him the benefit of the doubt, Hoffman."

I saluted him and left. I decided to make no mention of the new commanding officer for the time being, we had enough problems as it was without worrying about being led by a damned lawyer. I was glad I'd made the decision to keep it quiet, when I told them we were going into the Kursk salient the men were thought it was incredulous.

"They want us to invade Russia all on our own, do they?" Voss snarled. "It's a damned suicide mission!"

Mundt was uncharacteristically gloomy. "He's right, you know. The Soviets could have half of the Red Army packed in there, in fact they probably have. They know that an attack is certain once the rasputitza has ended. Our chances are not good, Sir, not good at all."

I tried to ignore the pessimism. "They're trying to locate us a guide, someone who knows the area well. When he arrives we'll go over the maps and find a good route in and out. We'll be fine."

"Or we'll be dead!" Voss snapped.

I took no notice and looked at Mundt. "Scharfuhrer, you'd better make an inventory of our weapons and equipment, we'll travel light so bear that in mind. We won't need the machine gun. The half-track is collecting us at six o'clock. We'll need rations for three days, as well."

"Three days?" he grimaced. "I thought this was to be in one night and out the next."

"You never know, Willy."

That evening I sat drinking vodka on my own. Eventually I drifted off to sleep, thinking that the men seemed to blame me, as if I'd volunteered for this mission. I drank too much and fell into a deep sleep and in the morning Mundt shook me awake.

"Our local guide is here, Sir," he said in a strange voice.

"What is it, Mundt, what's wrong with him? Is he eighty years old?"

"Not exactly, no. You'd better come and take a look."

I pulled on my boots, ran some fingers through my hair and buttoned up my tunic, I was ready to face another day on the Eastern Front. I looked for a mug of coffee to start the day and heard Mundt asking the guide to enter. She was nearer twenty than eighty, a very pretty young woman. She was of average height wearing rough, Ukrainian peasant clothes, woollen trousers, a cloth cap on her head and a short heavy woollen coat fastened at the waist with a belt. She unbuttoned her coat, she had a perfectly proportioned body, breasts that jutted firmly forward, slim waist and short, dark hair that shone as she removed her cap and shook it out. Her skin was smooth and cream-coloured, anything but peasant in appearance. A wide mouth, huge, dark brown eyes and fine cheekbones framed a face that could have broken a thousand hearts.

"This is Irena Rakevsky," Mundt said.

Voss looked up from the stove where he was pouring some coffee.

"What's she here for, is she taking over my cooking duties?"

He grinned, but I noticed her give him a venomous look.

"She's our guide," Mundt said, "she's taking us into the Kursk salient."

I knew I looked stupefied. I just couldn't help it.

"What's the matter, do you think women are not up to the task, Obersturmfuhrer?" she said abruptly. Her voice was slightly lower in pitch than I would have expected. I could have described it as sultry, but I doubted that she would appreciate me saying so. To gain time, I asked her where she learned to speak German.

"I trained to be an interpreter, I was at the University of Kiev when the war started."

"How many languages do you speak?"

"German, Russian of course and Ukrainian. I also learned some French and English. I was brought up outside the city of Kursk and I also know the countryside quite well. My father had his own estate, he used to hunt and I often went with him."

"I didn't think there were any landowners left in the Soviet Union?"

"He planned to become a member of the Politburo. He was a very powerful man."

"Was?"

"Yes, was. The Communists accused him of treachery and executed him, it was one of his local rivals, of course, he seized the excuse when the Germans invaded."

"So is this about vengeance?"

She laughed. "My father would have done the same thing

to him. It's not vengeance at all, for him it was just politics. For me I hate the Communists and I would anything to help bring them down. But you haven't answered my question, is a woman not good enough for you?"

I sighed. "It's not that, Miss Rakevsky. For us it's not so normal for women to fight, not in the SS, nor in any of the German armies."

"In that case you'd better make sure you don't us get into a fight, hadn't you? I shall be back later to go over the route with you. Make sure you have a good map, I don't want to waste my time."

She swept out of the room leaving us open-mouthed.

"My God," Mundt said, staring at the door, "that is some woman!"

"Damn right," Voss added. "I wouldn't mind having her guiding me, but not behind enemy lines."

I could see Miss Irina Rakevsky causing problems even before we left. Already my NCOs were feeling their testosterone levels beginning to rise.

"We'll have to treat her properly, all of us, just like she's one of the men."

The both looked at me incredulously. Yes, it was going to cause problems. But I had a feeling that the beautiful and feisty Miss Rakevsky was well able to take care of herself. Voss produced some breakfast, a thick potato soup with black bread and I ate it with ersatz coffee to wash it down. I spent the morning checking and inspecting the weapons and supplies. A trooper brought the packet of maps and I went over the whole area of the Kursk salient. It was obvious to me that we would attack, we had powerful, well-equipped armies deployed to north and south, it was equally obvious that the Russians knew and they would be well prepared. Shortly after lunch the girl came back. She picked up the maps without asking, looked at them closely and tossed them to one side.

"Is this the best you can do?" she asked. "They're not even accurate, look, the distance between Sumy and Kursk is much greater than they show here."

I felt the crazy need to defend myself from this fiery Ukrainian. "Miss Rakevsky, they're the maps that Division supplied, they're the best we have available."

"They'll have to do then, where do you intend to cross the lines?"

I pointed at the map. "Here, at Belgorod."

"No, not there. It's no good."

"Why not?"

"Because it's flat, open country. There is nowhere to hide, the Russians will see us coming from kilometres away."

"We'll be travelling at night, Miss Rakevsky, I doubt they'll see us at all."

"And when something goes wrong and we're stuck in the middle of the Red Army in broad daylight, what then?"

The men were listening intently and I had to concede

she had a point.

"What do you suggest?"

"Here! We can cross over fifteen kilometres south of Belgorod. I know that area well, I can get us through the Soviet lines."

I nodded. "In that case we'll do it your way. Are you armed, do you need a pistol?"

She reached under her thick coat and pulled out a long, vicious-looking hunting knife. "I have this, it is all I need."

"Good enough. All of you be ready to depart at six."

The half-track arrived an hour late, at seven o'clock.

"Engine wouldn't start, damp electrics," the driver said miserably. A sad looking SS-Oberschutze, he looked as if he'd sooner be anywhere in the world than here in Kharkov, about to go up to the front line. We piled on board, our packs laden with additional ammunition and food. For once, our Hanomag SDK 251 half-track clanked along the Ukrainian tracks without bogging down, the mud was obviously drying out. We already appreciated having the girl with us, she directed us along a route that was less churned up than the roads the military used. It took us two hours to reach our forward positions, after I had to convince a suspicious Haupsturmfuhrer that we weren't deserting and taking a valuable vehicle as a present for the Soviets at the same time.

"Don't be crazy, they'd shoot us full of holes if we tried to cross the lines in this noisy thing. We're on a straightforward recon mission, Haupt, we're not even taking the half-track with us."

"Alright, you can go forward. There's a Russian position about three hundred metres in front of us, if you go straight ahead you'll run straight into them."

"We're not going straight ahead," Irina said.

He looked at her keenly. "A woman?"

"Have you never seen one before?" she asked caustically. "If you men are finished chatting we need to make a start. If we're not well behind their front lines by dawn we'll be in trouble."

The officer raised his eyebrows and looked at me.

"She's a local," I said with a shrug.

We dismounted from the half-track and Irina led us forward, striding along confidently in the darkness of the steppe. Within a hundred metres we dropped into a culvert, it was heavily overgrown and we stumbled along out of sight of the enemy. They called them balkas in Russian, the ravines, dried up riverbeds that littered the steppes, some shallow, and some deep enough to swallow a regiment of Panzers. After another hundred metres Irina stopped.

"What is it?" I whispered.

"Russian sentry, he's about thirty metres ahead. Can't you smell the pig? He hasn't bathed for months! He's smoking Russian tobacco, it's called mahorka, smells like a garden bonfire."

Was she serious? I sniffed the air and sure enough the faint, rank smell of unwashed human body overlaid by the pungent stench of the Russian tobacco smoke assaulted my nostrils. I turned to the men.

"Willy, there's a sentry up ahead, take Bauer with you in case there are two of them. Knives only, no shooting, for God's sake!"

He nodded and signalled for Stefan Bauer to accompany him. We waited quietly while they slipped forward. After an agonising ten minutes, Mundt called out softly in the dark.

"It's Mundt, we're coming in."

They materialised quietly out of the darkness.

"All ok?"

He nodded. "No problems, there were two of them, we dragged the bodies together and put their bayonets in their hands as if they'd been fighting."

It was feeble, but it might confuse the enemy for a short time.

"Well done. Irina, take the lead, let's move on."

She knew the ground well, we were able to move along balkas and paths that were less muddy and better hidden than those that the military would use. Most of the ground around us was little more than quagmires waiting to trap those men and their machines that dared to try and traverse them. We saw the occasional vehicle that had been left stuck in the mud for later retrieval.

"In Finnish, they call this season rospuutto, it literally means roadlessness," she said quietly.

"I'll bear it in mind if I ever visit Finland, Miss Rakevsky."

She smiled. "You may call me Irina, Obersturmfuhrer."

"In that case you must call me Jurgen, Obersturmfuhrer is much too military for a pretty girl like you."

Did she blush? I couldn't be sure, but she quickly looked away and concentrated on the path ahead. We made good time and I estimated we'd covered around thirty kilometres on a northeast heading. We'd find somewhere to lie up during daylight, watch the enemy, and try to assess their strength. Tomorrow night we would head back and attempt to find at least one Soviet officer to take back with us for interrogation. Then we could cross back south of Belgorod. It sounded so easy, and perhaps it would be, for once. We found a natural place to make camp. It was in a shallow bowl at the top of a low ridge that would give us a good view across many miles of the open steppe. Dawn was breaking by the time we were all inside cover. I took the first watch and took out my binoculars to watch for enemy movements, that was when the cavalry came.

Willy Mundt saw them first. "Cossacks," he hissed.

I didn't need to give the order, we all ducked low, but clearly something had alerted them, they'd probably seen movement before we were all properly hidden. There were six horsemen, no, seven, one of them had a woman riding behind him. They approached from the north, the slope was steep and rocky making it impossible for horses to climb up to where we sheltered. They dismounted and the woman tethered their horses to a tangle of bushes while the men drew their sabres and started to climb, slashing the foliage out of the way as they came up. They looked magnificent, wearing dark blue breeches tucked into knee-high riding boots, standard Soviet pattern baggy brown tunics and dark grey Cossack Astrakhan hats. More worrying than the sabres, they carried PPSh sub-machine guns slung over their backs. A development of the older PP type, Georgi Shpagin had designed the new weapon for use by untrained conscript soldiers. The PPSh mounted a drum magazine loaded with the shorter 7.62mm pistol round. They were appearing in huge numbers on the Eastern Front, at close range they had proved to be devastating. The Cossacks came within close range and we could see their features distinctly. They all had large and fierce moustaches, some had beards, with dark-skinned weather-beaten faces. They looked magnificent, men who were born to make war. Mundt looked at me with his eyebrows raised and whispered.

"Any ideas, Sir?"

"Do all of the men have pistols?"

He nodded.

"We might just get away with a few pistol shots but if the enemy hears automatic fire they'll be all over us."

Our MP38s were fine weapons, like the PPSh they were also devastating at close quarters, but they differed from the Soviet weapon in that they had no single shot capability. All that was needed was a heavy finger on the trigger and the gun would blaze away all thirty-two rounds until the magazine was empty. Mundt spoke to the men quietly. "Pistols only, knives if we get close enough but I doubt we'll get past those sabres. Try and take your target out with a single shot. What about the woman?" he nodded at the woman at the bottom of the slope, tending the horses.

"I will take her," Irina said, touching her jacket where her huge combat knife lay hidden.

"Very well, let's do it. We need to wait until they almost trip over us. If we miss one and he uses his PPSh we're done for. Wait for me to shoot first."

We crouched low, keeping out of sight. Each of us holding a pistol, mine was a Walther PPK 9mm. I noticed that Voss had a Luger Parabellum, an expensive weapon normally carried only by more senior officers. I idly wondered where he had looted it from, but I didn't care, only that it fired when it mattered. We were covered in mud from the night's journey and the foliage hid us well so they didn't see us at first. They were swishing the bushes with their sabres, but not very intently, they obviously doubted that they would find anyone. One of them came up and stood only a metre away, sheathed his sword, unbuttoned his fly and started to piss almost on top of me. He was obviously having happy thoughts, perhaps about the previous night with an attractive woman. It would be his last. His eyes caught sight of something strange, his brow wrinkled in puzzlement, then he squinted and suddenly realised he was looking at a man, a soldier. He grabbed for his sabre with one hand, trying to tuck his cock back inside his trousers with the other. I shot him in the heart, I wasn't confident of a headshot at the sharp upward angle. Simultaneously five further shots rang out and the six Cossacks all collapsed to the ground. Two of them were still alive, one started to cry out but Mundt and Bauer had their combat knives ready, they swiftly knelt down and their knives slashed across the two throats, the Russians sagged to the ground lifeless. I could see Irina sprinting down the slope towards the woman who tended the horses. She was standing still, looking up at what had happened to the Cossacks. She was undoubtedly in shock and didn't respond to the woman crashing down the slope and just watched as Irina hurtled towards her. Even when she saw the raised combat knife she didn't move, our Ukrainian guide reached her and held her tightly. I looked around at the scene of bloody carnage.

"They're all dead," Mundt said. "We've been looking around for signs of the enemy, but I think you were right, a few pistol shots will most likely go unnoticed."

I looked at the bodies, the magnificent, outlandish

costumes, covering the lifeless corpses inside. Wesserman was gathering up the sabres and Voss their PPSh sub-machine guns. I spoke to Mundt.

"I'd better see how Irina is doing with that woman, Willy. Do you know anything about horses?"

He grinned. "I spent my summer holidays on a family farm, yes, I know my way around horses. What are we going to do about them, they're not easy to hide?"

"I've no idea, probably hide the saddles and let the horses loose, come and take a look at them."

We climbed carefully down the slope and walked over to Irina who was standing with the other woman, speaking in Russian, I assumed.

"What's going on?" I asked her. "I thought you were going to kill her."

"There's no need, Jurgen. She was a prisoner, they took her three days ago and used her as their whore. She was smiling when she realised that we were killing them all."

I looked her over, she was pretty too, no wonder the Cossacks had abducted her. Her features were not as fine and delicate as Irina's, she was slightly larger and heavier, but still very attractive. Her hair was blonde, her eyes blue, a genuine Slavic maiden.

"Does she speak any German?"

Irina shook her head. "Only Russian and some Ukrainian. I told her we wouldn't kill her."

I nodded. "Of course not, provided that what she told

you is true."

She shot me a venomous look. "I have told you the truth."

"Yes, but has she?"

She didn't reply.

"We'd better get back up the slope and out of sight," I continued. "I'll send two of my troopers down to deal with the horses."

"What will you do with them?"

Two of the men wanted to take the horses and disguise ourselves as Cossacks so that we could cover the ground quickly on the way back. I told them to forget it. In the end Mundt and Bauer went down to remove the saddles, and set the horses loose. They were local Panjes, better than the horses we brought in from Western Europe which were not able to last for long in the sub-zero conditions found in Russia. These shaggy, hardy Russian Panjes proved indispensable to both armies for transport in bad weather and as mounts for cavalry. Many of our larger horses had died from the cold, but these native breeds could survive in the open at almost any temperature. I shuddered to think of six German soldiers racing around behind enemy lines in broad daylight dressed as Cossacks, especially if we were caught. The Russians were tough enough on captured SS soldiers, but dressed in their own uniforms would mean an immediate bullet in the back of the head. I watched the two women talking quietly to each other.

"Irina, we need to send this woman back to her own people."

"Her name is Alina Gordievsky, Jurgen. Of course she would like to get back to her people. We were just discussing it. Her home is a small village of west of Kharkov, she was taken during a raid."

It was not unusual, the Cossacks had an almost free run of the territory during the harsh winter and the rasputitza that followed, they roamed the steppes with impunity, secure in the knowledge that pursuit was impossible. They would sweep in suddenly, often hundreds of them in huge formations, killing and looting and then disappear as quickly as they came.

"So she needs to get back across the front lines, you're suggesting she comes with us, aren't you?"

"Of course. What else can she do?"

"Very well, but make certain she keeps out of our way and out of sight until it's time to go."

As the day wore on, we took it in turns to either sleep or observe the broad steppe below us, we could see for ten kilometres to the north and east. What we saw was enough to take back to our intelligence people. In the distance tanks were on the move, hundreds of them, probably T34s, although they were too far away to be certain. There were teams of people digging tank traps and tank pits to hide tanks and artillery, half-buried in the earth where they could be used as defensive positions to shoot at enemy tanks with relative impunity. Some parts of the steppe were bare of enemy vehicles, just hundred of men working with shovels. Minefields, without a doubt! They knew that we were coming as soon as the rasputitza ended, that much was transparently clear. I was on watch as darkness started to fall and I woke Mundt.

"Willy, get the men moving. We've seen enough, this place is a death trap. If we can collect a prisoner on the way back our mission will be complete."

He smiled. "So all we need is to find a Soviet General to make our masters happy, is that what you're saying, Sir?"

"No, Willy. I'm sure a Colonel would be sufficient."

He grunted. "They may have to be happy with a Lieutenant."

"Provided that it's another of Stalin's sons, he would no doubt suffice," I replied drily.

Lieutenant Yakov Dzhugashvili, Josef Stalin's eldest son, was taken prisoner in Smolensk during the early days of Barbarossa when our German forces overran western parts of the Soviet Union. He'd been held since then in Sachsenhausen Concentration Camp until the news had emerged that he'd been killed, apparently shot while trying to escape.

"Has he got any more sons?" Mundt asked with interest.

I laughed. "I wouldn't count on it, my friend. Let's content ourselves with a senior officer."

As darkness fell we started to make our way back to the crossing point, fifteen kilometres south of Belgorod. At first the going was easy, Irina kept us out of the worst of the mud although we were still plastered with it. We almost ran into a Soviet encampment, a regiment of tanks were positioned across the track we'd used the previous night, the crews were working to camouflage them with huge nets stretched over each tank. Cossacks were dragging bushes and branches behind their horses, delivering them to the crews who threaded it through the netting. It explained why our reconnaissance flights had been unable to detect the enemy positions.

"I know a path that leads around this place," Irina whispered. "It means we will have to cross a shallow river."

She led us away from the camp, into a narrow balka that hid us and we detoured for two kilometres to the south before we were able to continue west again reaching the river, it was about twenty metres wide.

"How deep is it, do you think?"

"About a metre, no more. During the dry season it is completely empty. It is..."

I told her to be quiet and whispered to the men to be still. Irina murmured to Alina and held her arm. I could hear footsteps, pebbles being kicked aside as someone came nearer. A sentry? The sound of voices reached us, two men. A match flared and they both lit cigarettes, they were nearer now and we could hear their voices. Irina whispered to me. "They are talking about whether to build a hidden bridge under the surface of the river that their tanks could use to counterattack."

So they had to be officers, or at least one of them was. These would have to do.

"Scharfuhrer," I murmured to Mundt. "We'll take these two. Tell the men not to shoot, we'll jump them as they come past."

He nodded.

We spread out above the riverbank, invisible in the dark. As the two Russians walked past chatting happily to each other, we launched ourselves at them. Two troopers dragged each of them to the ground with a hand clamped over their mouths and a combat knife at their throats. Irina ran over and spoke to them urgently.

"It is alright, they understand that if they try to make any noise they will be killed, your men can let them up."

I nodded to Mundt and the two Soviets were allowed to get to their feet, their uniforms covered in mud from the riverbank. One was a major, the other a lieutenant. It was enough, if they were discussing a bridge they were almost certainly combat engineers, they should have a wealth of information for our intelligence section to extract from them.

"You'd better gag them, Willy, in case they get second thoughts while we're crossing the lines. Tie their hands too, we don't want them making a grab for one of our weapons."

They searched the two Soviets until they found strips of cloth, shabby white winter camouflage hoods that were stowed in their packs, they wrapped them around their mouths as gags. We had to take the lanyards from their pistols to tie their hands, I was about to tell them to toss the guns in the river when the men picked them up and they abruptly disappeared as if by magic. Souvenirs, of course, our armies had 'liberated' thousands of these Tokarev pistols during the early days of Barbarossa. They still held some kind of fascination for the men as a war memento, with a very practical use if the going got tough.

I asked Irina to come up and walk with me.

"We can't cross in the same place as we came over," I said to her. "We left two dead soldiers, they'll be more alert this time."

"Yes, I understand, I'll do my best to find another crossing point, but that one was the safest. Anywhere else will be much more risky."

"Then we'll have to take the risk."

She gave me an unpleasant look, "It's alright for you, you're a soldier", and then went back to join Alina. Women! Would I ever understand them? Probably not, but what more did she want from me? I could hard sprout wings and fly us over the lines. I could hear her talking in low tones to Alina, presently she came back to speak to me.

"Alina says there is a crossing point much nearer to

Belgorod, the Cossacks used it two days ago to raid into German-held territory. It would be a good place for us to try."

"Do you trust her?" I asked.

"As much as I trust you, Obersturmfuhrer," was the tart reply. It wasn't Jurgen anymore, I noticed.

"Very well, we'll go that way, would you ask her to come forward, she can take the lead and you will interpret. Warn her that if she is lying to us, she'll be the first one to get her throat cut."

She gave me a venomous glance and then hurried away to fetch Alina. The Ukrainian girl led us in a direction that I calculated would intersect the city of Belgorod. Although it was in German hands, a few kilometres outside the city were the Russian defences, manned by tens of thousands of Soviet troops and hundreds, maybe even thousands of tanks.

We could see the city buildings in the distance when we came upon a single-track railway line, she led us due west, following the path of the line. She spoke some words of Ukrainian or Russian to Irina.

"She says that this was a local line that closed many years ago, it was used by a quarry to take stone into the city."

"Ask her where the crossing is."

She questioned her closely. "She says that there is a tunnel that was dynamited when the Russians retreated, but there is a hidden way through. It runs underneath the front lines, we can go through the tunnel and come out on the German side. It is not defended, most people don't know it even exists."

We followed the line for two more kilometres until the ground rose into a series of low hills. The rails disappeared into the side of a hill, when we reached it the entrance to the tunnel was blocked with huge blocks of stone. Alina went to a tangle of debris leaning against the hillside twenty metres away, she asked Irina for help and we moved heavy sheets of rusting corrugated iron to one side. Irina pointed to a dark opening.

"That is the entrance of the old part of the tunnel, Alina says that fifty years ago there was a branch line that came in here but it was closed. We can go in through this entrance. She says to put the corrugated iron back afterwards, otherwise the Soviets may follow us."

The narrow tunnel was barely high or wide enough for a horse. Clearly the Cossacks had dismounted before they came through. Inside, we marched in single file, Alina first, Irina behind her. I followed them, and then Mundt, who had his combat knife ready in case they tried anything untoward, pushed along the two Soviet officers. The other men came after and I heard them replacing the corrugated iron. There was no light, I took out my small combat torch and played it over the walls. It was just as well, our narrow tunnel forked into the larger tunnel and we narrowly avoided sprawling over the broken steel of the old rails and the boulders that lay littered all around.

"Ask her how long this tunnel is," I said to Irina.

She spoke softly to Alina. "She says about a kilometre."

We stumbled on in the dark, aided by occasional flashes of my torch, until we saw glimpses of moonlight ahead of us. We finally came out into a dark, ruined building which even the roof had been destroyed.

"She says this was the factory where they crushed the marble, the trains came into here and unloaded and it was immediately put on to conveyor belts."

I looked up. The old conveyor belts criss-crossed the huge, empty space, almost like giant vines in some ghostly industrial jungle. We walked across the echoing, empty building until we came out into the open. We were near Belgorod, which was still in German hands, less than two kilometres away.

We soon stumbled upon two sentries from General Hausser's Second SS Panzer Corps. They were sceptical at first but after they contacted the Fourth Panzer Army Intelligence Officer we were allowed through and our own SS Intelligence arranged for a half-track to collect us and bring us back to Kharkov. It was dawn when we reached the city but it was already bustling. We went straight to the Regimental Office. I left the men to look after the women and the prisoners while I went inside to find Muller. His office door opened and a stranger emerged, with Muller trailing behind him. I saluted and Muller introduced us. "This is the new commanding officer, Standartenfuhrer von Meusebach. Standartenfuhrer, this is Obersturmfuhrer Hoffman."

At first sight von Meusebach did little to inspire me. He was quite short, his hair cropped close to his head. Unlike the Prussian officers whose style he obviously tried to emulate, he was also paunchy and somewhat round-shouldered, evidence of his sedentary occupation, at least until now. He wore thin, gold, wire-rimmed glasses, unusual in a line officer. He stared at me with a neutral expression. His uniform, the field-grey of the Waffen-SS was immaculate, perfectly creased, jackboots gleaming black. I saw him looking at my Iron Cross with an expression that looked almost like envy. Unusually for a senior officer on the Eastern Front, he displayed no decorations.

"You have just returned from a mission across the lines, Obersturmfuhrer?"

"Yes, Sir."

"In that case I will forgive your slovenly appearance, but next time you report to this office make sure you look like an SS officer, not a vagabond Jew."

I must have looked like an idiot. I was so astonished that I couldn't help my jaw drop. Did he think he'd been posted to a peaceful French city to enforce the traffic regulations?

"I'm sorry, Sir. It's the war."

As soon as I spoke I knew that I shouldn't have said it. He glowed bright red with anger.

"The next insubordinate remark you make will result in you being put on a charge, is that clear, Hoffman? I assure you that I am well versed in every aspect of military law."

"Yes, Sir, I'm sure you are."

He looked at me suspiciously. "Dismissed."

I saluted and he went back into his office, Muller accompanied us to the Gestapo Office. As we walked across the road we had to wait while a line of Panzers, perhaps twenty of our Panzer IVs clattered along, their tracks ripping up the cobbles as they travelled. They seemed pitifully few compared to the columns of T34s on the other side of the salient.

CHAPTER TWO

'The Eastern front is like a house of cards. If the front is broken through at one point all the rest will collapse'.

General Heinz Guderian

The last of the Panzers disappeared and we crossed over the road. Behind us four Tigers rumbled past, the Panzer VI, huge and daunting with their enormous 88mm gun, but they were still pitifully few to take on the Russians. We walked under the arched entrance and left the men in the courtyard with Irina, Alina and the prisoners. Major Ernst Brandt of Abwehr, army intelligence was talking to two security officers, one in plain clothes the other in the uniform of the Sicherheitsdienst, an SD Obersturmbannfuhrer who clutched a walking cane. When he turned around his face was one I recognised instantly.

"Obersturmfuhrer Hoffman, how pleasant to meet again."

SD Sturmbannfuhrer Walter von Betternich, with his equally unpleasant Gestapo colleague, Gerd Wiedel. Muller had previously brushed with the two security officers when they put him under a Schutzhaft, the Gestapo's protective custody order and he was clearly as unhappy as I was to see them. He elected to speak to Brandt, von Manstein's intelligence officer.

"They brought in two Soviet prisoners, Major, I believe they are both engineering officers."

"Very well, let's hope they have plenty to tell us."

"Hoffman, would you bring them in," Muller said to me.

I'd taken off their gags when we reached our lines and when I led them into the building one of them spoke angrily.

"Under the Geneva Convention we refuse to divulge any information other than our names, ranks and numbers."

Brandt looked at him coolly. "Has the Soviet Union now signed the Convention, Major?"

The Russian stared at him stonily, refusing to answer.

"No, I thought not. I've no doubt the Gestapo would like to discuss things further with you. Kriminalkommissar Wiedel, would you care to handle these two officers? You know the kind of information the Feldmarschal wants."

"Of course, Major. They will have plenty to tell us,

believe me. Hoffman, would your men kindly escort these prisoners to our cells."

I detailed the men to take the prisoners and Wiedel followed them out. The SD officer, von Betternich, spoke to me. "Hoffman, you've done well, how have you been?"

The last time I'd met the SD Obersturmbannfuhrer, he'd had a girl friend of mine sent to a concentration camp. It was true she had admitted to being a Jew and using a stolen identity card, but any Jew in Nazi Germany would be desperate enough to try anything to avoid the brutal fate that was meted out to them. I gave him a cold nod, refusing to answer him.

He smiled. "It wasn't my fault you know, that Jewess of yours. Besides, I did offer you the chance to join our organisation. Perhaps you could have saved her."

He looked at me for a moment, then shrugged and limped away on his cane. "We'll get together another time, Hoffman," was his parting shot.

I thought that with any luck a Russian sniper would get him first and save me the trouble of meeting him again. Major Brandt, the Abwehr officer, looked up from his notes.

"Hoffman, tell me what you found over the other side."

I explained to him about the defences. "They're formidable, Sir, the Russians are expecting us, there's no doubt about it," I added.

"Many tanks, you say, artillery dug in, mines, did you

see many infantrymen?"

"Not many but the salient is hundreds of square kilometres, it would be impossible to see everything, Sir."

"So it may not be as well defended as you think, not across the whole salient?"

"You're wrong, Sir, the Russians are preparing defences everywhere, they're just waiting for us to make a move."

He smiled. "You are an inexperienced officer, Hoffman, so I doubt you would understand everything there is to know about Soviet defences. However, the Gestapo will interrogate your prisoners and perhaps we'll get some more answers. I'm afraid that you have rather overestimated the Russian preparations, I'll put it all in my dispatch to von Manstein."

He smiled and left the office.

"Major Brandt didn't believe a word of what I said," I remarked bitterly to Muller.

"He's under a lot of pressure, Hoffman. Von Manstein is determined to press home this next attack and he doesn't want to hear about insurmountable Russian obstacles."

"So they only want the good news, do they, Sir?" I sneered.

"Now you understand it, my friend, it's all politics. Listen, you need to start packing, we're moving tomorrow to the railhead at Podvirky, we'll be guarding the railway depot bringing in the new armour and supplies. It won't be as comfortable as the city, but hopefully we'll be away from the snipers."

I wasn't sure which part of the city of Kharkov he'd found comfortable, but it certainly wasn't the part where we were quartered.

My men were waiting for me outside with both women, they'd managed to scrounge coffee from the Gestapo kitchen and the hot liquid refreshed me. Sadly even the Gestapo didn't have real coffee.

"Were they impressed with what we brought back, Sir?" Mundt asked.

I grimaced. "They didn't believe me, Willy. Thought I was exaggerating or made it up."

"So it was all for nothing?"

"I hope not, but I just don't know." I finished the last of my coffee and we started the short walk across town to our quarters. "We're moving out tomorrow, we're to reinforce the garrison at Podvirky."

"Damn it," he scowled. "It's a shithole out there, just a railway depot and a few greasy peasant houses, what they call Isbas. In Germany we call them hovels. As if Kharkov isn't bad enough they send us out there."

We passed a curious sight in the city square, a company of tanks, all bearing the usual German military symbols, the German Cross and the Swastika together with Divisional markings. What was strange was that they were all Russian T34s. A Sturmscharfuhrer, a Sergeant Major, saw me looking at them, he was wearing the usual black

German tanker's uniform but I half expected him to speak Russian.

"Not what you expect to see in our army, Obersturmfuhrer?"

I smiled. "Not really, no, a present from Josef Stalin?"

"We captured these during the battle for the city. There were so many that we've formed a T34 company within the Fourth Panzer Army."

I gazed at the enemy armour. "Are they any good, these things? Our tankers say they cause them a lot of grief."

He shrugged. "They're not as good as our own heavy tanks, although they can be useful in a scrap. The problem is spare parts. We have to cannibalise other T34s when repairs are needed, it's not always easy. Of course, in the T34 the commander has to operate the gun as well as observe and command the tank, it makes life complicated in action."

"The Red Army seems to do alright with them," Mundt said, looking with avid interest.

"Sure they do," the NCO replied. "You send five hundred T34s against a hundred of our own tanks and they're sure to do wicked damage."

"They don't have that kind of numerical advantage, do they?"

Even as I asked the question I thought of the massive Soviet preparations in the Kursk salient, hundreds of tanks in only that one small area, perhaps many thousands across the whole salient.

The tanker stared at us solemnly. "We'd better hope they don't, hadn't we? If they do, we're buggered."

We nodded and walked on. Irina was holding Alina's hand, since we'd killed the Cossacks she seemed to be utterly dependent on Irina for support and protection. I asked her what she was planning to do with Alina.

"She will stay with me until I can arrange to get her back to her village. She will be safe."

"Good. We're leaving Kharkov in the morning but we won't be far away. I want to thank you for helping us."

"It is no problem."

"I'd like you to have dinner with me this evening, Irina, there must be at least one restaurant in the city that is still functioning."

She smiled. "That is very kind of you, Jurgen," before I could go on, she said, "but I have already arranged a dinner date, so it is not possible."

I felt suddenly deflated. "I see, who with, one of the men?"

"No, it is with Alina."

I looked down and saw that they were still holding hands tightly. Alina was looking at her with something very close to adoration. So that was the way it was, I'd certainly misread the signs.

"I hope you enjoy a pleasant meal, then."

"I'm sorry, Jurgen."

I nodded. Irina and Alina left, Irina had her hand around Alina's waist. Mundt grinned. "No chance with either of those two, Sir. Shame."

I looked him directly in the eyes. "Willy, shut up!"

He stared at a point ten centimetres above my head, as regulations demanded when addressing a senior officer, "Yes, Sir," but he was grinning like a circus clown.

"We've got a couple of hours to get cleaned up and rested, we're back on duty this afternoon, we need to prepare to move out tomorrow. You'd better get some rest."

They walked away with broad smiles. Damn, I'd fancied my chances with Irina, what a waste. I walked to our quarters thinking about those T34s. If their performance was inferior to our own tanks, particularly the newer types like the Tiger and Panzer V, why were we using them? Were we so desperate that we had to use second-rate Soviet armour? Then again, I had seen the T34 in action, they weren't as poor as the tanker had suggested, they were quick and powerful, lethal except when faced with our Tigers and perhaps the newer Panthers which could stand off at a distance and pick the T34s off almost at will. There was only one explanation. We were running out of resources. With a front line stretching thousands of kilometres, it was proving impossible to both attack and defend along the entire length. I considered the formidable defences that I'd seen in one small corner of the salient and what it would mean to an attacker. Unless our leaders faced up to what we were up against it was going to be a very costly action indeed. The leadership of course meant Adolf Hitler, head of OKW, Oberkommando der Wehrmacht, the Supreme Command of the Armed Forces. In view of his intransigence with the Sixth Army at Stalingrad, resulting in its encirclement and defeat at the hands of the Red Army, I wasn't optimistic about him having a change of heart about the Kursk salient. Neither was I certain that our armies could withstand another shock defeat like Stalingrad. I could only hope that we could smash through the salient and push on eastwards, but in my head I knew it wouldn't happen, couldn't happen.

We spent the rest of the day preparing our equipment for our move to the railway line. It was a miserable thought, despite the problems of snipers and occasional shelling by the Russians, the night bombing raids and the sudden partisan attacks, we'd become used to our lice infested quarters in Kharkov. The idea of camping out in a damp muddy field next to a railway yard was not a happy one. During the evening the men passed around bottles of schnapps and we drowned our sorrows. Voss asked me if I had a date tonight, I threw an empty bottle at his head and he ducked to avoid it to roars of laughter. But I slept badly. I couldn't get the past forty-eight hours out of my mind, our mission into enemy territory. In view of the High Command's refusal to accept what I'd reported back it had all been for nothing. My intentions with Irina were just as doomed, this was not a high point in my life.

In the morning I put on a clean uniform as ordered, at least, one that was slightly less ragged and filthy than the previous one I'd worn, we boarded the half-tracks and drove through the mud to Podvirky. We did not need to sleep in tents, we were to be quartered in the railway village, a squalid collection of wooden huts, isbas, most of which had been partially destroyed by the Red Army. When we attacked the Soviet Union in 1941, Joseph Stalin had ordered both soldiers and civilians to initiate a policy to deny the invaders basic supplies and shelter as they moved eastward, known as 'scorched earth'. They burned and destroyed everything, houses were dynamited, woodlands and fields burned, the whole countryside denuded of foodstuffs, livestock and crops. Fortunately a few buildings had escaped destruction, Mundt went looking for suitable accommodation for the platoon while I attended the CO's briefing.

Our new HQ was in the only comfortable building in Podvirky. It had formerly belonged to the mayor who probably had intervened to stop its destruction. Von Meusebach had established his new quarters in the upstairs rooms, downstairs was the Regimental offices. Outside, near where his black Mercedes car waited, a group of Hiwis were working to lay a hard bed of broken stone and boiler ash to make a hard stand to keep it out of the mud. Another Hiwi was scrubbing at the mud and filth that coated the Mercedes as well as everything else in this theatre of war. I went into what had been the dining room where a map was pinned to the wall. The other officers were already waiting.

"Ah, Hoffman, you decided to give us the benefit of your presence."

"Sir."

He squinted at my uniform, evidently considering whether to find fault, but as his other officers were no better dressed, in some cases worse, he kept quiet. He had a long stick that looked like a billiard cue and he used it to point at the large-scale map of the local area.

"Our patrol area is from here to here," he pointed at Podvirky and at the next village along the line, about ten kilometres away. "We will be conducting a patrol each night, Hoffman, your platoon can begin tonight. Remember, I intend to run a tight ship, that means I want you and your men looking like soldiers at all times, on or off duty. A smart regiment is an efficient regiment, understood?"

We all nodded like puppets. He looked at Hauptsturmfuhrer Glasser's boots. They were a pair of brown leather paratrooper's jump boots.

"Those boots, Glasser. They're not regulation, are they? Why are you not wearing regulation SS jackboots?"

"It's the Russian winter, Sir, mine fell to pieces and these are much better than the new ones that are like cardboard, they just fall apart."

"I don't want to hear excuses about our equipment, Glasser. Get yourself regulation boots!"

We all envied Glasser his warm, practical boots. He'd soon notice a difference going back to wearing uncomfortable jackboots. Ours were perpetually wet and failed dismally to keep our feet warm.

"Yes, Sir."

"Hoffman, I want a written report on my desk in the morning."

"A report of what, Sir?"

"Your patrol of course. I want you to account for every hour, what happens, what doesn't happen. By nine o'clock, clear?"

"Yes, Sir."

"Very well. I shall be dining in Kharkov this evening, if anything requires my attention, you can send a dispatch rider to find me."

Muller coughed discreetly.

"Well, Muller?"

"We don't have a dispatch rider, Sir, he was killed and his motorcycle destroyed by a Russian mortar shell."

Von Meusebach sighed theatrically. "In that case find another motorcycle and detail a man to ride it, deal with it." He checked his watch. "I need to get changed for the evening, dismissed."

We started to walk out. Von Meusebach called out to

me. "Hoffman?"

"Sir?"

"When you bring your report in the morning, I'll inspect your platoon. Make sure they look smart, not like a band of partisans. That's all."

I had to stand outside and take a few deep breaths to contain my anger. He obviously thought he was on the parade ground at Lichterfelde, our SS training barracks in Berlin. He was in for a rude shock when the Soviets attacked. Mundt was waiting for me nearby, he took me to the building they'd found, one of the squalid wooden isbas, the shacks that the peasants lived in all across the Soviet Union. This one was slightly larger than some. Apparently it had once been used as the local inn. It had only one large room for cooking, eating and sleeping, just like our quarters in the city.

"There's no booze left," Mundt smiled, "but otherwise it's not too bad. The roof wasn't badly damaged and it's dry enough for us to sleep in."

"We're due to go out on patrol tonight, Willy, so you'd better tell the men to get some rest. The new CO wants to inspect the platoon too, at nine o'clock tomorrow morning, he's a stickler for smartness."

The men looked at me with expressions of alarm.

"He's deadly serious, you'll need to be clean shaven and best uniforms."

There was a chorus of moans.

"Obersturmfuhrer, we haven't had much sleep for two nights, it's fucking ridiculous," Wesserman snapped. "Why is he doing this to us?"

"It must be the war, Schutze Wesserman, I can't think of any other reason."

The others laughed at his misery.

"I suggest we all try and grab a couple of hours sleep, we've been on duty for a long stretch. If we don't keep alert we'll be easy meat for the partisans."

That sobered them up. They laid out their gear and settled down to get some rest. I tried to do the same, but I didn't sleep, my brain was still racing after our journey into the salient.

Hauptsturmfuhrer Glasser was waiting for us when we reported to begin our patrol. He'd been the second in command until von Meusebach arrived and had hoped to make the position permanent, like Muller he was disappointed at the arrival of the Berlin lawyer.

"You can see the railway line one hundred metres to the north, Hoffman. Take your men and patrol to the west, you should reach Lyubotin, there is a small station there. Make sure the station is clear of the enemy and then get back, it should take you about six hours, I'll expect you back here before dawn."

"Is there much partisan activity in the area?" I asked him.

"You've been away on a recon mission so you wouldn't

know, Hoffman. The night before last two platoons of regular infantry were wiped out three kilometres west of here, that's why we were brought in. Does that answer your question?"

At ten o'clock we marched away and reached the railway line, then we turned to follow it to the west. It was very dark, the moon hidden behind thick clouds.

"Make sure your machine pistols are ready to fire and keep them pointed away from the rest of us, I don't want any accidents," Mundt shouted.

"Scharfuhrer, try and keep it a bit quiet, if there are partisans around it might be best if they didn't hear us coming."

"Sorry, Sir."

The men took the hint and we walked on in relative silence. I was thinking about Irina, mourning the fact that I'd missed out on having a pleasant evening with her as well as a tumble in her bed. I smiled inwardly. In view of what I now knew if she had a tumble with anyone it would not be a man. We'd travelled about five kilometres and I must have been on the verge of falling asleep. I flinched, as a hand touched my shoulder, it was Mundt.

"Be quiet, I heard something."

I was instantly still. The wind was coming from the west, which is why Mundt had heard them before they realised we were in the area. I whispered to the men to get off the line, we'd been walking along the sleepers to make the going easier. We melted into the scrub at the south side of the track and crept forward. It was heavy going, the ground was soaking wet and I could hear my jackboots squelching as I walked. I prayed that whoever was up ahead couldn't hear the noise. Their voices started to reach us, men murmuring quietly in the unfamiliar cadences of the Russian language. Partisans, it couldn't be anything else.

"Scharfuhrer, pass the word to the men," I whispered. "If they use grenades keep them away from the line, we don't want to do the partisans work for them. As soon as we get nearer we'll drop to a crawl. No one is to shoot until I do and watch out for sentries, they're sure to have them posted."

He passed the word along to the men and we crept nearer, then I motioned with my arm and we dropped down onto the muddy ground. I was conscious of the wet mud, soaking through my uniform to my underwear. Stupid thought, I told myself, concentrate on the job in hand, these people would be watching for us. It was sheer luck that put the wind in the right direction for us to hear them first. I heard faint noises, someone was digging, a shovel pushing into the ground and throwing the mud to one side. Then I saw the first one, a sentry, he was sitting on the steel line, staring all around him, occasionally he darted a look up the railway line towards us, but failed to see us low on the ground in the darkness. The other men were about ten metres further behind him and were digging, presumably burying a mine under the line. I had no choice as I was at the front. I took out my combat knife and turned to Mundt, who was behind me. He saw the knife and nodded, then I started to crawl forward, nearer and nearer, each time the sentry turned to look away I crept nearer until I was within four metres from him. It seemed incredible that he hadn't seen me, but it would be his last error of judgement. He looked away from me again and I rose swiftly and ran the four steps towards him, he heard me coming and whipped around but I launched myself at him, aiming at his head I clamped one hand around his mouth and with the other, slashed across his windpipe. He struggled for a few moments then slumped. I lowered him gently to the ground and crouched low, waiting for the others to come up. I looked along the line, a short distance away the group was huddled around a hole in the ground, muttering quietly. I started as something touched my leg, but it was Mundt, alerting me that the men had come up. He pointed to his machine pistol and I nodded, feeling on my back for my own MP38 and pulling it to my front. We were ready, I looked at Mundt, and he inclined his head slightly. I jumped up and ran, my men either side of me. We got five metres nearer before they suddenly looked up and grabbed for their weapons. It was too late, I pressed the trigger and sent a stream of bullets into the partisans. I counted ten of them. Only one thing mattered and that was to kill them fast before they had a chance to start shooting back at us. Two men went down and the rest of my platoon opened fire, it was devastating, streams of 9mm bullets pouring into the group, knocking them to the ground. Within seconds they were all down, dead or wounded, but as the shooting died away we distinctly heard the sound of footsteps, someone was running, knocking the grass and scrub aside as he rushed through the night, seeking safety from our murderous gunfire.

"Mundt, Bauer, come with me, the rest of you check the area for any more of them and dismantle their explosives."

I ran in the direction of the footsteps, the other two followed. The route took us onto a path of some kind, drier than the swampy ground that surround the railway line, the going was a lot easier and we hurtled along, trying to close the gap. Fortunately he was making so much noise that it was not difficult to follow the fleeing partisan, then we saw him, the moon appeared from behind a cloud, lighting up the scene. He was about fifty metres in front of us, we surged forward, encouraged by sight of our target. Someone behind me fired a burst from a machine pistol, it missed the partisan but he swerved off the path and started to flounder across the soft ground. It was a fatal mistake, we quickly came parallel to him and the three of us fired on full automatic, he went down in full flight, his body rolled and tumbled to land in a muddy puddle. We went across to inspect it and make sure he was dead, but we were in for a shock, it wasn't a he, it was a she. A young woman of about eighteen years old, attractive too, I reflected that she should have been in school or university, not planting bombs on an obscure Ukrainian railway line in the dead of night.

"Silly bitch," Bauer said. "What a fucking waste, a girl like that."

"She was defending her homeland, Stefan, wouldn't you if Germany was invaded?" I said quietly.

"We all would, Obersturmfuhrer," Mundt said. "But we wouldn't send our wives and girlfriends to do it, neither is our homeland a shithouse like this one."

I shrugged. "They just think differently to us."

One of them muttered, "Fucking barbarians." I thought it was Bauer but it was too dark to tell.

We walked back to where my men were carefully pulling out the explosives from the hole dug by the partisans under the line. We'd been lucky, they were almost finished, another thirty minutes and they'd have completed their work and vanished into the night. The bodies of the partisans were lying like discarded sacks. My men worked as if they didn't exist, they were forgotten already. Voss was pulling out the last of the explosives.

"That's about all of it, they hadn't set the fuse so it was quite an easy job. We'll take the explosives with us?"

I nodded. "We don't want to leave them for the locals to try again."

"I doubt that they're short of supplies," Voss said.

"They seem to have plenty of everything."

I thought of the tens of thousands of troops, the hundreds of T34s in that tiny area of the Kursk salient and mentally compared the image of our hastily thrown together company of captured Soviet tanks. There was a conclusion to be drawn there, but not a comfortable one. The men had no such reservations.

"So how come they seem to have so much equipment and we're always running short?" Wesserman asked plaintively. "Look at their clothes, Christ, they've got padded jackets and trousers, fur caps."

"We haven't seen the Soviets using captured German armour or vehicles against us either," Voss added. "They don't need our captured soldiers to fight for them either, someone said that the Sixth Army at Stalingrad was let down because we had so many second rate Romanians and Italians fighting for us. Some said we even had Russian Hiwis in the front line."

"The Russians have no shortage of manpower, Wesserman, they have a huge population from which they can recruit more soldiers and workers for their factories to make tanks and guns, that's why they always outnumber us."

"So why did we go to war with them, Sir?" he asked.

"I have no idea," I replied, it was a lame answer, but of course, the truth was that the German perception of the Soviet Union was of a severely weakened giant. Adolf

Hitler had gone on record as saying about Communist Russia, 'You only have to kick in the door and the whole rotten structure will come crashing down'. We'd certainly kicked in the door, but the structure was proving to be much stronger than our Fuhrer had anticipated.

We returned to Podvirky and I wrote out my report in our squalid isba. At nine o'clock I handed my report to von Meusebach and he listened intently as I described our brush with the partisans.

"Very well, Hoffman, we are expecting trains day and night along the line so it was lucky that you stumbled on them. I'll have my orderly type up your report and you can sign it, then it will be sent on to Vinnitsa."

I was puzzled at such a complicated procedure for a routine report, but made no comment. He was a lawyer, after all.

"Excuse me, Sir, I think we should consider only running the trains during the day, after dark it's very risky. If they detonate those explosives as one of our trains goes over them the damage could block the line for several days."

"Don't be stupid," he snapped. "The trains have been ordered to run day and night, our army needs the new Tigers and Panzer Vs. You'll just have to lose some sleep and double the patrols, that'll put a stop to the partisans."

We had hundreds of kilometres of railway track running through partisan-held territory, operating trains at night would clearly be an invitation to disaster, but I said nothing. He wasn't the kind of officer to invite suggestions from his junior officers. He glared at me, then snapped, "I'll inspect your platoon now, Hoffman!"

He stalked outside, pulling a face when his gleaming jackboots sunk into the mud. Mundt had the men lined up, they had made some small effort but they still looked a shambles, as did every other soldier on the Eastern Front. Except for von Meusebach.

"You're a disgrace to your uniforms, all of you, you look like pigs! Next time you report for duty, make sure you shave and wear clean uniforms. The SS needs men, not scarecrows, to fight battles. Remember, we have won every battle on every front. The German soldier will always win with a combination of personal pride and discipline. Don't let it happen again!"

I wondered what he called the Sixth Army's huge defeat at Stalingrad. He stalked back into his HQ, I left the men muttering dark threats about what they'd like to do to von Meusebach and went to get some rest. The massive build-up of men, armour and equipment would mean a lot of sleepless nights for those of us already here. The arrival of the CO could only make a bad situation worse. Hopefully he'd have second thoughts when the shooting started.

During the afternoon a train stopped with a line of flat cars, each one held a Tiger tank, the huge, battle winning behemoths slumbering on their steel transporters waiting to be unloaded and sent to the assembly areas. Crews and mechanics swarmed over them. In order to move them over the Soviet railways the wide tracks had to be replaced with narrower transport tracks. Once the tanks were unloaded the tracks had to be changed back to the wider tracks that were necessary for manoeuvre in battle. All afternoon the tanks were unloaded and crews prepared them to move, as they became battle ready they drove away to join their units. When darkness fell the engineers used overhead lights so that the maintenance crews could keep working. We returned to our billet in the semi-ruined isba.

"I wish they'd turn those damned lights out," Mundt said. "We're sitting targets for every Soviet fighter bomber that happens in this direction."

It was normal to have a blackout at night and we were lit up for the whole of the Red Air Force to see, it sometimes seemed to me that our High Command were oblivious to the realities of the front. I slept uneasily that night, I doubted that anyone got much sleep around the railway yards of Podvirky with so much noise and so many lights blazing, but we were lucky, the Soviets did not attack. No artillery barrage came screaming in to smash the area to rubble, no Soviet fighter bombers came swooping down to destroy us with bombs, cannon and machine gun fire. Even the U-2 biplanes, the night bombers stayed away. The following morning we went out on patrol, but we returned without seeing any more of the partisans. I hadn't expected to, they mostly operated after dark, but of course we had to keep up the patrols regardless, they would be watching for any kind of a gap in our defences. During the evening I managed to find a ration truck that was returning to Kharkov. The driver agreed to give us a lift into the city but wasn't keen on bringing us back out to Podvirky at the end of the evening, until I bribed him with a 'liberated' Nagant M1895 revolver. The Nagant M1895 Revolver was a seven-shot revolver designed and produced by Belgian industrialist Leon Nagant for the Russian Empire. I'd taken it from a Soviet Major who had been captured during our battle to recapture the city of Kharkov. It had become a dead weight in my pack and I was glad to get rid of it, besides, either there'd be plenty more where that one came from or I'd be dead and it wouldn't matter. There was no sign that the Russian war was going to end anytime soon and a night out in the city was beyond price, something that might not be repeatable for some or all of us in the forthcoming days, weeks and months.

We clambered off the truck and I arranged to meet the driver at midnight. I kept the pistol in the pocket of my tunic, I had a suspicion that if I parted with it now he might 'forget' to return later to collect us. The bar we went into was packed with men, Wehrmacht, SS, a few Hiwis, a couple of Luftwaffe infantry. A band was on a low stage at one end of the room, enthusiastically playing traditional Ukrainian songs with a collection of accordions, violins and even a saxophone. Sadly their passion for their music was not matched by their skill, but nobody seemed to mind and the whole room was buzzing with life, a welcome change from the war outside. We downed three glasses of local beer in quick succession and then Mundt suggested we move somewhere else.

"It's much too crowded here, besides, there's nothing to look at."

"You mean women," I smiled.

He nodded. "It would be nice to see one or two pretty faces."

We left and walked along the main street until we spotted a bar in a side street. It looked a little dark and away from the regular areas patrolled by our Feldgendarmerie, but I agreed to give it a try.

"Are you all carrying side arms?" I asked them.

They nodded and I looked down to check that they did indeed all have holsters on their belts.

We walked down the street and into the bar, it was totally different from the previous establishment, here they had a band that played in tune, passable versions of American New Orleans jazz. And there were women, at least a dozen of them, admittedly most were already with a partner but at least we could look. It was Bauer's turn to get the drinks and we sat at a table while he ordered the beer. A buxom waitress brought a tray of foaming glasses and set them down, we all looked hungrily at her cleavage, artfully displayed inside her low-cut Ukrainian traditional dress. We gratefully drank the beer and looked around the bar, we were the only German soldiers in the room, there was a small dance floor and several couples were attempting to dance some kind of a folk dance to the raucous jazz. Then the music slowed and the men and women held each other close and smooched around the floor. I felt sad, hungry for the physical and emotional connection with a girl. It made me think of Irina and I thought I was having an illusion when suddenly I spotted her face as a crowd of people parted. She saw me at the same time and came across to our table.

"Aren't you going to invite me to dance?" she smiled

She saw the confusion on my face. "It's ok, Jurgen, I haven't got Alina with me."

I got up and went with her to the dance floor. Despite everything, it felt good to hold a soft, warm, female body in my arms.

"How is Alina?"

"Alina? She's fine, I think. She went home this morning so I doubt that she'll be back."

"That's a shame, I thought you were very close."

"I suppose we were," she said, "but I rather fancied you too, I thought you might have contacted me before now."

She must have seen my jaw drop. "What, you thought

that I only liked women? In this war, Obersturmfuhrer, you have to take anything you can get."

I didn't reply for a few moments, I had never been so confused in all my life. I was about to answer when there was a commotion at the door. I tried to clear my mind from the alcohol and the heady confusion of this pretty young woman. A group of civilians had walked in, four of them. Stupidly I wondered why they were armed with Soviet PPSh submachine guns and then it dawned on me. There were partisans, in the bar. A voice rang out in perfect German.

"Everyone stay where you are, you Germans put up your hands!"

I slowly put up my hands and looked across to our table. Two partisans had submachine guns pointed directly at my men. While I watched, one of them relieved them of their pistols, then came over to me and took my Walther automatic. The German-speaking leader, the gaunt young man standing in the middle of the room with his PPSh covering us, looked directly at me.

"You, SS officer. Are there any more of your people in here? Answer me honestly or I'll kill one of those men at the table!"

I shook my head. "No, this is everyone. What do you want?"

He didn't reply. "Andriy, check the front door, make sure there are no soldiers nearby. Pavlo, get everyone to move away from the Fascists."

They herded the crowd of customers away from us and the leader looked warily around the bar. Andriy looked outside and then closed the door. "It's all clear, Petro."

"Good. You, fascists, you will come with us. Andriy, go to the back, we'll go out that way. Pavlo, you and Olek make sure they make no noise. You, fascists, do not make any trouble or you will be killed!"

I had no doubt that we were about to be killed anyway. Mundt looked across at me, but I shook my head, I was out of ideas.

They moved us to a narrow, dark passage that led out of the bar, I knocked against a wooden shelf as we walked through and something snagged in my pocket. The Nagant, the Russian pistol, I still had it in my pocket. It was loaded with six bullets, it wasn't much against four PPSh machine pistols but it was all I had. I turned so that they couldn't see what I was doing and palmed the pistol. I was trying to work out the best time to start shooting when a row erupted in the bar. It was Irina.

"You, Petro, what are you doing with these German soldiers?"

"What is it to you? Why do you want to know?"

"I want revenge on them, I've lost a brother to these people."

The partisan hesitated, but a pretty girl was not easy to say no to.

"Very well, you may accompany us, but keep out of the way."

We walked through the door and they held us at gunpoint in the yard outside. I kept behind Mundt so that my hand holding the pistol was out of sight. "I have a pistol, be ready when I start shooting," I murmured quietly. I saw his head incline in a tiny nod.

Petro their leader stood to one side of us with Irina next to him. Did I know her well enough to trust her motives for coming out with the partisans? Yes, probably, she had every reason to hate the Soviets, so she must be on our side. I'd have to trust her. The three other partisans were in front of us, barely two metres away. I wondered how accurate the Nagant was while I whispered to Mundt, "When I start shooting, go for Petro, I think Irina will try to spoil his aim."

Another tiny nod, it was time, I brought up the pistol and shot the first man in the stomach, the other two started bringing up their guns but I shot both of them in quick succession, all three were down and Bauer sprinted forward with his combat knife out. Mundt and Wesserman had rushed over to help Irina with the leader, Petro. As I'd hoped, she'd held his arm, stopping him from aiming the weapon, but with an angry shout he threw her off, brought up his PPSh, and pointed it directly at her to kill her, shouting curses in Ukrainian. I knew it was too late when the noise of a volley of automatic fire split the night, but Petro merely toppled, shredded by the 7.62mm Soviet bullets. Bauer had snatched up one of the weapons from the felled partisans and pulled the trigger, in an instant stopping Petro.

We stood frozen for a few moments with the sudden violence that had come to this backstreet bar, our near brush with death, before we came to life again. Mundt and Bauer checked the bodies of the partisans, one of them had our pistols in his backpack and Bauer retrieved them and handed them back to us. Astonishingly, Petro was still alive. When I stood over him he stared back at me with hate-filled eyes. He tried to say something, but blood was oozing out of his mouth and eventually he gave a loud sigh and his eyes closed forever.

"Irina, thank you for helping us." I said. "He nearly killed you."

She was trembling. She must have expected her body to be riddled with bullets from Petro's gun. She tried to speak but couldn't get her words out.

"Would you like me to take you home?"

She nodded. Mundt was holstering his pistol, still holding one of the PPShs.

"Scharfuhrer, give me one of those, just in case they have any friends around the corner. I'll see Irina to her home and try to catch our lift back later. You know where to meet the truck?"

"Midnight, same place as he dropped us off."

"Yes, you'd better give him this."

I handed him the Nagant M1895. "If I don't get back you can tell him it came in useful but it may need reloading."

"You'll be ok?"

"Yes, but cover for me if I'm delayed. We'll go out through the bar, I don't want anyone thinking that a bunch of partisans got the better of the SS."

We walked through the back door and into the bar. The whole place went silent when they saw us carrying the partisans PPShs. The message was obvious, stay away from the Waffen-SS. Our drinks were still on the table, we picked them up and calmly finished them off to make the point.

"We'll stay here for a while, I should think it's safe now," Mundt said, "I'll see you later."

I took Irina's arm to take her home. The band was taking a break and the barman had the radio on listening to the news from Radio Kiev, a Ukrainian station approved by the German occupiers.

"Here is the news on May 13, 1943. The war in North Africa is over. German and Italian forces have surrendered to the Allies in Tunisia, ending the campaign of Rommel's Afrika Corps."

I felt all eyes in the bar on me. Much of the Ukraine was nominally sympathetic to the German cause, having suffered so many years of famine and purges at the hands of Stalin. However, this was the second major defeat of German arms, following so closely the surrender at Stalingrad three months before. Our next major test of arms was about to occur in the Kursk salient, I had seen the massive preparation of both sides. We couldn't afford to lose another big battle. The collapse of morale after Stalingrad was palpable, like a damp fog settling all around us. If we lost here, I doubted the ability of our troops to carry on. It could be the beginning of the end of our efforts to conquer the Soviet Union.

"Let's go, I don't want to hear any more of this," I said to Irina.

She moved closer to me, as if to give me some comfort at such a miserable time. She still hadn't spoken to me, she looked pale and I could feel her body trembling. It was an astonishing change from the girl who had guided us into the Soviet sector so confidently, who then seemed to turn away from the company of men for the voluptuous Ukrainian girl we had brought back with us. More than anything I pitied her, she should have been dating a boy, or perhaps a girl in a university bar, not dodging bullets and having to see bodies piled on bodies in her own backyard. We threaded though the dark streets, when we reached a junction she pulled me in the direction of her home, but still she didn't speak. We walked along deserted streets, past parked Panzers, waiting silently for the coming battle. Finally we turned into a cul-de-sac on the outskirts of the city, she opened a gate, and we walked up the path to her front door. The house was in darkness, but most houses in Kharkov were without lights, even those that possessed them didn't want to attract the bombers or the artillery shells. I let her arm go and said goodnight, then turned away to go back to my unit. Only then did she speak.

"Jurgen. Please, stay with me tonight."

I considered for half a second at most. Heterosexual, lesbian, bisexual, I didn't really care. It was true. In war you took what you could get. Just before we went inside I heard a massive, low rumble, like the sound of engines. We both looked up, but there were no signs of any aircraft. The wind had changed direction to blow from the east, the noise was tank engines warming up, Russian tank engines from inside the salient, hundreds of them, perhaps thousands. I looked eastwards, but there was nothing to see, the Russians were probably making the noise at night to unsettle us and lower our morale, they were masters of psychological warfare. Their point was well made, they were there, ready for us, thousands of tanks and guns, mines and traps waiting for us to come to them.

CHAPTER THREE

'With amazement and disappointment, we discovered in late October and early November that the beaten Russians seemed quite unaware that as a military force they had almost ceased to exist'.

General Blumentritt

I never found out where her family were, but Irina's house was empty. She led me up to her bedroom and left me for a few moments. When she came back, she was naked. I kissed her, tasting her warm lips, our tongues intertwining while my hands caressed her breasts and felt around her body and she stiffened as my hand slipped between her legs. She was touching my body, a soft, tantalising touch that I found shockingly arousing, then began to stroke my penis. I was hard and erect, all thoughts of the war had fled and I gently probed between her legs and touched inside her. She was wet, soaking with the wetness of her own arousal, she moaned as I pushed my fingers in further and then lifted her onto the bed, one hand behind her back, the other pushed inside her. She pulled me down onto her and guided me into her, then we made love, not the gentle erotic exploration of two new lovers but the animal need of two of war's victims. It was harsh, rough and incredibly exciting. Soon, she was screaming, or maybe it was both of us and within a few short minutes we both reached an orgasm. We lay together holding each other, saying nothing. For two hours we were silent, there was nothing to say, the night had brought us its quota of blood and death and our sexual union was just a way of blotting out the terrible realities of those four corpses lying bloodied and broken against the wall behind the bar. Still without a word she started to kiss me, then bent down to lick my body until she reached my groin and took me into her mouth, sucking until I became hard again. I reached for her and stroked her, we made love again, but this time we had spent the bitter anger, stress and frustration of the war, and we wanted more, an emotional bonding. We gently gyrated our hips and I pumped in and out of her, perhaps half an hour elapsed before she reached a climax and I had my second orgasm of the night. After holding her to me for another ten minutes I gently removed her arm and got up.

"Irina, I have to get back, otherwise I will be disciplined for desertion. I'm sorry."

"You remind me of Bizet's opera, Carmen," she said with humour in her voice. "You know, when Jose, the corporal, has to leave Carmen to go back on duty. She tries to persuade him to desert, would you like me to try to persuade you too?"

"Did the opera end well?"

"Not really, no, she finds another lover, the toreador and Jose kills her in the final act."

"Perhaps I'd better go back then. Irina, I'd like to look you up again when I get back into the city."

"Are you sure? Tonight was just desperation, Jurgen, two people in each other's warmth."

"I'm sure. How do I contact you?"

"You can get a message to me at that bar we were in, it is called The Dive. They will pass a message."

"I'll do that."

I kissed her and we held each other briefly, then I went down the stairs, out of the house and found my way back to the city centre. I checked my watch, it was nearly four in the morning, and I had time to get back if I could find a lift. I started walking out of the city I was lucky, there was an incredible roaring noise and a clatter of tracks. I turned to see a Tiger tank rumbling towards me along the main street. It stopped alongside me and the commander looked down.

"We're headed to Podvirky, do you need a lift?"

"That's marvellous."

I climbed up onto the hull of the Tiger and clung to the barrel of the machine gun. The commander gave an order into his microphone and the tank started forward again.

"How did you know where I was going?" I asked him, shouting above the roar of the engine.

He laughed. "There are only two destinations in this direction, Podvirky or Germany. I assume you're not deserting?"

"The only thing I'm deserting is a beautiful girl tucked up in bed!"

He nodded. "I thought that might be the case. What are you doing at the railway, anti-partisan duties?"

"We are yes, at least, until the battle starts. Why are you taking this tank to Podvirky, surely it came from there only recently?"

"It did, yes. The turret mechanism is faulty so they're sending another one in. It's due some time today. We'll just use the railway crane to swing this one off and the new one in place. It's the easiest way. Damn turrets weigh a lot, they're not easy to transport."

"It's lucky for me you came along, there's not much traffic on the road at night."

"It's the damned partisans, they come out like rats in the darkness. Have you had any brushes with them?"

"Some, yes," I admitted, but I didn't want to give him

any details, it had been a strange night. A night of warm companionship and then sudden violence, blood and death, followed by sex with a girl who I had thought was a lesbian. Yet strange didn't seem a word strong enough to describe it. Outlandish possibly. Surreal definitely.

I thanked him and jumped off near our quarters, the half-ruined isba. I managed to get an hour's sleep, then the noise of the camp woke me, men shouting, engines starting up, a railway engine's steam whistle sounding, the crash of ramps as they started to unload the first of the new Tigers that had arrived. I put my head under the cold-water pump in the yard and tried to clear my tired brain. After breakfast I reported to HQ for orders. There was no sign of von Meusebach so I spoke to Muller, once again the second in command. He handed me my typed up report and I was about to sign it when something in his eyes made me look at it again. It had been subtly altered to give the impression that von Meusebach was actually leading the patrol, not tucked up in his bed.

"I can't sign this, it's nonsense."

Muller sighed. "I think you should reconsider, Hoffman, he can make all our lives difficult if we don't carry out his wishes. It's only a damned report, for God's sake."

"It's only a damned lie," I replied quietly, but I knew I had no choice and I scrawled my signature.

"We've got more Tigers and a couple of the new Panzer V tanks due in today, it'll be a bitch getting them unloaded just as we were getting used to rolling the Tigers off and changing their tracks. Now we have a new set of problems, why the hell they don't settle on one good tank design I don't know. The Tiger is a real winner, the finest armour on the whole of the Eastern Front."

His second in command, Glasser, coughed to interrupt him. "Sir, they say that these new Panzers Vs are even better than the Tiger, much better performance, better armour, they're very good, so they say."

Muller grunted. "That's just propaganda, Glasser. I've heard that they're unreliable and don't pack the punch of the Tiger, although they're faster, I grant you. No damned good being fast if you've broken down, is it?"

"I'm sure they'll sort out the problems, Obersturmbannfuhrer."

"They need to, that's for sure. Why are they delaying the attack, Glasser? The ground is drying up, we should be attacking now, not sitting here on our backsides tangling with partisans."

"We may not attack at all if we don't find out who is passing information to the enemy, Muller."

We all looked up as two men walked through the door, two men I recognised. SD Obersturmbannfuhrer Walter von Betternich and Gestapo Kriminalkommissar Gerd Wiedel.

"What do you mean?" Muller asked.

"It's quite simple, we believe that someone is passing

information on our entire order of battle, unit dispositions, in fact we believe that the entire Operation Zitadelle could be at risk if we can't plug the leak."

I was mystified. "Operation Zitadelle?"

"Yes, Zitadelle," Muller said irritably. "I suppose there's no reason why you shouldn't know, it is the name of the operation to eliminate the bulge in the lines between Orel and Kharkov, the Kursk salient, so that we can shorten the front line. Once we have taken Kursk we can continue the drive to Moscow."

Von Betternich nodded. "Yes, Model's 9th Army will attack southwards from Orel whilst Hoth's 4th Panzer Army and Army Group Kempf will attack northwards from here at Kharkov. The two armies will meet near Kursk but if the offensive goes well, the armies would have permission to continue eastward on their own initiative. With luck we can establish a new line at the Don River, much nearer to Moscow."

He looked at us. "The problem is that if we can't find the traitor, we may have to delay the offensive indefinitely. I need hardly tell you that the Fuhrer is unhappy, most unhappy. He's threatened to send every last member of the Intelligence units to the front armed with only a shovel."

"Are you sure that someone is passing information to the Russians?" Muller asked.

"We've intercepted the signals, there can be no doubt. We can still retrieve the situation, there's much that the

Russians don't know, but first we have to find the traitor. Muller, I will be needing an escort, can you release Hoffman and some men of his platoon again?"

"You'll need to clear it with the new CO. We're struggling to cope with the partisan attacks, they're a real threat, not some mythical traitor that may or may not exist."

"Von Meusebach will not object, I have an direct order from the Reichsfuhrer SS. Hoffman, I trust you have no objections?"

I hesitated. If there was anyone I'd like to hunt down and shoot it was von Betternich himself, but I was trapped by SS discipline, and by the oath I'd taken to the Fuhrer when I was commissioned.

"No, Sir."

The SD officer was smiling broadly, I'd worked with him before and discovered that he had an uncanny ability to virtually read minds, probably because of his long experience as a Berlin policeman. He stared at me silently for a few moments until I began to feel uncomfortable.

"You blame me for that Jewess, don't you, Hoffman?"

"Do I, Sir?"

"You know damn well you do, man. Listen, even if she was the sister of the Fuhrer, God forbid, once she was found out to be a Jewess using false papers stolen from an Aryan German there was only one possible way it could end. Were you in love with her?"

"That's none of your business," I muttered.

"In the case of an SS officer enjoying a relationship with a Jewess it is emphatically my business, but I'll take that as a yes. I'm afraid you must put that behind you, my friend, we have important work to do, far more important than any Jewess, in fact more important than anything else on this front. This spy is forwarding our communications and plans to Stalin almost as quickly as our own commanders are informed. Have you heard of the name 'Lucy'?"

I shook my head.

"That is the name by which this group of people are known, we have no idea why. Perhaps it is a woman named Lucy who controls the group or perhaps it is something else. Last year we arrested a number of people involved in a spy ring called 'Die Rote Kapelle', the Red Orchestra. We were lucky, in July the Gestapo uncovered a radio operator named Johann Wenzel and it all started to unravel from there. That was when we first heard of this Lucy spy ring, but we have made little progress in identifying them. Until now, that is, when we made the connection between Army Group South and the plans for Zitadelle. As soon as the message was passed to von Manstein's Headquarters the Russians began reinforcing key areas in the Kursk salient, areas that exactly match the points we planned to attack. It is too great a coincidence, they must have been told our exact intentions."

"Does that mean the attack may be cancelled?"

Wiedel the Gestapo man, pointed at one of the maps

on the wall. "Look at this, Hoffman. The salient more than doubles the length of our front line and we don't have enough troops and tanks to defend it all, let alone restart our offensive on Moscow. Cancelling the attack is out of the question, but it is not too late to modify the plans, provided we can stop this Lucy spy ring. If they find out we have changed our plans they will just re-site their defences and we'll fall into the trap. We have to find the traitor!"

"You must put aside your anger at what happened to your girlfriend and put all of your efforts into catching this spy," von Betternich continued. "It is more important than any of us, Hoffman."

"What do you want me to do?"

If the Russians knew in advance where we were to attack the result would be unthinkable, tens of thousands of men wiped out unnecessarily. I'd put the business with Heide out of my mind, there would be a time and place later when I would settle accounts.

"We have a funkwagen, a radio detection truck in Kharkov. We know that the transmissions are made after dark, between the hours of nine and ten o'clock, so that's when we shall concentrate our efforts. To begin with, I want you and three of your men to follow the van at a discreet distance and be ready to go in and make the arrest if they detect any transmissions. You can use a Kubelwagen to get into the city. I'll give you the requisition before you go. We will need to visit Army Group South Headquarters at Vinnitsa too. There are some enquiries that I need to make there."

I was surprised. "Surely security at Army Group South is locked up tight, I can't imagine that the leak could come from there."

He smiled. "Security is so tight that only five weeks ago there was a plot to assassinate the Fuhrer at Feldmarschal von Kluge's Army Group Centre in Smolensk. We understand that it was only luck that prevented the bomb from going off. "

"The Fuhrer? That's unbelievable! Did you arrest the people responsible? Was it a Soviet spy?"

"It was no Soviet, it was a group of our own officers, they planted a bomb in a case of champagne, when the bomb failed to explode they managed to retrieve the bomb, so we have no direct evidence. We haven't arrested them yet, we are still making enquiries."

I was about to question him more, it was very, very odd that an assassination attempt against Adolf Hitler would not be investigated and concluded immediately. There was only one answer, the answer that bedevilled every aspect of German life, politics. It meant that for some reason they did not want to look too closely. Did someone want the Fuhrer dead? No, that would be too incredible.

"You are surprised that our own officers would make an attempt on the Fuhrer's life, are you not?" von Betternich continued.

I nodded.

"There have been at least thirty attempts on the life of the Fuhrer in the past ten years, almost all from his own people. However, that is not your concern. This Lucy spy ring takes priority over everything else. Is that clear?"

I nodded.

He handed me an official SD document. "This is a requisition for the vehicle. Report to the Gestapo office in Kharkov with three of your men at eight thirty, in time to accompany the radio truck. That's all."

I found the platoon and gave them the good news. Most of them groaned.

"Do we still have to mount the anti-partisan patrols," Mundt asked.

I nodded. "I'm afraid so, yes, I doubt that von Meusebach will relieve us of that duty. I need three volunteers to come with me tonight."

As expected, Willy Mundt put up his hand. Bauer and Wesserman volunteered too, but that left a problem. Who would be in charge of my platoon in the absence of myself, and my sergeant, Scharfuhrer Mundt? The best junior NCO was Beidenberg and he'd performed well lately.

"Sturmann Beidenberg, you will take over the platoon while we're away, I'm promoting you to Unterscharfuhrer as from this moment. I'll need to get it confirmed, but in the meantime, congratulations."

He broke out in a broad grin and the men patted him on the back, there were no sour faces so I thought I'd probably made the right decision.

"Willy, here's the requisition for the Kubi, would you collect it after lunch and get it checked over, make sure the tank is full of petrol and so on. If they detect this damn spy I don't want to find that the engine won't start when they ask us to go in and arrest him."

He took the document. "I'll take care of it."

"Good. We're due back at the railway siding, they're bringing in more armour today, there's also an ammunition train due in. Muller wants tight security when it turns up, if the partisans hit the ammunition it'll blow up half the town."

Someone murmured 'and good riddance' but I ignored it. We walked over to the railway line, it was empty but already tank crews and mechanics were assembling. In the distance a plume of smoke gave advance warning of the arrival of the train. It gave the Soviets ample warning too, as the train came into view a flight of Sturmoviks came roaring overhead, they'd crossed the lines at low level and followed the railway track. Abruptly the peaceful countryside marshalling yard descended into chaos.

The anti-aircraft guns were the first to respond, streams of tracer bullets and cannon fire arced up towards the aircraft. The first Sturmovik reached the train and two bombs detached from under the wings and straddled two Tigers sitting impotently on the flatcars, still several hundred metres from the unloading point. The bombs sent up showers of earth and stones but appeared to do little damage. There were four Sturmoviks, the second fared no better than the first but the third scored a direct hit on the train, the flat car lurched off the track and the Tiger slid down to one side. The fourth Sturmovik dropped its bombs nearer the engine, obviously intending to strand the train so that a further raid would finish it off. The bombs dropped almost next to the train, one missed completely, the other smashed into the coal tender and started a fire in the combined coal and oil tanks. Muller shouted at us.

"Get that tender disconnected so they can move the train clear! The rest of you start unloading those Panzers. Hurry, before the next attack comes in!"

We started forward, but Mundt stopped me. "They'll need oxy-acetylene to cut the tender away from the engine, there's a set in the mechanic's workshop."

"What are we waiting for, Willy? Let's go."

He led the way and I followed the men into the old barn that served as a workshop. Next to the bench were two tall, heavy steel cylinders and a set of long, rubber pipes, ending with a heavy brass nozzle. They were mounted on a trolley, Mundt shouted orders and the men half rolled, half carried the equipment across the rough ground. The stricken tender was blazing, tethered at each end to both the engine and the long train behind, locked by a tangle of steel couplings. The anti-aircraft guns started firing again and I looked up, the Sturmoviks were coming back to strafe the area, they'd offloaded their bombs, now they wanted to deliver the coup-de-grace.

"Take cover, the Sturmoviks are back," I shouted.

The men threw themselves to the ground but some were too slow as the Russians machine-gunned the area remorselessly. They were armed with two fixed forward-firing 23mm cannons, two 7.62mm machine guns and a 12.7mm machine gun in the rear cockpit. It was enough to cause massive death and destruction, bullets and cannon fire swept across the railway yard like a tornado, men flung bloodied and broken to the ground, buildings and vehicles riddled with bullets and torn apart by cannon fire. The anti-aircraft guns scored a hit, one of the Ilyushin IL-2s went down in flames to the four-barrelled 2cm Flakvierling 38. Mounted on one of the flatcars it was a fearsome anti-aircraft weapon, sending streams of heavy calibre shells up at enemy aircraft. As the Russian dived into the ground the others turned away to head back east. The Flakvierling switched targets and managed to score a hit on another Sturmovik, but the aircraft was heavily armoured and was able to make its escape, trailing smoke. I stood up to survey the damage. The biggest problem was the tender. It was burning fiercely, threatening to overwhelm the engine.

"Willy, get that cutting equipment over there fast, the

rest of you, grab the fire extinguishers, we haven't got much time!"

It was hard dragging the heavy gas cylinders over the rough ground but we made it at the same time as the men ran up with the extinguishers. They sprayed water and foam over the area of the coupling while Mundt got the cutting equipment started. He waded through water, smoke and flames until he was at the coupling. While he burned through the heavy steel, we kept the extinguishers playing over Mundt and the area he was working in, but it was obvious that we didn't have enough capacity to keep going for long, already one of the extinguishers had run out. I looked up seeking inspiration and noticed the trickle of steam coming from the engine. Of course, steam, water, they went together, didn't these huge steam engines carry water tanks?

I leapt up onto the engine, the heat intense even though it was several metres from the fire. The engineers looked startled.

"We need water on the coupling to protect the man trying to cut the engine free, do you have a hose connected to your water tank?"

They looked at each other. One of them shrugged, "Sure, we've got the drain hose." He nodded to the other man. "Hans, hook it up and spray water on the flames. We can't use too much of our water, Obersturmfuhrer, otherwise we won't have enough to get up steam."

I sighed with exasperation. They'd stood watching the flames threatening their engine and done nothing while they had a tank full of cold water and a hose.

"If we won't get that fucking tender uncoupled you won't have any need to get up steam," I shouted at them. "We need to get that fire put out!"

Hans connected a long piece of rubber hose to a nozzle and the engineer turned a steel valve. Water poured out and he started to spray the tender.

"Cover the coupling with water, that's where my Scharfuhrer is working to cut you free," I shouted. He redirected the hose and steam rose in the air as the water hit the hot metal, but it was enough, I jumped down and saw that Mundt had nearly cut through the steel. It only took another four minutes and the steel coupling dropped free. I shouted up to the locomotive and told the crew to move their engine away from the train. There was a hiss of steam and the great locomotive started forward, picking up speed until it was away from the immediate danger zone. Once they got to Kharkov there would be more anti-aircraft fire to protect them. Some of the other soldiers had started to form a bucket chain, together with some Hiwis they passed buckets of water along the line and poured them onto the burning coal tender.

"Willy, leave it to them, they've got the fire under control, we need to help unload the armour, we're not safe yet, the Reds may be back."

We started on the first of the flatcars with the tank perched helplessly its length, impotent until they were unloaded and on the ground. Even with the special narrow tracks for rail transport they were vast, steel giants of the battlefield with the immense 88mm gun pointing rearwards. The crews were waiting for us, they had taken shelter inside the tank and battened down the hatches when the air attack started but now they came out to help us unload.

"Willy, we need the unloading ramps in the yard, can you take some men and bring them," I said to Mundt. "You'll probably need more men to help." He nodded.

I didn't envy them their work, the ramps were huge lengths of steel, massively heavy that they positioned for the tanks to roll off the flatcars. While he went to bring the ramps we continued preparing the Tiger. With a roar, the engine started and as we released the last of the security chains, the driver slewed the giant vehicle around, locking one track and driving around with the other until it pointed at ninety degrees to the side of the flatcar, as Mundt came up with the ramps. There were ten men to each of the long lengths of steel. They positioned them under the Tiger tracks, hooking them over the lip of the flatcar. Mundt waved to the tank commander and we jumped clear as the driver engaged the gears and gently drove his Panzer onto the ground. He waved a thank you as he went past and I looked at Mundt who had come up beside me. One side of his scalp was almost bald where the fire had burned away his hair and his uniform was charred and ripped.

"That was damned fine work, Willy, we could have lost the engine."

He shrugged. "It was nothing, someone had to do it, Sir."

"But the someone was you, Willy, I'm putting you in for a medal, you could have burned to death."

"Put someone else in for a medal, Sir, I'm not interested in all of that fuss," he said, but I could see that he was both embarrassed and proud of the praise for his courage. We looked around as the yard supervisor came running up to us, a tubby, bald German railway worker who had undoubtedly been promoted several times above his abilities just because he was a civilian who had volunteered for service in Russia. He may have been brave, but his management skills were not in evidence.

"What are you men doing standing there idling? The rest of the Panzers need to be unloaded, you soldiers are all the same, lazy swines! Hurry up!"

The only sign that he had been involved was the sheen of sweat on his forehead and baldpate. Other than that his uniform was unmarked. I couldn't help it, I swung at him and connected with his jaw, a punch that sent him sprawling to the ground. Mundt and I bent down to pick him back up and I put my face next to his.

"Listen to me you little piece of shit, while you were hiding from the air attack my men were fighting the fire and risking their lives to release the locomotive and begin unloading the tanks. You talk to another of my men like that and I'll have you drafted into the SS and sent to the front."

He tried to get away, I could feel him trembling, but we had a firm hold of him.

"Do you hear me, answer me?" I shouted.

"Yes, yes, my apologies."

"Go away and do your job then."

We released him and I gave him a push that almost sent him sprawling again. He regained his balance and walked hurriedly away.

"I'm not sure you should have done that, Sir," Mundt said, but he was smiling.

"Nasty little bureaucrat, skulking in the rear areas is one thing but insulting the soldiers that do the fighting is another, it's unacceptable. But I'm afraid he's right in one respect, we do need to make better progress on unloading these tanks."

We called the men to move the ramps to the next flatcar and continued with the heavy, backbreaking work of unloading the armour. At one stage we had a scare when we heard the roar of aero engines, but this time it was the Luftwaffe. I heard someone shout, "It's about damned time. We never see them these days!"

The commander of a Tiger we were unloading leaned down. "It's not always their fault, they're short of everything. Pilots, aircraft, ammunition, everything! Petrol is the worst, we only have enough to drive these tanks fifty kilometres."

"You can't be serious? You'll barely get to the front with that amount of fuel, surely they're refuelling you before you deploy?"

He shrugged. "We hope so, but if not they'll have to drain the tanks of the more obsolete tanks to fill our own, it's getting critical."

"What are they doing with the petrol, I thought we had plenty of fuel?"

"We've never had plenty it's always been a problem for tanks and aircraft because we burn so much. We failed to take the Caucasus oilfields and apart from that small oilfield at Maikop we haven't had the success we needed in finding oil. They've even tried making synthetic fuel from coal, but it's not entirely successful, most of our shortfall is brought in from Romania. Even the Romanians are not so free with their supplies these days, they still blame the Fuhrer for leaving their troops in the lurch at Stalingrad."

"How will you cope in the coming offensive?"

"They'll bring in supplies from somewhere, I expect, they always do, but it will mean taking it from somewhere else where it's not needed as much."

Mundt grimaced. "What a way to fight a war. They

can always use the Tigers as fixed artillery if they get desperate."

"If that becomes necessary, we ought to use the new Panther V tanks in that role," the commander laughed. "They've had problem after problem, they still haven't worked out how to stop the engines catching fire."

Mundt and I exchanged glances. The tanker was describing an army in chaos with massive shortages, unreliable armour and even now the Luftwaffe failed to defend the vital railhead. We worked on until the last of the Tigers was unloaded and finally went back to our HQ to find food in the cookhouse. There was silence while we ate, the combination of exhaustion after the efforts together with the terrible picture painted by the Tiger commander left us all dispirited. None of us wanted to say the unthinkable, that the war was at risk of being lost, here, in the smoking pyre of the Eastern Front. We'd seen massively increased numbers of Soviet aircraft overhead and more frequent absences of the Luftwaffe. We'd suffered from artillery barrages as the Russians moved nearer to our positions and our guns seemed incapable of sufficiently accurate counter battery fire to deal with them, and we'd seen the massive reinforcements of tanks and men that the Soviets were bringing into the Kursk salient. Russia had rapidly become the most inhospitable, unwelcoming place on earth for us German soldiers, almost a graveyard. They could keep their Lebensraum, the living space that Adolf Hitler had espoused since the days of his book, Mein Kampf. They could keep their fields of wheat in the Ukraine, their oilfields and their massive mineral resources. We were coming to an end and a new mood of pessimism was sweeping through the German military. Even in our elite Waffen SS formations there were few who still believed that victory was possible. We could win an overwhelming victory in the Kursk salient, but if we didn't have enough petrol to drive on to Moscow, it would be a hollow victory indeed. But for most of us, the prospect of that victory was receding fast, it seemed that the best we could hope for was to minimise our losses. And what then? At that moment, I didn't believe many of us wanted to think the unthinkable.

I checked my watch, I had half an hour before we needed to drive to Kharkov for the first of our evening patrols with the funkwagen. I needed a clean uniform, we all stank of smoke, soot, coal and exhaust fumes. It would be uncomfortable spending the rest of the night like this, yet I'd used my only spare after von Meusebach's order to clean up. I'd have to manage with what I was wearing. We had no hot water so I stood naked in the yard at the back of the inn while Bauer played a cold stream of water on me from a hosepipe. I went back in feeling refreshed, although when I dressed in my dirty uniform I felt grimy again. At seven-thirty I joined Mundt, Bauer and Wesserman and we drove into Kharkov in the Kubelwagen with Bauer at the wheel. The city seemed ever more grey and dismal, even the bright spring evening couldn't add any lustre to the bomb damaged streets and buildings. There were soldiers everywhere, evidence of the build-up for the coming battle. We passed tanks, dozens of them, Tigers, Panthers and smaller, more obsolete models, most parked along the main streets as if their crews had driven them into the city for a shopping trip. We drove to the Gestapo Office and went around to the enclosed courtyard. The funkwagen was parked inside.

It was an Opel Blitz, normally used for transporting infantry and supplies, but this one had been converted to have a square, boxy cabin built on the back. On top of the cabin roof was a strange looking device, like a network of rods that had been assembled to make a giant frame. I knew the principle of how these things worked, the operator inside the cabin rotated the array on the roof, the stronger the radio signal the louder the tone heard inside the operator earphones. In this way he could guide the truck to the source of the radio signal. There was no sign of von Betternich, but when I went back around the front of the building Wiedel was waiting in the foyer.

"Hoffman, excellent, are you all ready?"

"What do you want us to do, Wiedel?"

His rank of Kriminalkommissar was the Gestapo equivalent of my SS rank, Obersturmfuhrer, the correct mode of address to an officer of the same rank was to use the surname.

"Follow the truck, don't let it out of your sight but try to be a little discreet. If there is a chance to catch these bastards in the act, I'd like to take it. Listen, if you do manage to grab anyone I want them taken alive, do you understand? There are many questions that we would like to put to this traitor who is sending our secrets to the enemy."

"I'll do my best."

We went back around the building and into the courtyard. The crew of the funkwagen, the radio truck, were warming up their equipment, the engine was running and someone inside was doing something with the radio, periodically the aerial array rotated and we could hear strange crackling and squealing noises. The operator finally peered out of the door and looked at Wiedel.

"It's all functioning, Sir, if he transmits we'll get him."

"Very well, it's almost time, you may as well proceed."

We followed the radio truck in the Kubelwagen. It was a boring hour spent slowly following the lumbering truck as it attempted to sniff out the radio signals of an enemy spy. At the end of the hour we seemed to have seen every dingy back street in the city, every burnt out building, as well as numerous prostitutes lounging on the street corners waiting for trade. The funkwagen eventually drove back to Gestapo HQ and we parked nearby. The Kriminalassistent in charge of the radio came across to us.

"Not a whisper tonight, I'm afraid. We'll try again tomorrow, maybe we'll have better luck."

I nodded and wished him a good night. We climbed into the Kubelwagen and started out of the city back to Podvirky. We almost ran into a young woman who was stumbling along the road, Bauer halted the vehicle. At the last moment I had recognised Irina.

"Jurgen, thank God, I need you to help me!"

She was dishevelled, her face streaked with dirt and tears, her clothes obviously thrown on quickly as her coat wrongly buttoned.

"Irina, what's wrong, why on earth are you running along the road at this time of night?"

"It's my parents," she said, "they have been arrested!"

"You mean the police?"

"No, it was an SS police unit, they called themselves Einsatzgruppe C."

I felt a sense of foreboding. Most of us knew of the Einsatzgruppen and what we knew was nothing good. They were the very dark side of the SS and most of us in the Waffen SS wished that they wore a different uniform. This group was based in an old school close to Gestapo HQ, Kharkov.

"Irina, there's nothing I can do tonight, you must get home. I'll find out what is happening tomorrow and let you know. Please, go home now. We'll give you a lift, you shouldn't be out on your own on a dark country road."

She nodded her agreement, climbed in and squeezed next to me. She held my hand tightly all the way back to her house, as she got out she looked at me with huge, damp eyes.

"Jurgen, please do what you can to get them out, they haven't done anything wrong."

I kissed her and promised to do my best, but as we drove back to Podvirky I had a feeling that it may not be enough.

On the way back we passed more lines of Panzers, assault guns and hundreds of support vehicles, limbers for the field guns, half-tracks, armoured reconnaissance vehicles, trucks and motorcycles. It seemed that every tracked and wheeled vehicle on the Eastern Front was here, waiting. I had no doubt that inside the Kursk salient the mechanised forces of the Red Army would be similarly prepared, together with their colossal reserves of infantry, minefields and tank traps that they were strengthening and extending every day. The men looked at them silently as we rolled past, the question on their minds the same as the question on the mind of every German soldier in this sector. When would we attack and why were we waiting when every day we waited was a gift to the Soviets?

CHAPTER FOUR

> *'The enemy holds every trump card, covering all areas with long-range air patrols and using location methods against which we still have no warning. The enemy knows all our secrets and we know none of his'.*
>
> *Grand Admiral Doenitz*

I'd split the platoon for the night patrols so that we would at least get sleep on alternate nights whilst we were doubling up with escort duty for the Gestapo funkwagen. Mundt took the men out and got back in the early hours without incident. In the morning I found an excuse to go back into Kharkov, Bauer drove the Kubelwagen and I went to the Einsatzgruppe C building. When I walked in there was no sentry, not even anyone walking around the corridors. I heard voices coming from behind a closed door, knocked, and walked in. The Sturmbannfuhrer who sat behind the desk looked up, surprised to see a visitor. Two other soldiers were in the office, an Obersturmfuhrer and an NCO, a Scharfuhrer. I saluted.

"Sir, I've come to enquire about the parents of a friend of mine. Mr and Mrs Rakevsky, you arrested them yesterday."

He picked up a clipboard from his desk and looked through several sheets of paper. "Yes, that's correct, they were picked up in an anti-partisan sweep. What do you want to know?"

"It's a mistake. Their daughter has acted as a guide for my Waffen SS unit, taking us into enemy territory. The whole family are friends of the Third Reich, they are definitely not partisans."

He shrugged. "So? What do you expect me to do about it?"

The two other men both laughed, when I looked at them closer I could see they were very scruffy, unshaven and flabby, more like concentration camp guards than front line troops.

"What I'd like is for you to release them to my custody, Sir. I'll have a word with them, but as I say, they are not partisans."

He stood up, hands on hips, looking angry. "Look, Obersturmfuhrer, I don't know what kind of war you are fighting here, but our job is to deal ruthlessly with partisans.

That means making arrests and carrying out sentences straight away. It's a hard, dirty, dangerous business and we don't mess around. As soon as we knock down one partisan unit, there's another one to be dealt with around the corner, so we have to move fast."

"I'm sorry, I don't understand." There was something in his voice, the way he spoke, a kind of subtext, a hidden meaning.

"Then I'll make it clear to you. We arrested them for treason and sabotage. They were both shot an hour later. Was there anything else you wanted?"

"Shot? Are you sure?"

He sneered. "We always shoot traitors immediately, my friend. Why would we waste time on them?"

I walked out of their building in a daze. It was wrong, terribly wrong, but what could I do about it? I was close to Gestapo HQ, on an impulse I went inside. They showed me through to Kriminalkommissar Wiedel.

"Ah, Hoffman, no luck on the wireless detection?"

"Not yet, no. I've come to see you about Einsatzgruppe C."

He looked up warily. "They're not the best people to tangle with. What have they done now?"

I explained about Irina's parents. "She helped us, guided my platoon across enemy lines, now this."

"Hoffman, it's way above my jurisdiction. The Einsatzgruppen were created under the direction of

SS-Obergruppenfuhrer Reinhardt Heydrich and they're separate from the Gestapo, a different department. Since Heydrich's death, RSHA has kept tight control of them. Their principal task as you know is to deal with the Jews, gypsies, partisans and Soviet political commissars. The important thing for you to bear in mind is that they are Reichsfuhrer Himmler's pet project. Nobody interferes with the Einsatzgruppen, nobody, they are almost a law unto themselves. Take my advice, leave this alone and get back to your unit."

"But surely there is something..."

"You haven't heard me," he interrupted, "they cannot be controlled. Even the Gestapo or the SD can't intervene, I'm afraid you just have to accept it, otherwise you'll find yourself under arrest and put in a camp, or worse. Look, they're both dead so forget it, go back to Podvirky."

I got up and stormed out of his office. It wasn't his fault. It was the fault of the whole, rotten Nazi system that I was fighting for.

We Germans were an advanced civilisation. We had music, philosophy, science and a world of culture behind us. Why were we allowing these murderers and thugs to blaze a trail of wanton death and destruction amongst the civilian population? Wasn't it enough that we were fighting at the front, where at least it was soldiers fighting other soldiers? Did we have to go into innocent people's homes, drag them out, and murder them? For one mad moment I thought about making a formal complaint to Reichsfuhrer Himmler, but I recalled the fate of others who had criticised the Reich. The concentration camps were full of them. Instead, I asked Bauer to drive to Irina's house. She was at her home, still tearful and very pale.

"Jurgen, did you find anything out about my parents?"

I shook my head. "I did, yes, but it's not good, I'm so sorry!"

"You mean they have been sent to a camp?"

"No. No. They were shot."

She screamed with terrible anguish. Then she started beating me on the chest, punching me, she slapped me around the face. "You fucking Germans, you come here and invade my country, even when we try to help you all you can think to do is murder us. That is your culture, is it?"

"No, it is not, Irina, you should understand that..."

I didn't get any further.

"Get out, I never want to see you again! Don't come here! Don't ask for my help! Just go away. I hope the Russians come back and shoot you all. Go on, get out, now!"

Miserably I walked away, back to our Kubelwagen. Bauer gave me a sympathetic glance.

"Not good, Sir?"

"The worst it could possibly be, Stefan. Let's get back."

We returned to Podvirky and I spent the rest of the

day numbly supervising the men as they helped unload more armour from the flatcars, as we unloaded crates of armour-piercing ammunition. A funkwagen lumbered up and Wiedel climbed out.

"Hoffman, I'm glad I caught you, this is our new truck, we're working with two vehicles tonight, can you bring your men in straight away, we've got a lot of work to do."

"Sorry, Wiedel, I can't do that. We're too busy here. Why not ask your friends in the Einsatzgruppe to help you?"

He smiled. "Still bitter, eh? You know there's nothing we could have done about it. But I need you in the city, here is the order from von Betternich." He handed me a document. "You will see that it gives him total authority over you and your platoon, you can show it to the CO if you wish, but make it quick."

He drove off. The men were watching me carefully.

"I wouldn't push the Gestapo too far, Sir," Mundt said. "They can be touchy bastards at times."

"I don't care, Scharfuhrer, they can do their worst as far as I'm concerned, they're all a bunch of crooked thugs."

"No doubt they are and I'm sure you don't care. But we all have to be careful. Go easy on them."

I found von Meusebach in his HQ building. Outside, a trooper was busy polishing his black Mercedes. He was inspecting the map on the wall. He nodded as I saluted.

"Well?"

I handed him the order that Wiedel had given me. "They want my platoon in the city now, Sir."

He gave me a sharp look. "I can't spare one of my platoons just on the Gestapo's say so, Hoffman. Denied." He tossed the letter aside.

"I believe it's the Reichsfuhrer's say so," I replied, deadpan.

He looked at me suspiciously, snatched the letter up and reread it.

"I see. You'd better hurry then."

"Yes, Sir."

I gave him a perfect salute and walked out of the building. I was still angry at the way he'd altered my report to suggest that he had been in action. It was by no means unknown, senior officers taking credit for the actions of their juniors, but it was regarded with distaste by all ranks. I had other problems on my mind, though, Mundt was right. Whatever difficulty I had with the Gestapo, the SD or the Einsatzgruppen, I should be careful not to push them too far, they made dangerous enemies, much more so than the Soviets. We drove past the street where Irina lived and I felt even more miserable, but it was too late to do anything about it, they were dead and she hated me for it. When we reached Gestapo HQ both funkwagens were in the courtyard, both had their engines idling quietly. Von Betternich was talking to Wiedel, the two men walked over and I saluted.

"Hoffman, one of the funkwagens is going out north of the city, the other to the south, each will be stationed about ten kilometres away. Both trucks are in direct radio contact so if we do get a fix on a transmission we can pin the location down in seconds. Wiedel is in the northbound truck, can you send two of your men with him, we'll go south and you can follow with your men."

I detailed Mundt and Wesserman to go with Wiedel, they climbed into the back of the truck. I would go with Voss and Bauer in the Kubelwagen. We left the courtyard in convoy, when we reached the main crossing point next to Kharkov Central Square Wiedel's truck peeled off and went north, we turned south. We drove out of the city and into the suburbs and then stopped on top of a low hill. Von Betternich climbed out of the truck and I joined him.

"We need to triangulate his position from here, as soon as he starts to transmit we'll get our first fix and then start to drive into the city. Wiedel will be working on his own fix and will radio us when he has it, we mark it on the map and we have him."

I nodded and was about to join Bauer when he said, "Hoffman, I heard about the Einsatzgruppe, it was outside of our control, that problem with the girl's parents."

"It always is, I'm beginning to wonder who the real enemy is, Sir."

He stared at me coldly. "I suggest you keep that kind of thing to yourself." He looked up. "Ah, my radio operator is signalling, I think we may have some custom tonight."

He limped away and I went back to our Kubi. "Better get started, Stefan. They've got something coming in."

Von Betternich was waving and shouting at me and I went back over to the truck.

"Get in here, Hoffman, Wiedel has run into problems."

The operator passed me the headphones. I heard Wiedel's voice.

"We've run into the whole fucking Red Army, we're completely surrounded. Our truck crashed and overturned, I have two casualties, Scharfuhrer Mundt may have broken an ankle and my radio operator has broken legs and other injuries, neither is able to walk. We're at coordinates 50, 34, 66, please advise."

I looked at the large-scale map on the planning table. Von Betternich was already checking.

"I've found it here, a place called Velikyy Berlun," he said, pointing to spot on the map.

"But, that's behind Russian lines, they can't be there."

We checked the coordinates twice more, but it was inescapable. They were approximately five kilometres behind the Soviet front lines.

"Do you have any suggestions?" von Betternich asked me. For all of his police experience, he was out of his depth where front line operations were concerned.

"As far as I know, that area is occupied by Malinovski's 50th Army, there's something like twenty thousand men surrounding them. Perhaps surrender would be worthwhile considering."

"Surrender? An SS NCO and a Gestapo officer, you know what they'll do to them?"

The Russians shot most Gestapo and SS captives on sight, just as we did with their commissars and partisans.

"You're right, we'll have to help them. I can take a team in to try and bring them out, but it won't be easy."

I was calculating how we'd manage to get two wounded men across the lines, men who were unable to walk, when von Betternich spoke again.

"Make the arrangements. Hoffman. I imagine using a Kubelwagen is out of the question, it's going to be hard to get those injured men back?"

I smiled at him. "We wouldn't even get past the front line in any kind of a vehicle. What is really needed, and we don't have them, is horses. They can cross muddy ground at speed where nothing else can. Besides, if the Russians saw a cavalry unit moving they would assume it was their own Cossacks. However, in the absence of horses we'll just have to manage, I'd better go and inform Standartenfuhrer von Meusebach that we'll be crossing the line again." I started to walk back to our Kubelwagen but he called out and stopped me.

"We do have horses, Hoffman. A company of Cossacks surrendered to us during the battle for Kharkov. We have their horses and equipment in a stable near here."

I cursed myself for even mentioning horses. I'd intended it as an example of how the Soviets could move around in these awful conditions when we were usually stopped by soft, muddy ground. Even the Panzers bogged down on occasion.

"Well, Obersturmfuhrer, can you do it or not?"

"Let me see the horses. Bauer, Voss, you'd both better come with us."

We drove back into the city. We walked along a lane behind the Gestapo building and across a small, shabby square. An old fountain, long dried up, stood in the centre. Two ancient Ukrainian women enjoying the sunny evening sat outside a small house in one corner of the square, watching us carefully. Von Betternich limped forward and led us to a narrow track between a shuttered, half-ruined hardware and agricultural shop and a government office, its windows now shattered and broken office furniture littering the ground outside. Ten metres down the track there was the unmistakeable odour of horse dung. He opened a side door and strode in. A startled Unterscharfuhrer leapt up and stood to attention.

"Relax, Wegener, we're only here to look at the horses. Take us through, would you."

Wegener took us down a narrow corridor and through a door into the stable, which was surprisingly large and clean, better than our quarters, I thought ruefully.

"The local communist party elite used this place to

stable their horses before we arrived, so it's got the best of everything. Plenty of room for the horses, the only roof in Russia that doesn't leak and it has good drainage. What did you want, Sir?"

Von Betternich ignored him and we looked at the lines of animals. A Hiwi stood quietly grooming a magnificent chestnut brown Panje, it looked at me with mournful eyes. There were at least fifty horses in the stable, all were obviously well looked after and I wondered what they were used for. As if to read my mind the Unterscharfuhrer said, "They've been here for several weeks, they're kept here for the Brass to use, you know, the Prussian officer types who miss riding around their country estates."

"Well, what do you think?" von Betternich asked.

"They're certainly fine looking animals. I don't know, Voss, Bauer, either of you know anything about horses?"

I'd ridden horses when I was younger, many of us did, but what was being proposed now was something very different. Voss looked at me excitedly.

"I've done a fair bit of riding, Sir. They look like they'll do the job."

"Bauer, are you up to it?"

He nodded. "I've ridden a few horses, yes. There's one problem, Sir, we haven't a Russian speaker between us, it could make it difficult."

"I speak Russian," a voice said from behind us, we looked around. It was the Hiwi, a big, brawny man of about thirty-five. He had unkempt, wavy dark hair and a long, straggly beard that reminded me somewhat of the pictures of Rasputin. Grigori Rasputin was the Russian mystic who was perceived as having influenced the Emperor Nicholas II as well as his wife Alexandra and their only son Alexei. Rasputin had often been called the 'Mad Monk', while others considered him a 'strannik', a religious pilgrim as well as a psychic and faith healer. Maybe we could have done with the real Rasputin, we were definitely going to need some help to make a success of this foray behind the lines.

"Who are you?" I asked him. "A Russian?"

"My name is Felix Gusava, yes, I am Russian. I was conscripted into the Red Army, but I managed to escape and desert to your German army."

"So you've no liking for Stalin's regime, then, for Communism?"

He laughed. "For Stalin? I used to have a wife and two children. My wife tried to protest at the way some of her relations were treated. They were better-off peasants, you know, the Kulaks. They killed her."

I nodded. According to the political theory of Marx, the Kulaks were class enemies of the poorer peasants and were described by Lenin as bloodsuckers, vampires, plunderers of the people and profiteers, who fatten on famine. Marxism dictated a revolution that would liberate poor peasants and farm labourers alongside the industrial workers. It meant that the planned economy of Soviet Bolshevism required the collectivisation of farms and land to allow industrialisation of large-scale agricultural production, farms owned by the Kulaks. Stalin had a simple way to remove any obstacle to his Communist revolution. Mass murder.

"What about your children?"

"Taken by the local Communist Party bosses, they sent them away and I was never able to find out where. All I am left with is my hate."

I looked at Wegener. "Would you mind if I take your Hiwi, Unterscharfuhrer?"

"Not at all. Felix knows everything there is to know about horses, he will be valuable to you."

"Well, can you do it, Hoffman?" von Betternich said. "I'd like to get my men out."

"Yes, I'd like to get my own men out too. I'll give it a go, but time is wasting, we need to get started straight away. There'll be four of us and four men to bring out, Wiedel, Mundt, Wesserman and your radio operator."

"His name is Heinrich Foch, he is one of the most skilful radio men on the Eastern Front, possibly in Germany. He is very valuable."

"I'll do my best. We'll take ten horses, that'll give us two spares if one or two goes lame, or gets shot. Felix, would you saddle up your ten best, quickest mounts."

He nodded and went amongst the horses to start

preparing them.

"We'll need to let the Regiment know, Sturmbannfuhrer Muller, of course."

"I'll handle that when you've gone," von Betternich said. "What else do you need?"

"Extra ammunition for our machine pistols, hand grenades, that's about it. If we get into a running fight, we're finished anyway. You'll need to give Felix a sidearm, I notice he doesn't have one."

"Our policy is not to arm the Hiwis, Hoffman."

"I don't care. If he's going to risk his life, he'll need to be armed. He'll also need a machine pistol."

He nodded. "Anything else?"

"They'll have first aid supplies with them on the truck?"

"Yes, they will."

"In that case, we'll take rations for two days, that's about it. We need to get moving."

Twenty minutes later we were saddled up and the horses were loaded with supplies, even a Cossack sabre was strapped to the side of one of the saddles. Felix Gusava, now armed with a Walther PP pistol and an MP40 machine pistol, had chosen well. We had ten horses in prime condition, their coats gleaming, whatever else failed us on the mission it would not be the horses. Felix had contrived to ride the horse with the sabre strapped to the saddle. Maybe he had some Cossack blood in him? Or perhaps he just wanted use it to hack a way through the

Soviets. I'd need to watch him.

"I've requisitioned a motorcycle and sidecar to accompany you to the front, Hoffman. I'll be coming that far, I've brought your documentation. I don't want someone shooting at you before you even start."

I grinned at the thought of the SD man riding a motorcycle, but when the BMW R75 drew up he took the offered waterproof coat from the rider, buttoned himself into it, donned his steel helmet, and sat in the sidecar behind the machine gun. He looked at me and I nodded. He shouted to the motorcycle rider, "Let's go."

It was a hectic journey out through the suburbs of Kharkov and through the darkened countryside until we reached the front, the motorcycle kept the speed down but we still needed to canter the horses to keep up. A sentry stopped us and von Betternich showed him our papers. He waved us through and we found ourselves in a muddy farmyard. Two Wehrmacht officers came out of the farmhouse to meet us.

"We're from the Two Hundred and Fifty Fifth Infantry Division, this is Leutnant Moer and I'm Major Klement. We're scouting the area to look for potential attack routes for the Panzers. As far as we know there are no significant troop formations nearby."

We shook hands. "What about insignificant troop formations?" I asked them.

He smiled. "None, as far as we know."

"Very well, we'll go straight across. We'd better lead the horses on foot for the first stage, we can feel our way over and avoid any obvious problems."

"Good luck, Hoffman," von Betternich shook my hand.

I nodded. "We'll do our best."

I let Gusava lead the way. I'd forbidden them from wearing their helmets, or even carrying them, so as not to immediately give us away. Even so, a sentry that failed to recognise who we were would have to be blind, but it would perhaps give us a few seconds edge while they made up their minds. The horses snorted occasionally that could easily have alerted a Soviet sentry, but we hit no problems and no one challenged us. Once I judged we were well behind the lines we mounted the horses and rode towards our objective, the crashed funkwagen. We rode along a muddy track, the mud was about twenty centimetres deep and our horses were perfect for traversing its entire length, about three kilometres. At the end of the track we saw lights ahead, obviously an encampment and we dismounted and led the horses quietly in a wide circle away from the tents. Even had they heard us, it would be as I'd said, they would assume that it was one of their own patrolling Cossack units. We stayed off the track now, besides, there looked to be a whole army camped nearby. We could see hundred of tents, lines and lines of tanks, scores of trucks, obviously it was a combined arms unit which the Soviets used increasingly in this campaign. Instead of as our Panzer Grenadiers, some of their units relied on tank riders, troops who held on to purpose-built handholds on the T34s to ride into battle. I wasn't sure about the soundness of their philosophy, apart from becoming a target for enemy anti-tank fire, the T34s carried drums of diesel fuel on the tops of their hulls. When one of our shells hit the fuel the men were instantly transformed into flaming pyres, often the tank was destroyed too. Still, the Soviets seemed to have unlimited replacements and little regard for the lives of their soldiers, so they could get away with it. As well as the T34s and their tank riders, they combined motorised infantry to keep pace with the armour and units of anti-tank guns and artillery, all designed to fight and move as one unit.

I checked my bearings with the compass I carried and risked the torch to take a quick look at the map in my saddlebag. We were going in the right direction, the crash site about a kilometre away. We remounted the horses and trotted away along a smooth path of hard packed mud, the going was much easier until a sentry stepped out into our path and shouted something, presumably in Russian. I was about to give an order to take him when Gusava spurred forward calling out something in his language. The sentry answered but as he spoke, Felix ripped out the sabre and in one huge, wide slash brought it down across the sentry's neck, almost decapitating him. He didn't stop, just slowed his horse slightly as he kicked the dead man into the long grass at the side of the path. I said nothing. It was quick, neat and brutal. Five minutes later we arrived at the map coordinates, at first we saw nothing. A little further on the funkwagen lay upside down at the bottom of a shallow ravine. I signalled them to dismount.

"Felix, you'd better take care of the horses, the rest of you, make sure your weapons are ready in case it's a Soviet trap."

I cocked the bolt of my MP38 and led the way to the edge of the ravine. At first there was no sign of any life. Had the Reds captured them? Was a machine gun about to open fire and spray us with machine gun bullets?"

"Hoffman?" a voice whispered.

I recognised Wiedel's voice as he walked up to us.

"Are you all ok?"

"So far, yes, we've had a few near misses but no one has seen us yet. Am I seeing things or have you come on horseback?"

"We've formed a Cossack unit of the SS, Wiedel. We've got horses for all of you, we need to get you in the saddle and start moving back to our own lines."

"We'll need a hand with Mundt and Foch, they're sheltering in a small farmhouse behind those trees. I didn't want to leave them with the truck in case the Soviets found it, they'd hack them to pieces."

I thought of Felix Gusava hacking the sentry out of his

path. "Yes, they probably would."

I sent Bauer and Voss to help, made certain that Gusava was keeping a good watch and then we followed them to look at the injured men.

We went around the edge of the ravine, pushed along a narrow path through a small wood and there stood a farmhouse. Its roof missing, we walked through the open door space. A man in the uniform of the SD lay on the ground, his legs tied between pieces of wood, Voss and Wesserman were trying to help him get to his feet. Mundt lay there, his ankle swathed in torn rags that someone had torn up to bind his ankle. A girl was bending over him, giving him a drink of water. When she stood up I saw that she was quite short, petite and pretty, what people would describe as gamine. Unlike many Russian women I'd seen who tended to be taller, stouter and tougher, perhaps to survive their terrible winters. I looked at Wiedel with raised eyebrows.

"It's ok, Hoffman, she's helping us."

"Is she Russian?"

"She is, yes, but she's definitely not a Red."

"How can you be sure?"

He smiled. "Her name is Nadia Vlasov, she was trapped here when the Red Army arrived. Is the name familiar?"

I shook my head.

"Her uncle is Andriy Vlasov. Lieutenant-General Andriy Vlasov. After his army was surrounded in July last year,

Stalin insisted that he should escape by aeroplane. The General refused and hid in German-occupied territory, but a local farmer betrayed him to our troops. General Georg Lindemann interrogated him and then had Vlasov imprisoned in Vinnitsa, but Vlasov claimed that he was totally opposed to the Bolsheviks and believed that Stalin was the greatest enemy of the Russian people, so they let him go. You can imagine how that went down!"

"Jesus Christ, they must have gone crazy in Moscow."

"They did all of that. We're talking to Vlasov about forming a Free Russian Army, although I don't know if anything will come of it. But if they get their hands on his niece it won't be very pretty."

"Yes, they'll execute her, it's the way the Communists punish traitors, by murdering the relatives."

I didn't add that our own Nazi leaders operated a similar policy.

I left him and looked at Mundt, he seemed cheerful enough.

"Did I hear something about horses, Sir?" he asked me.

I nodded. "The mud is still pretty bad, horses are about the only thing that can move with any freedom."

"For invalids with broken ankles and legs, you mean."

I smiled. "That's true, but they saved us a long walk to come and get you."

"Getting out may not be so easy, Sir."

"They don't know we're here, so provided we move

fast, we can be out before they realise."

I stood up and looked at Wiedel.

"What do you plan to do about the girl?"

"She comes with us, of course. If we leave her for the Russians, they'll kill her, or use her as a bargaining chip. Besides, Vlasov would never forgive us if he found out we'd left her. Have you brought spare horses?"

I nodded. "We brought two extras, so no problems there. We need to get moving, we haven't much time."

I got up and asked Bauer to bring the horses around to the farmhouse. Ten minutes later he was back with our mounts. We got Mundt onto one of the horses and Foch to another, his broken legs would be useless with stirrups so we fastened him down with straps and told him to hang on. If he fell off he risked a compound fracture, but if we didn't get him out of here he risked rather more, a Soviet bullet and a shallow grave at best. The rest of us mounted up and headed back towards the German lines.

Perhaps it was the noise of our horses hooves that prevented us from hearing them, but halfway back we ran into the worst possible foe, a genuine Cossack squadron. They came on us suddenly out of the darkness, one moment we were alone on the desolate plain that led west. At first they didn't recognise us and one of the leading horsemen shouted to Gusava , who replied in Russian. The Cossack acknowledged and they were about to go past when one of them looked closer, recognised our uniforms and opened his mouth to shout. We were lucky as they had their rifles slung, not expecting trouble. We had our machine pistols ready, I pulled the trigger and the first two horsemen were thrown off their horses in the hail of 9mm bullets. There were fourteen others, if they'd turned tail and ran they would have survived and brought reinforcements, but they were Cossacks. One of them shouted a single word of command, as one man they whipped out their long, wicked sabres and charged us. It was slaughter as we were armed with semi-automatic weapons. Despite the speed and ferocity of their assault we hammered at them with our six machine pistols, a hail of lead that plucked them from their saddles and hurled them to the ground. Only two were left unscathed, they had been at the rear of the charge but were almost on us, my MP38 was empty but I drew my Walther PPK and fired, emptying the clip at the two Russians, Gusava fired too. One of them fell, the other flinched, wounded, but rode on towards us. I tugged at the reins to move my horse out of his path but abruptly I was shoved aside as another horse charged forward, Felix Gusava, sabre drawn and raised to parry the Cossack's blade. The sabres struck with a clang and a shower of sparks, the two riders circled each other, swords whirling and clashing together as each tried to gain the advantage. I reloaded and heard the clicks as the rest of the men put fresh clips into their weapons, but strangely we sat on our horses and watched the epic struggle.

It was like being transported back to the last century, to the time when Napoleon's elite cavalry swept all before them on the battlefields of Europe before the English Duke of Wellington and our own Prussian Marshal Blucher finished the French Emperor's dreams for the last time. On the field of Waterloo sabre fought with sabre, and so it was on this dark, miserable Ukrainian field. Gusava was clearly outclassed, fighting more with savage ferocity and hate than any real skill. The Cossack was a disciplined and trained swordsman, but his horse suddenly stumbled, probably in a rut created by a tank track, and in order to regain his balance he dropped his guard for less than a second. It was enough, as he was bringing his sabre up again to slash as Gusava struck, using the point to skewer him low in the guts, just above his groin. The man screamed in agony, and then slowly toppled from his horse. Gusava leapt off and stood over him, then hacked down on his neck finishing him. Voss clapped ironically.

"A good kill, Russian, but couldn't you just have shot him?"

"It was a Cossack that killed my wife with a sabre, I wanted to give him a taste of what she had."

"That's enough," I said to them urgently, "We've made a hell of a lot of noise, they'll be around here shortly to check it out. Let's move, and fast!"

I forced the pace hard, taking the lead away from

Gusava. If we ran into any Russians now, it was too late for talking. We hurtled across the Soviet-held countryside. Perhaps the only thing that saved us was that no one would believe that anyone other than a Cossack unit would be on horseback in this area. At one stage, as we were crossing a patch of open terrain and moving into a small forest, someone shouted. I twisted to the side and saw that we were riding adjacent to the edge of a Soviet encampment, but no shots were fired. It was impossible to tell when we crossed the lines but suddenly we were clattering into the farmyard, von Betternich stood next to the BMW motorcycle and sidecar and watching us come in. The motorcyclist was standing next to him and both had their pistols out, as if they would have been of any use had we been a real Cossack raiding party. Behind them were two of our military ambulances. Von Betternich had obviously been busy.

We dismounted and shook hands. While the men were helping the two casualties down from the horses he greeted Wiedel, then looked questioningly at Nadia Vlasov. The Gestapo man explained her presence and he nodded his agreement.

"But how the hell did you wind up in Soviet territory, Wiedel?"

"It was my fault," he said with a grimace. "Our driver felt ill and I said I'd drive, but I took a wrong turning. Before I realised what was happening, we were already behind the lines and a Soviet unit had manoeuvred in behind us. I just drove on hoping to circle around and get back. Then we ran into that damned ravine. Fortunately Miss Vlasov was there to help us, and of course our radio was undamaged so we were able to call for help."

We watched one of the ambulances drive away with the casualties.

"This doesn't help us find the Lucy spy ring, Wiedel. Now we're short of a truck. Do you have any ideas?"

He shook his head.

"Damnit, we're back to square one," von Betternich sighed.

"Look, Sir, I don't understand this," I said to him. "The Russians are waiting for us in strength, probably in far greater numbers than we can ever hope to have. Isn't it folly to continue with the attack? I know about the military advantages of taking the salient, but it seems to me that they must be outweighed by the massive numerical superiority that the Russians have got over us."

He smiled. "There may be something in what you say, Hoffman. But you see, the Fuhrer does not think so. Look on the bright side, if we can find the spy it will mean that we can change our deployments and hit them where they least expect it, that way we could defeat several Soviet armies if we can only surprise them. It's still possible."

He seemed to be thinking about something else, his mind obviously far away.

"Yes, perhaps we can do this in a different way. We need to find accommodation for Miss Vlasov. Wiedel, put her up in the Hotel October."

He nodded. "Yes, Sir."

"That radio code that the Soviets were able to break, do you still use it to spread false information?"

"We do, yes."

"Good. We'll send a message from von Manstein's headquarters, advising that Miss Vlasov has been accommodated in the Hotel October, use that code so that we know they will hear it. Perhaps that will lure them to us."

They both smiled, two arch-conspirators satisfied with their dark scheme.

"Wiedel, when get back to Kharkov set up the ambush at the hotel, if we're lucky they'll fall into our laps. Make sure you capture them alive when they come to kill her. We might just get a lead from them to Lucy if we can find out how they get the information passed to them."

I couldn't help but overhear. "You're using an unarmed civilian as bait, what about Nadia Vlasov, she could be killed?"

The SD man shrugged. "What about it? When Vlasov finds out that the Soviets have murdered his niece he'll have even more of an incentive to fight for us."

I went to the second ambulance and told the driver to follow us back to the city, then ordered Voss and

Wesserman to go with him. Gusava led the horses away and I climbed into the back seat of the Kubelwagen with Nadia. Bauer got in the front with Wiedel beside him and drove off, the ambulance pulled away behind us.

"You heard that you are to be billeted in the Hotel October?" I asked Nadia quietly.

"I heard it all, Obersturmfuhrer. I hope they catch the people they are looking for."

I was quiet for a few moments. Then I leaned nearer and said, "They'll do their best to protect you, I'm sure. I'm sorry, it wasn't my idea."

She smiled tiredly. "You know, when they came to our town, the Communists, they arrested many of our people, most of them Kulaks. I was young then, but my father was in command of a company of the Red Army. Our neighbours were arrested and marched towards the station to get on a train bound for Siberia. You know what that means, the Gulags?"

I nodded.

"They saw my father, his company were also at the railway station, they were there to prevent any trouble, any riots or demonstrations. Our neighbours saw him and the wife ran across to speak to him, she begged him to help, at least to spare their children, there were four of them, the youngest was only four years old. Do you know what he replied?"

I shook my head.

"He said, 'I'm sorry, it wasn't my idea'. You reminded me of him, please, spare me your false sympathy and spare me your help. I will protect myself. "

I looked at her in surprise. "Are you armed, Miss Vlasov?"

"Yes, I have a pistol hidden in my jacket. Is that a problem for you?" she asked fiercely.

"No, it's no problem."

She'd obviously been through a lot and was undoubtedly a survivor. Perhaps she would best the Russians if they did come to kill her, maybe she didn't need protection. But I looked at her again, a small, almost childish figure of a young woman, if Russian partisans or Special Forces attacked she'd stand no chance. It was a bitter pill and I found it very, very hard to swallow.

As we drove back the Panzers, the assault guns, the trucks and field guns were in the same places and still hadn't moved. Troops were all around, casually doing routine maintenance tasks, there was no urgency. I'd noticed in the salient that the whole of the ground was cut up with the distinctive marks of tank tracks and wheel ruts, it was obvious that the Red Army was not taking the same relaxed attitude to the coming offensive. I felt that I wanted to drag out the commanders and shout at them, tell them what they faced the other side and how it was getting worse with every day that they delayed. But of course, without the order from von Manstein they were going nowhere. And the Feldmarschal couldn't give the order until he himself received the order from the Fuhrer. And Hitler would not give the order, certain in his superior knowledge of strategy and tactics, knowledge that seemingly he alone possessed, or believed he did. It was as if the Soviets did not exist, that our armies were positioned here like some ancient mariner, fearful of crossing into uncharted waters where all that was marked on his map was 'There be monsters'. It was an apt analogy. There certainly were monsters only a few kilometres away, monsters that grew bigger and more powerful with every day that passed.

CHAPTER FIVE

'The officers of a panzer division must learn to think and act independently within the framework of the general plan and not wait until they receive orders'.

Erwin Rommel

"Damnit, Hoffman, I'm not happy about you wandering off without permission!"

I was standing in von Meusebach's office, he was distinctly unhappy. Muller stood behind him, fixing me with a sympathetic glare.

"I'm sorry, Sir."

This was the SS, excuses were worthless, obey orders and win battles, that was all that mattered. Except that we hadn't won the battle yet, the battle that would be fought around Kursk. Von Meusebach had the order from

Himmler, however, and he couldn't go too far with his criticism for fear that it may be construed as criticism of the Reichsfuhrer. He suddenly looked thoughtful.

"Hoffman, I understand you did a good job for the Gestapo and of course you rescued the men that their stupidity had put them behind the lines. Perhaps you would like to transfer to the Gestapo if you prefer working for them, I could sign a recommendation?"

He was clever, he could achieve more with a stroke of his pen than my platoon could achieve with their machine pistols.

"No, Sir, I don't wish to transfer."

"Very well, in future keep me advised of every move you make." He'd evidently decided he'd pushed me hard enough. After all, the order from Himmler was not to be taken too lightly. "Look, Hoffman, you've had a difficult time. You should catch up with some sleep, report to Muller later, dismissed."

I saluted and left the office. Bloody SD, bloody Gestapo, bloody von Meusebach, and their silly games! I did as he suggested and went to my quarters. Fully dressed I tried to get some sleep, but it was impossible, the noise from tanks being offloaded, troops marching, orders being shouted and the thousand and one other sounds that are part of an army preparing to go into battle were everywhere. I dozed for two hours and then got up and put my head under the cold-water pump outside our isba. I was thinking about

Nadia Vlasov, the beautiful, enigmatic Russian girl that was being offered by the Gestapo as a sacrifice. When I went back inside I found Voss and Wesserman had woken up and were brewing coffee, apparently they'd been unable to sleep much either.

"Are we on radio truck duty tonight?" Voss asked.

I realised that I'd no idea what they had planned for us. They still had one intact funkwagen after all.

"We'd better go into the city and find out, Oberschutze."

It would be a good excuse to get away from the squalor and misery of the stinking, noisy railway yard. We still had the Kubelwagen parked outside and Podvirky was getting on our nerves. There was nothing here except grime, noise and von Meusebach. Kharkov, for all its war damage, shabby populace and dirty streets at least offered something more than this stinking backwater. We drove into the city and parked outside Gestapo HQ. I left the men with the vehicle, there was no sign of von Betternich but Wiedel was in his office. He looked up in surprise when I walked in.

"I was going to send a messenger for you later. You've only been back a few hours, couldn't you sleep?"

"Not next door to a railway marshalling yard unloading Tiger tanks, no. Are we needed tonight for the funkwagen?"

"No, we have something different planned. Von Betternich has driven to Vinnitsa, the headquarters of Army Group South. He is sending the message about

Miss Vlasov's whereabouts, so if they make a move on her, we'll be ready for them. How many soldiers can you muster in your platoon?"

With Mundt injured I was down to eleven men. He was surprised. "So few? I thought platoon strength would be much higher."

I grimaced. "Not since they've been pulling men out of regular units to form the new divisions, we're all desperately short of men."

He nodded. "In that case, we'll have to manage. Do you need an order for your CO?"

I smiled. "I think the Standartenfuhrer would appreciate that, Wiedel."

He wrote out the Gestapo form, handed me the order. "Hoffman, it's important that we catch these people alive."

"If they come," I replied.

"We think they will. Stalin is reported to be incandescent about Vlasov's treachery, whoever manages to kill or kidnap his niece will certainly get into his favour, they'll jump at the chance. Remember, we're not worried about the girl. It's the Russians we want. We can interrogate them and find out where their orders came from and it should lead us to the spy."

"I'll remember."

I walked out of his office, determined that whatever happened, I'd do my utmost to protect the girl.

I decided to stay in the city so I sent Voss and Wesserman

back to Podvirky with the order for von Meusebach.

"I want the platoon back here by five o'clock," I told Voss. "If you can't find transport, they'll have to march here. Just be at Gestapo HQ for five."

They drove off in the Kubi, I had only one destination in mind. I walked into the centre of the city and got directions for the Hotel October. When I walked through the entrance, the clerk looked up and glanced at me with disdain. I caught sight of my reflection in a mirror behind the desk. I looked like a gypsy.

"I'm sorry, we're full."

"I'm looking for Miss Vlasov, she is a guest here I believe."

"Miss Vlasov, yes, she checked in this morning. I have a request not to disturb her until two o'clock. She is in room 412."

"I'll call back."

I left and found a bar opposite the hotel where I was able to sit at the counter and get coffee and a bowl of thin soup. I was starving hungry, as I hadn't eaten much in what seemed like days. Four Wehrmacht officers came in, sat down at a table and started drinking heavily. Before long they were making jokes about the SS, 'Himmler's toy soldiers, where were they when they were needed at Stalingrad?' One of them came up to the bar and leered at me, I just ignored him and carried on eating my stew.

"Are you lot going to disappear again when the Reds

come to attack Kharkov?" he snarled.

I looked at him in amazement, wasn't he aware that it was the SS that had retaken the city and not the Wehrmacht?

"Sergeant, just take your drink and go back to your table before you get into trouble."

He didn't move. His face was only ten centimetres from mine now.

"Are you going to make me, SS man?"

He smiled broadly and put a hand on my chest as if to push be backwards off my stool. There was no choice, I punched him hard on the chin and he spun to the floor. His friends jumped up and ran to help him up.

"Are you ok, Werner?"

"I will be when we knock this SS bastard's head off. Let's get the swine."

All four of them jumped me and although I struck out in all directions with my fists and boots, I went down under a hail of blows. As a boot kicked me in the head I took hold of it and twisted it, sending the soldier sprawling to the floor. He landed next to me and I punched him in the face for good measure, but there were still three of them doing their best to beat me to a pulp. I kept lashing out, but it was a losing battle and I felt my consciousness starting to fade. I was desperate to find some way out of this bar room brawl but my strength was draining fast. I had given up all hope of getting out of it in one piece when a shot rang out and the boots kicking me abruptly ceased. I shook my head to clear it and tried to look up, but my vision still blurred.

"Gestapo, what's going on here?"

I recognised the voice. Wiedel. My vision finally cleared and I could see him standing there, leather coat, trilby hat, Walther PPK in one hand, his metal Gestapo identification disc in the other. The NCOs started to protest that I'd set on them. Wiedel looked at them coldly. "Get out and don't come back. You're lucky I don't have you all arrested. This bar is now off limits to all of you. Now go!"

The one I'd hit, Werner, started to protest but Wiedel held up his hand. "If you wish to discuss it, come down to Gestapo Headquarters and you can file a complaint."

He looked at his friends, they were obviously keen to avoid the Gestapo and he took the hint and left.

"How the hell did you find me?"

"The clerk at the Hotel October saw you come in here. We need to set up this ambush for later, where is your platoon?"

I told him that they had been ordered to report to Gestapo HQ in the afternoon.

"Very well, we'll go over to the hotel and speak to Miss Vlasov. How are you, by the way, did they do any permanent damage?"

I smiled. "Nothing I can't live with. By the way, I tried to visit Miss Vlasov earlier, she's not to be disturbed by anyone until two o'clock."

"This is Gestapo business, she'll see me."

We walked across to the hotel where the receptionist was still behind the counter in the dingy lobby. Wiedel stared at him. "I want a room opposite Miss Vlasov's room."

The man held out his hands in an exasperated expression. "We're full up, the room opposite it occupied."

The Gestapo man stared at him for a few moments. When he spoke his voice was as icy as the Russian winter. "I'm not interested in who is in the room, get them out and give me the key, you have twenty minutes! Move!"

The receptionist looked shocked, but Wiedel reached across the counter, took him by the jacket and dragged him towards him. "If I see you still standing there in five seconds I'll put you in a Gestapo cell."

The man ran towards the stairs, we followed him and climbed up four flights, the lift was not working as usual, Wiedel banged on Nadia's door. It took five minutes of heavy knocking, but she came to the door looking dishevelled and frightened. He pushed past her. "We need to check the security in this room, are there any other entrances?"

"Of course not, only the window."

"Hoffman, check outside the window, make sure there are no convenient fire escapes or drainpipes they can use."

I opened the window and looked out, it would need a ladder to climb up the sheer side of the building. There was a knock at the door and I drew my Walther and opened it, but it was only the clerk with the key to the room opposite.

Six hours later I was ready with the rest of my platoon. Von Betternich had returned in the afternoon, he told us that the message had been sent and he confidently expected the Russians to take the bait.

"This damned Lucy ring is so fast that they often get messages out to Moscow even before our own local commanders receive them. The fake signal states that she will be here for one night only and then we are sending her back to the Reich to join her uncle, General Vlasov. If they're going to try anything, it will have to be tonight."

The platoon arrived during the late afternoon and I assigned them to their positions. Six of them were in the room opposite, under the command of Unterscharfuhrer Beidenberg. They were the arrest squad. Two were dressed in hotel uniforms and played the role of porters and bellhops. The other three were in the room with me and Nadia Vlasov, Voss, Bauer and Wesserman. Nadia sat in the corner of the room looking bored and miserable. I kept peering through cracks in the curtains, but there was no sign of enemy activity. The door knocked and someone shouted 'room service', the men hurriedly picked up their machine pistols but I told them to relax, I'd recognised Schutze Vellermann's voice. I opened the door warily.

"I thought you might like some refreshments," he said

cheerily. He was pushing a trolley loaded with an urn of coffee and a huge plate of sandwiches.

"Bring them in, Schutze, you're a lifesaver."

We sat contentedly eating our unexpected meal, I asked Nadia to join us but she declined, just sitting quietly in the corner. Was she afraid of what was to happen? She was clutching her bag to her stomach and her pistol would certainly be inside it. Hopefully she wouldn't have to use it. The evening wore on and the night was pitch black, with no moonlight to give us a good view of anyone approaching the hotel. By midnight we were all starting to feel very tired and bored, it was difficult to stay awake. The hotel was utterly silent which is why I was able to hear the faint squeak of a loose floorboard.

"They're here," I whispered.

They held their weapons ready, pointed at the door.

"Only shoot if it's unavoidable, remember, we want them alive. Nadia, get behind the bed."

She ignored me and pulled her pistol out of her bag, cocked it and waited. I shrugged, if that's the way she wanted to play it she could carry on, it was her they'd come to kill. We heard the door opposite fly open and Beidenberg's voice shouting at them to surrender, and then there was an explosion and a burst of automatic fire. Men screamed. I couldn't tell who they were and then another explosion shattered the night.

"They're using grenades, our men opposite are probably

outgunned. It's time we joined in. Bauer, guard Miss Vlasov, you other two be ready when I open the door. If you have to shoot, aim low, we want prisoners."

Voss and Wesserman pointed their MP38s at the door of the room. I looked at them and they nodded. Then I ripped the door open in one savage motion.

Two Russians stood in the corridor, each holding a PPSh machine pistol. The third was kneeling down, about to attach some kind of charge to the door of our room. The first two men raised their weapons as soon as they saw us, but Voss and Wesserman were ready. They totally ignored my instruction to aim low and both of the enemy went down in a hail of bullets. They were obviously finished, the third man had his weapon on the floor while he was working at the door, he whirled to pick it up and I launched myself at him, knocking him over and away from the PPSh. He punched me in the stomach, a hard blow that knocked the wind out of me but I brought my legs up and kneed him hard in the crotch. He screamed in agony and I took the opportunity to punch him hard on the nose, there was a crack as his nose broke and blood streamed out, but he wasn't beaten, he rolled to one side, grasping for his pistol in its holster on his belt. I'd dropped my machine pistol when I dived for him, my own pistol was in its holster and there was no time to get it out before he opened fire. It was as if in slow motion, I saw him whip up the pistol, even saw his finger tightening on the trigger, then Beidenberg rushed out of the room and knocked his hand to one side, sending the shot into the wall. The Unterscharfuhrer gripped the man's arm and twisted it behind him, up to his shoulder blade and even further until with a loud crack it dislocated. The man screamed again, Voss and Wesserman rushed out and held him and I got up, retrieved my machine pistol and looked around at the carnage. The first two Russians were dead. Inside the opposite hotel room two of my troopers had been killed, caught in the grenade blasts. A third man was lying on the floor, bleeding from a stomach wound, I bent down to look closely but it did not appear to be deep. I took out a field addressing and applied it to the wound to stop him bleeding to death.

"That'll do you for now, I'll get the medics up here quickly, you'll be ok," I said to him soothingly.

He nodded his thanks and I went back out to look around. Schutze Vellermann was walking warily towards me, his weapon pointed ready to fire.

"I was in the stair well, one floor up when I heard the shooting, Sir. I can't see any more of them."

"Very well, go to the end of the corridor and make sure no one else gets past, unless they're ours, if anyone tries it. Shoot them! Before you do anything else, call for a medic, we've got some men down in here."

He nodded and walked quickly away. I checked out our prisoner, he looked like a partisan in shabby civilian clothes, dungarees and a torn jacket, but underneath he gave me the impression of being hard and fit.

"Bring him into the room, let's see what he has to say before the Gestapo gets here. You'd better search him for documents and weapons."

He carried no papers other than an old, expired Russian pass bearing the name of Vasily Chernenko. He looked annoyed when they found the piece of paper in an inside pocket of his coat, he obviously hadn't meant to have it on his person.

"So, Vasily, do you speak German?"

His eyes flicked in recognition of what I'd said and I assumed he understood well enough.

"Who told you that Miss Vlasov would be here?"

He didn't answer. But when Nadia stood up his eyes widened with hatred.

"Vasily," she shouted. "You came to kill me?"

"As I kill all traitors to the motherland."

"You know him?" I asked her.

"Yes, he was one of my uncle's sergeants, I thought he was loyal. Vasily, you know that it was not me that joined with the Nazis."

"That is not the way I heard it," he said viciously. "The NKVD has evidence that you were complicit in an attempt to persuade more of our troops to desert."

"That's nonsense," she cried. "Those bastards, they twist everything!"

I took hold of his wounded arm and he winced as it moved slightly against the torn shoulder joint.

"Tell us how you got the message, Vasily. We know about the radio."

He looked away abruptly, avoiding eye contact.

"Where do the messages come from?" I persisted.

He refused to look back at me, even when I twisted his arm and saw beads of sweat running down the side of his face. But I couldn't do any more to him, torture was the Gestapo's province, not mine.

Almost as if they'd heard my thought, Wiedel appeared at the end of the corridor. Von Betternich was behind him, limping painfully along after the climb up four flights of stairs. His eyes gleamed with satisfaction when they saw the prisoner.

"Excellent, Hoffman, well done. Is he the only one to survive?"

I nodded.

"He'll do, bring him along to Gestapo Headquarters. We'll have a talk to him there."

"Sir, Miss Vlasov is unhurt."

He looked puzzled. "Really? So we could use her again, that's interesting."

He looked around at the battle damage for a few more moments and then turned away limping back to the stairs, Wiedel followed him. I detailed two men to take the Russian with them. A group of medics appeared with stretchers and our casualties were carried away.

"Voss, Bauer, you'd better station yourselves outside the room for the rest of the night. I'll take the men back to Podvirky, I think the excitement is over for the night. I'll send transport for you in the morning. I went to walk away but Nadia Vlasov walked over and put her hand on my arm.

"Obersturmfuhrer, thank you for protecting me. Can you not stay for the rest of the night? I fear there could be a further attack."

"I need to get the men back to their post in Podvirky, you'll be fine with these two men to guard you."

She looked disappointed. "I see, again, thank you."

On an impulse, I said, "I'll come sometime tomorrow and make sure you are safe."

She flashed me a small smile. "I would like that."

I glared at Voss and Bauer who were grinning like imbeciles. "Shouldn't you two be in the corridor, setting up a guard post?"

"Yes, at once, Obersturmfuhrer."

They sauntered through the door.

I assembled the rest of the men and took my depleted platoon outside the hotel to walk back to Gestapo HQ to collect the Kubelwagen. The night was still black and very quiet, all I could hear was the tramp of our jackboots on the cobbles, but something caught my eye, just a flash of movement, possibly innocent but it was as if we'd appeared unexpectedly and someone had responded in a panic. More partisans?

"Beidenberg, Wesserman, I think I saw something, that cottage over there."

I pointed to a small house set back from the main street. They nodded and we rushed over to the front door, giving each other cover as we went forward. The windows were shuttered, I wasn't certain what I'd seen, perhaps someone leaving in a hurry. Wesserman and I covered the door with our weapons, Beidenberg kicked it in and we rushed inside. It was a stinking, dirty peasant dwelling, there was a smell of something in the air, I sniffed and said, "It's lamp oil. Someone light a match and see where the lamp is."

There was the scratch of a match striking, dimly illuminating the room. Wesserman saw the lamp immediately lit it. The whole room was alight now, a filthy hovel with a bundle of straw in the corner for a bed and an old wooden crate as some sort of rough table. But what was on the table was of more interest, a radio transmitter, fitted in a brown canvas backpack. A wire aerial was strung from the radio and hung out of a back window, or rather a hole in the wall covered with a loose piece of oilcloth. Wesserman kept watch on the radio while we searched the surrounding area, but whoever had been in the room had heard us coming and was long gone.

"You'd better bring the radio back, we'll take it to Wiedel, maybe he can use it to help find the traitor," I said. "There's no chance of catching anyone here, they're long gone, we'd better get back."

Wiedel was ecstatic at our haul. He woke up his radio technician and told him to inspect it for clues. I took the opportunity to make our escape from the Gestapo and catch a lift back to Podvirky on a supplies truck heading to the railway yard. When I got into my bed I had no trouble sleeping that night. The next morning my platoon were all together, Voss and Bauer from guarding Nadia Vlasov and Mundt discharged himself from the sick bay, although he still walked with a decided limp.

"I can't stand those doctors, I'd sooner take on the Russians," he said grimly.

We spent the next two weeks struggling with every other available man to free Panzers and STuGIII assault guns from the mud. The Sturmgeschutz III assault gun was a powerful mobile gun, built on the chassis of the Panzer III. Initially intended as an armoured light gun for infantry support, we widely employed the STuGIII as a tank destroyer. Our self-propelled assault guns had proved invaluable. We often deployed them by night, hiding them behind camouflage or in specially dug pits or even in the thousands of narrow ravines that littered the steppe. Their fast, accurate fire had proved devastating and decisive in battle after battle and they were considered as vital as any of the Panzers. We were going to need every one we could get when the battle began. The pace was quickening everywhere as the High Command built up their forces for the coming battle. It was the middle of May and the spring rains and consequent mud were ending. We knew that it would be vital to attack before the Russians built their defences into overwhelming strength and were eagerly waiting for the order to deploy into the forward positions.

We returned to our shabby billets in Podvirky at the end of one particularly hard day. While attempting to lay a roadway of logs to prize a Panzer IV out of the wet clay that gripped it, we were suddenly attacked by low flying Soviet fighters. Fortunately they hadn't carried bombs, but after the flight of four aircraft had finished shooting up the area with machine gun and cannon fire dozens of our men lay dead in the brown, Ukrainian earth, never to see their homeland ever again. The constant fear of attack, the delays in setting a date for our own assault on the salient and the constant filth, grime and shortages of the Eastern Front was taking its toll. The air attack seemed to knock the stuffing out of all of us. Why can't we just attack the bastards? That was the question on everyone's lips. When we got back, von Meusebach was waiting for us together with another SS officer.

"Men, this is the commanding officer of our Second SS Division Das Reich. Gruppenfuhrer Walter Kruger has a few words to say to us."

Kruger stood to address us. He was lean and hard, every inch the fighting soldier, his Knight's Cross with

Oak Leaves and Swords a testament to his bravery.

"You have all worked hard to prepare for this attack and there is no doubt that we shall unleash a storm that will drive the Soviets back to Moscow and beyond, a storm they will never forget!"

A few men cheered, but most of us had heard it all before.

"The attack has been postponed for several weeks."

He was drowned out by a series of shouts, groans and catcalls. He held up his hand.

"This is by order of the Fuhrer. I know you are disappointed, but we are awaiting deliveries of the new Panzer V. When these new tanks are deployed we will be smash through the Soviets, we'll beat them and drive on to Moscow!"

He paused, waiting for applause for his fighting rhetoric. There was silence. He had effectively told us that the High Command was giving the Russians more time to prepare their massive defences. I hoped that the Panzer Vs would be as effective as they hoped, and that they would be able to cope with the hundreds more T34s that we were giving the Russians time to produce and deploy on the battlefield. Kruger carried on talking for a few minutes more and then quickly ended his talk.

I was weary of the constant battle to wrestle the armour off the flatcars and then to be called to wrestle them out of the mud that seemed to trap the unwary driver at every opportunity. I decided enough was enough. I was going into the city for the evening. I put my head under the cold pump and enjoyed my usual cold shower, Mundt cranked the handle for me so that I could crouch down and let the ice cold water pour over my head. I put on my uniform, brushed it off, wiped a rag over my jackboots and went outside. Mundt was waiting in the Kubelwagen with Bauer and Voss.

"We need to drive into the city to collect the mail, Sir, I thought you might like a lift."

"I thought the mail came yesterday?"

He kept a straight face. "I'm sure that more will have arrived today."

I couldn't help but smile, it was the flimsiest of excuses, but it would have to do. I climbed in and we roared off.

"We need to return before midnight, Willy, otherwise we could all be posted AWOL."

"I know that. We'll collect you at eleven, shall we say outside the Hotel October?"

I nodded. The Scharfuhrer could be a mind reader sometimes.

The reception clerk in the hotel confirmed that Nadia Vlasov was still staying at the hotel, they'd moved her to room 417 while they repaired the damage done to room 412. I thanked him and ran up the stairs, I didn't even bother with the lift, even if they'd got it working it would probably break down. Nadia answered the door when I knocked, her eyes widened with surprise.

"Jurgen, you took your time getting back."

"It's the war, Miss Vlasov."

"Call me Nadia." She reached forward and pulled me into the room, her mouth clamped on mine. "I've been expecting you."

We undressed each other with shaking hands. I showered her with kisses and stroked her beautiful, perfect but tiny body. Then we made love, a warm journey of pleasure and exploration as we each discovered the other's body. Afterwards, I lay on my back and she put her head on my chest.

"Can't you move into Kharkov, Jurgen? We could see each other more often, I've been lonely here on my own."

I looked down at her face, I only wished I could. Our dirty little hovel in Podvirky was hard to bear, but I explained to her that we didn't have much of a choice where we were posted.

"Why not join the Gestapo, then? Those two men, Wiedel and the one with the limp have been here talking to me."

"That's von Betternich, he's SD, not Gestapo."

"What's the difference?" she asked.

"It's slightly complicated, but here goes," I grinned, enjoying our conversation. She was perceptive enough to know how much I loved talking and explaining things to her. "The RSHA, the Reich Main Security Office known as the

Reichssicherheitshauptamt is an organisation subordinate to Reichsfuhrer Himmler in his dual capacities as the Chief of German Police, Chef der Deutschen Polizei and Reichsfuhrer-SS. The duty of the RSHA is to fight enemies of the Reich both inside and outside the borders of Germany. The organisation is divided into seven main offices, or Amts. Amt IV, Geheime Staatspolizei is the Gestapo, headed by SS-Gruppenfuhrer Heinrich Muller. Amt VI, the SD, is led by SS-Brigadefuhrer Walter Schellenberg. It is the foreign intelligence service of the SS."

I smiled, it sounded long-winded. "But I guess they do much the same job, they don't usually tell me much of what they're up to."

She put her hand up and stroked my hair. I wished we could stay like this always, that there would be no war raging outside this room.

"They seem to know a lot about you, Jurgen, they've mentioned you several times."

I was about to ask her what they'd said when there was a hammering on the door. I put a towel around my waist and jumped up to answer it, Mundt stood there. "It's a general alert, the Soviets have counterattacked at Belgorod. We're needed." He smiled at my semi-naked body.

"I'll be down in one minute, Willy."

I raced to throw my uniform on. "I don't know when I'll see you again, Nadia. If the Soviets break through, get out of the city fast."

She nodded. "I'll do that, try not to get yourself killed, Jurgen."

"I only wish the Russians would listen."

I pulled on my jackboots, grabbed my weapons and helmet and rushed down the stairs and outside. They were waiting in the Kubi with the engine running, I leapt in and we roared off. The journey back to Podvirky was chaotic, armour and infantry trucks driving at high speed towards Belgorod. We bounced and slewed all over the road, trying to avoid the worst of the potholes, but the mud had mainly tried. Why hadn't our Intelligence units alerted us before that an attack was now possible? We screeched to a halt, left the Kubi in the vehicle park and ran to the assembly point outside HQ. Von Meusebach was shouting streams of orders to men who ran in what seemed like random directions. He saw me and shouted.

"Hoffman, where have you been?"

"Gestapo business, Sir."

He nodded. "Very well, get your platoon into your half track, you're just in time, we leave in five minutes."

Mundt was already herding the men together, we ran for the half-track and climbed in, Bauer started the engine and we were ready to leave. The men were still putting on their kit, webbing belts, helmets and gas mask containers, although most of those contained other things, the threat from gas didn't seem likely to materialise. Von Meusebach stepped carefully through the mud and boarded his armoured reconnaissance vehicle, the SD 232 Six wheeler. Armed with a two-centimetre gun in the turret and additional MG34 machine gun, the vehicle carried a large radio aerial array over the turret that would enable the commander to keep control of his forces by radio. The CO's head stuck out of the turret, he presented a very heroic figure with his cap set at a jaunty angle, evidently deciding to forego the security of a steel helmet for the time being. We were all waiting lined up outside the Regimental HQ without engines running, waiting to leave when two men dashed out with cameras, they were SS-Kriegsberichter, war correspondents and photographers. They spent several minutes taking pictures of the head of the column, especially von Meusebach, they then waved and disappeared back into the building. The CO removed his cap, donned his steel helmet and dropped down into the turret, closing the hatch with a clang. The armoured car drove away and we followed, none of the men said a word about delaying the column for the photographs, but a very definite picture of von Meusebach was emerging.

We reached the outskirts of Belgorod and stopped, we were parked in a large, open area with several squadrons of Panzer IVs and Tigers and two StuGIII assault guns. The CO popped open his hatch and climbed down to speak with the tankers and then came over to us.

"The Red Army is trying to break through on a five

kilometre southern flank of the city, our task is to support the Panzers while they drive them back. Keep a tight formation on my vehicle. I want half of the regiment in front of me and half behind. I will keep control from the centre. Form up, we'll follow the Panzers in."

We boarded our half-tracks and waited, but not for long. The Panzers' engines roared and they surged away along a narrow lane that skirted the southern part of the city. We travelled for three kilometres without incident when abruptly we ran into the Soviets, a column of T34s complete with tank riders heading straight for us. Our units went straight into action, the STuGIIIs deployed one to each of the flanks, the Tigers formed a diamond formation and the Panzer IVs tucked in behind the security of the Tigers' heavier armour. They were already firing, shells landed amongst the Russians and the T34s started hitting back. Bauer pulled the wheel over and we steered for the shelter of a nearby ravine, a shallow dried up riverbed that would offer us some protection from the worst of the Russian fire. I jumped down to look for Soviet anti-tank guns or infantry carrying man-portable anti-tank rifles. The tank riders were already jumping down off their tanks, disappearing into shallow dips and holes in the ground. It was our turn to take action, our Tigers and Panzer IVs would be decimated if they organised their anti-tank fire.

Then it happened, the Soviet infantry started to push

the distinctive long barrels of their PTRDs out of the foxholes ready to engage our armour. The PTRD-41 Soviet Anti Tank Rifle was a single-shot weapon which fired a 14.5mm round. It was too light to penetrate the frontal armour of our tanks but it could penetrate the thinner sides of our smaller, more lightly armoured tanks and self-propelled guns.

I pointed to a nearby Russian position, Bauer swerved the half-track out of the ravine and we charged towards the enemy. Too late, they were concentrating on one of our Panzers and we were on them before they realised we were there. Mundt and Voss poured fire down onto them from our front and rear mounted MG34s, then a hail of bullets slashed at us from another foxhole that was only ten metres from us. We ducked down as the Soviet gunner emptied his clip and us, fortunately they hade a Degtyarev light machine gun, the one we nicknamed the record player. It was lethal in use, but when the 47 round pancake magazine ran out it was very slow to load. The gunner was inexperienced and his burst went wide of us, I peeped over the top of the half-track and saw him start to reload. I pointed to Beidenberg, "Bring three of the men, let's get them now!"

I didn't wait for him to acknowledge, we only had seconds to act. I leapt over the top of the half-track and started to run, within seconds I was almost on them, the gunner was still reloading but there were three other infantrymen in the hole. I pointed my MP38 and pulled the trigger, but in the heat of the action I'd forgotten the cardinal rule with Hugo Schmeisser's iconic design. The long clip of ammunition that extended under the weapon was not a good fit and the slightest movement meant that bullets would not feed into the chamber. I'd gripped the gun by the clip and when I pulled the trigger nothing happened. It was like a moment frozen in time, I stood there stupidly holding my useless machine pistol, the Russian machine gunner frantically rammed the new pancake clip onto his gun, his three companions brought up their cumbersome Moisin Nagant rifles ready to shoot. I dived to the side just as the first of the bullets whizzed through the air past my ear. The other two riflemen stood up to aim at me as I rolled away, but Beidenberg and the other troopers rushed up and fired repeatedly at the Soviets. The four of them were hurled to the floor of the foxhole, Josef helped me up and we ran back to the relative safety of the half-track.

Two more of our STuGIII self-propelled guns had arrived and were picking off the T34s one by one as the Tigers and Panzer IVs roamed the battlefield like game beaters, pushing them out of concealed pockets, breaking up their formations and blasting them with highly accurate bursts of the Tiger's powerful 88mm gun. We didn't have it all our own way, the Soviets set up a battery of heavy anti-tank artillery on a distant ridge and started to pour fire on our armour, a Tiger and two Panzer IVs exploded before the STuGIIIs turned their fire on the ridge and started to punish the Russians. The T34s started to retreat, it had been a scrappy affair and they had never looked like breaking through our armour, at least not in our small sector of the Soviet attack. As I looked anxiously around the battlefield for any signs of Soviet survivors, I saw the CO, von Meusebach, or at least I saw his armoured car, sheltering in a deep ravine, the hatches battened down so that they would have found it impossible to take any active part in the battle. It seemed that our new CO was not particularly keen to risk taking any enemy fire, or indeed on firing on the enemy himself. Apart from his caution, we had inflicted casualties on Russian men and armour, for their part they no doubt succeeded in what they were looking to achieve, an estimate of our fighting strength and abilities with which to judge their tactics for the coming battle.

We pulled away slowly, careful to watch for possible Soviet trickery, they were adept at throwing men and machines into pointless attacks so that they could draw out attention away from their real objective. I half expected another part of our front to be under attack, Kharkov or even the important railhead at Podvirky, but when we returned it was all quiet. The Tigers dispersed around the village for both camouflage and to defend the railhead, the crews had set up a barrel of beer that they'd 'liberated' from some local bar. They invited us to join them for a drink and we stood swilling down the local brew, it was alcoholic but there was nothing else to commend it.

I chatted to a Tiger commander from one of our SS Panzer battalions, a Sturmscharfuhrer August Just, both of us pulling faces at the appalling flavour of the Ukrainian beer.

"I think we all got a good taste of what is to come."

He grimaced. "If it ever comes, the talk now is of postponing it until July."

I nearly choked on my beer as a gulp went down my windpipe. It was astonishing news.

"Which bloody idiot made that decision? We're almost giving it to the Soviets on a plate. Don't they know what's going on over there in the salient?"

"I believe his name if Adolf Hitler," the tanker replied drily.

I looked around, but no one seemed to be listening to our conversation. "So he still insists on waiting for the deliveries of these Panzer Vs, he won't budge?"

He shook his head. "No chance. Every commander in this theatre of war has tried to persuade him to move, von Manstein even. Paul Hausser flew to Berlin to make the case, but Hitler still insists that we must have the Panzer Vs before we move."

"Look, August, I've been over the other side on reconnaissance missions, they're building defences up like you wouldn't believe. Now that the muddy season is ending they'll be redoubling their efforts, it'll be sheer hell when we go over there."

"I know that, we all know that, but we're stuck here until we get the order to go."

He looked me in the eye and I knew exactly what he meant. The waiting would result in massively higher casualties. Neither of us really expected to survive the coming battle against the massed might of the Soviet mechanised hordes.

CHAPTER SIX

'The battle is going very heavily against us. We're being crushed by the enemy weight...We are facing very difficult days, perhaps the most difficult that a man can undergo'.

Erwin Rommel

The tracks had hardened as the rainy season completely ended and the warmer weather dried out both the armies and the terrain. We had spent the past weeks alternately patrolling the railway line and in fruitless chases around Kharkov for the supposed traitor, the 'Lucy' spy ring that was like a festering sore to our intelligence people. It was already the twenty ninth of June and many of us doubted that the offensive would ever begin. Soon we would be into July. Even so, the preparations continued, more and more equipment was offloaded day after day and even the much-vaunted Panzer Vs arrived to everyone's relief. Except that when their crews took them out on local manoeuvres they repeatedly broke down and had to be towed back or repaired on the spot. The worst problem was engine fires, probably in the depths of winter it wouldn't have been a problem but as the temperature increased the engines overheated and fires broke out, immobilising the vehicle and threatening to explode the fuel tanks. Von Meusebach spent little time with his regiment, seeming always to find that he was needed elsewhere, usually somewhere cleaner and smarter where there was the chance of a good dinner and high-ranking company. It was almost a relief when I got a message from von Betternich and went into the city to meet him.

"We're going to Vinnitsa, to Army Group South, I need your men to escort me and Wiedel there to talk to the local SD and Gestapo people. Obviously we can't do this on the communications network, we have no idea who is listening in, but we think we've narrowed the leak down to certain Abwehr officers both in Berlin and here in the Ukraine. I want you back here at eight o'clock tomorrow morning, you'll need a half-track and six of your troopers, that should be enough."

"Sir, what if the offensive starts, surely it must come soon? My men will be needed here, we're Panzer-Grenadiers, not bodyguards."

He smiled gently. "I can assure you my friend that

Zitadelle will not start for at least a week and we shall be back in three days. It is essential that we catch these treacherous scum before we start the attack, otherwise the Russians will know our every move."

As I drove back to Podvirky I reflected on what he'd said, 'At least a week'. That meant that the pincer attack on the salient would begin within days, after the weeks and months of waiting. At least the long period of idleness would be over, except that I was confident that the Russians had not been idle at all. It was not going to be an easy fight by any means. Most of us were convinced that all of our Eastern Front operations were hanging on the outcome of Kursk.

Von Meusebach was as scathing as usual as he looked at my documents, including a telex from Himmler's RSHA in Berlin.

"So while we're working day and night you'll be swanning off with the Gestapo to von Manstein's HQ, is that correct?"

"Essentially, yes, Sir." I hadn't actually ever seen our CO working very much at all, but it would hardly be tactful to remind him of that fact.

"Make sure you get back as fast as possible, don't waste any time on the local night life, we have a war to fight here."

I saluted and left, it would be interesting to see how he coped with the smoke and horror of a major battle, what

I'd seen so far was not very encouraging. I doubt I was the only one hoping a Soviet tank gunner would range in on von Meusebach's vehicle. We packed ammunition and supplies for five days, just in case, then spent the evening drinking the local vodka and speculating about what we would face in the salient.

"It's not just the tanks," Mundt said. "I remember the drive on Moscow, when they counter attacked in that first winter. Wave after wave of the bastards, it was like the First War in the trenches. They came at us, lines of them, tens of thousands, we machine-gunned them, shelled them, we used mortars, hand grenades when they got near and still they kept coming. I can even remember their officer mounted on a horse, charging towards us in the middle of his men."

He paused to take a heavy draught of vodka. We were listening enthralled to the veteran of those first heady weeks and months when it seemed as if we were unstoppable.

"We shot him, of course, he was one of the first to go, but they kept coming. A vast army in those long brown coats, I remember the fur hats most, though. Whenever we could we would strip them off the bodies and wear them to keep out the cold, I remember going home on leave and some civilians mistook me for a Soviet."

"Did you beat them back?" Bauer prompted him.

"Eventually, yes, but they were like rabid animals. We

afterwards found out that half of them weren't carrying rifles. Their orders were to pick up weapons from those who fell. We couldn't believe it, but their capacity to obey the most murderous orders was amazing. When we'd killed most of the first wave the second one came in, then the third and the fourth. We killed them all," he finished soberly. There was sadness in his voice as he recalled so much death.

"Didn't they have commissars driving them on, Willy?" I asked him.

"They did, yes, but it wasn't just that. These people seem to have an infinite capacity to take orders, even when it means marching onto our machine guns and minefields. I tell you they're not like ordinary human beings. You've seen the way they live in the Soviet Union. They're treated worse than dogs, yet they'll defend their crappy patch of beaten mud as if it was a royal palace. It beats any normal understanding, and their wounded, we'd never seen anything like it."

He paused again and drank more vodka, as if the disturbing recollections were painful enough to need a drink to talk about them.

"The wounded, too, you wouldn't believe it, they never made a sound. They just lay there, suffering in silence. You could see it in their eyes, the pain of men who lay there with limbs blown off, guts hanging out through wounds in the stomach, just lying on the ground as if they'd lost the capacity for making any kind of noise. It's uncanny, I tell you. These people are not like us."

"You make them sound like supermen, Willy," I joked. "Brave, tough and capable of taking infinite punishment and yet still attacking when they know everything is lost, what are they, rabid dogs?"

They laughed nervously. I wished I hadn't spoken as Willy looked at me and said quietly, "Yes, that's a fair description."

I finished off the last of my vodka and lay down to try and sleep. In my nightmares I was surrounded by hordes of savage Russian soldiers, I was on my own and they attacked with rifles fitted with bayonets, all aimed at my belly. When they got near, they had faces covered in fur like wild animals and I woke up abruptly drenched in sweat. Damn those old soldier's tales. I'd have to take Willy to one side and ask him to desist, even if they were true.

At dawn we loaded the half-track and set out for Kharkov, von Betternich and Wiedel were waiting and we gave them the safest and most comfortable seats in the centre of the vehicle. The journey to Vinnitsa was long, hard and tiring. The track that took us there was well beaten and we were able to make good time, although it was bumpy and uneven, like most roads in the Soviet Union it was unpaved. But the flies and mosquitoes attacked us all the way through the thick forest that we had to cross, it was nerve wracking enough being constantly alert for partisan attacks and we kept both MG34s constantly manned. When we came out of the forest we were bitten all over and exhausted from watching every second for the partisan attacks. Fortunately the rest of the track to Vinnitsa was through open ground and we were able to relax. Until we drove into the city and realised that we'd come across a hornet's nest, something was clearly up. Every street was guarded with troops, tanks patrolled up and down and above us the Luftwaffe kept up constant over flights. There were checkpoints too, as we got nearer to headquarters of Army Group South they were manned by grim faced SS Leibstandarte and Feldgendarmerie, accompanied by Gestapo officers in long leather coats. I itched to ask them what was going on, were they expecting an imminent attack, but I resisted the impulse. The two security officers sat calmly in the middle of the vehicle ignoring everything, giving me the impression that they knew in advance that the city would be heavily guarded. Finally we reached von Manstein's HQ, established in a former barracks in a lightly wooded area on the outskirts of the city. We showed our documents to the final guard post, drove into the vehicle park and helped our passengers down from the half-track.

Von Betternich was smiling contentedly. "You know what all this is for, don't you?"

I shook my head.

"The Fuhrer is visiting Vinnitsa, Hoffman. His aircraft

is due to land shortly. Perhaps you will meet him, who knows."

At least that explained it. We weren't about to be attacked by the armoured legions of the Red Army. He limped into the building and we waited outside, enjoying the chance of relaxing after the long, jolting journey. We still had to beat off the flies, but their numbers were thankfully less than in the depths of the dark forests that we'd crossed.

"He must be coming to finalise plans for the salient," Mundt said. "At least we'll know where we stand."

"If we don't find this traitor, Willy, the Russians will know too, which would be a disaster."

We managed to find a signals unit making coffee and we shared out some black bread and cheese and washed it down with the hot brew. Wiedel came out and found us.

"We are invited to the airfield to watch the Fuhrer's aircraft land, Hoffman, it's quite an honour. Von Betternich will be with us in a few moments."

I didn't reply, I had my own view of the honour our Fuhrer was doing us. My opinion of him had deteriorated massively since we'd sat outside the Kursk salient allowing the Russians to build up their massive defences. The SD man came out five minutes later and we drove to the airfield. It was under even heavier guard and above us Messerschmitt 109s flew constant patrols, on the ground at least a hundred soldiers of the Leibstandarte Adolf Hitler waited patiently.

We all turned and looked as a long, black Mercedes staff car came through the checkpoint and into the airfield. When it stopped an adjutant leapt out and opened the door. Feldmarschal Erich von Manstein climbed wearily out, followed by the more nimble figure of Feldmarschal Walter Model, commander of the Ninth Army, part of Army Group Centre. We watched the sky avidly, waiting for the first sign of the Fuhrer's aircraft. Then a tension seemed to set into all of us, a slight noise in the distance that grew and grew until in the distance we were able to make out a small group of aircraft. As they came nearer they resolved into a Focke Wulf Fw200 Condor, the Fuhrer's personal aircraft codenamed Immelmann III, surrounded by a squadron of Me109s. The Focke Wulf dropped lower and lower until it swept over the runway and dropped gently to a feather touch landing. As it taxied to a stop troopers rushed up pushing a stairway and they locked it into position. A squad of the Leibstandarte Adolf Hitler rushed forward and took up their positions either side of the foot of the stairs and von Manstein and Model walked over to stand nearby. The aircraft door opened cautiously, first a few centimetres and then it was pulled fully aside and the Fuhrer stepped out to stand motionless at the head of the stairs as we all saluted. He waited a few moments more and delivered his familiar casual salute, then carefully climbed down the stairs. Behind him was another man in uniform that I didn't recognise, which was strange. The Nazi bigwigs were always in the news, and well known to every German citizen.

Reichsleiter Martin Bormann," whispered von Betternich, "he's the Fuhrer's private secretary."

Unlike Hitler, Bormann was quite pudgy and overweight. I guessed that as a secretary his work would largely be sedentary, with little opportunity for exercise. Then they descended the stairs and the Feldmarschals shook hands with their Supreme Leader, ushered him into the black Mercedes and they drove off. In front and behind the car were half-tracks laden with heavily armed Leibstandarte troopers. Finally we relaxed, he had landed and nothing had gone wrong.

"We can follow them back to HQ now," von Betternich said. "I need to speak to our people there and see if we can't track this 'Lucy' traitor. Just think, if we could uncover them while the Fuhrer is here, that would be something."

I climbed into the half-track and ignored him. I knew what he meant, praise from Hitler, pats on the back, promotions, medals, sometimes it seemed as if the whole of the Reich was dedicated to pleasing one man, hardly a healthy way to run such a huge empire. We drove back to Headquarters and left the security men to meet their counterparts while we found the army kitchen and got on with the more important business of getting something to eat. We were enjoying the early evening sunshine when a corporal came up to me and saluted.

"Compliments of Obersturmbannfuhrer von Betternich, Sir, you are invited to an informal reception for the Fuhrer this evening, it is due to start at ten o'clock in the main hall."

He turned about and left, I was stunned. I looked down at my stained, ragged uniform and automatically tried to brush off some of the dust. The men were grinning, probably thinking of their ragged scarecrow of a platoon leader rubbing shoulders with the high and mighty of the Third Reich. As usual, Willy took matters in hand.

"Don't worry, we'll help you get cleaned up, Sir. We may even be able to sew up the rip in the shoulder of your tunic, it happened when you went after those Russians in the foxhole."

I hadn't even noticed, I took off my tunic and my God, there was indeed a rent about fifteen centimetres long at the back of the shoulder. Willy took a needle and thread out of his pack and patiently sewed it up, another man had a sharpened razor and I did my best to scrape off my stubble. I finished off with a wash in a sink of cold water, wet down my hair and smoothed it back, put on my tunic and cap and stood in front of my men for 'inspection'.

"Those boots will never do, one moment," Willy said.

He reached under the axle of our half-track and came out with his hand covered in glossy black grease. He smeared it over my jackboots and rubbed them off with a piece of dirty rag, sure enough they looked clean and shiny.

Mundt nodded. "It'll do, we're not in Berlin so they can't expect any more."

I thanked them and left. The Leibstandarte guards checked my documents carefully, relieved me of my pistol and allowed me to go inside. The hall was packed with about a hundred officers, the Fuhrer was at the furthest end away from me which suited me fine, the last thing I needed was to be caught up in the machinations of the Nazi hierarchy.

I was quietly drinking a glass of fine Mosel when I heard a familiar voice.

"You're not enjoying it, are you?"

It was Wiedel, the Gestapo. I nodded to him.

"Not really, no. Politics never did to anything for me and I've seen too many blunders on this front to be overly impressed with this gathering."

He smiled. "Military strategy comes from only one source, Hoffman, it sounds suspiciously like you are criticizing the Fuhrer."

But he smiled as he spoke. It was some kind of black Gestapo humour.

The buzz of conversation got louder and I looked up to see that Hitler had moved nearer to us, he was standing talking to Feldmarschal Model.

"These troops of yours don't impress me," I heard him saying. "The men of 1943 are not of the same calibre as those of 1941."

He was referring to our massive armies that had invaded the Soviet Union, storming through Poland and the Ukraine to the gates of Moscow. But Model went bright red with anger at his Supreme Leader, formerly a corporal in the Great War.

"Of course they are not, my Fuhrer, the men of 1941 are dead, scattered in graves all over Russia."

There was a deathly silence, Hitler went pale with anger, then snorted and turned away to speak to von Manstein. Wiedel and I looked at each other. No comment was necessary. To agree with Hitler would be cowardly, to agree with Model could mean arrest. Neither of us had Feldmarschal rank to support us. I wanted to leave and go outside to smoke and chat with the men, smoking in the same room as the Fuhrer was forbidden, but leaving the reception before him was equally impossible. Von Betternich joined us and he was smiling.

"You wouldn't believe the gossip I've picked up in this room, Wiedel, I could have half the General Staff arrested tomorrow morning."

"In that event who would fight the war, Obersturmbannfuhrer?" I asked him.

His smile broadened even more. "That's a valid point, my friend. Do you have any suggestions for us, or should we ask the Fuhrer?"

"Ask him when we can attack the salient, that would be

more useful."

"Ah, yes, Kursk. Just wait, there is to be an announcement shortly."

I wondered how he seemed to be so well informed, until I saw him exchange glances with Bormann, the secretary. Of course, it was politics, quite simply the shifting balance of power and allegiance that was so all pervasive inside our Nazi-led administration. Like many SS officers I had never joined the Nazi party, I had little interest in or enthusiasm for politics. The more I saw of it, the more I found it corrosive and damaging to the heady ideals of the Third Reich before the war, when I had made my decision to become a professional soldier.

"Achtung!" Someone shouted across the room and there was instant silence. The Fuhrer stood on a low dais that had been placed in the middle of the hall and look coldly at his assembled officers.

"You have been waiting for many weeks to be given the order to attack the Kursk salient. I can now tell you that I will convene a meeting of my generals at the Wolfschanze on the First of July. At that meeting I will announce the date of the offensive. Decisions have been made that will affect the whole course of this war. Decisions that will see our armies once more sweep victorious to Moscow and beyond. Our new Panzers are now in place and will spearhead the advance. All of your questions will be answered and your fears laid to rest in the next few days.

The world will shake to the mighty roar of our armies and our Panzers will once more begin our crusade to the east. You have my word that you are on the eve of a great and resounding victory!"

The room erupted to Nazi salutes and shouts of 'Sieg Heil! Sieg Heil!'. It was heady stuff and I almost got caught up in it until I looked at von Manstein and Model, both wore expressions that were anything but enthusiastic, sour would be a more accurate description. And von Betternich was smiling openly, clearly enjoying the show. I had the uneasy feeling that this whole affair was being stage-managed. Politics!

The Fuhrer stalked out of the room with Bormann close behind him. Most of the officers stayed to enjoy the food and drink but I'd had enough, I left to go back to my platoon. I'd only been back for half an hour when Wiedel came to find me.

"We need you now, all of you, we've detected a transmission. This could be what we've been looking for. Come with me."

We followed him to the headquarters radio room. A furious looking Abwehr major was standing outside the door, protesting that he'd been thrown out of his own office. Wiedel ignored him and we went inside, there were banks of radio equipment with operators sitting in attendance with headphones clamped around their ears. We walked through to an office where an operator in plain clothes, obviously Gestapo, was adjusting a suitcase-sized radio. Von Betternich was watching him carefully.

"We've got a similar set at Kharkov so that with any luck we can triangulate between the two points, Wiedel explained. "How are you doing?"

The operator looked up. "I think it's him, I've been in touch with Kharkov by telegraph and they say the same, it's almost certainly our man."

"Excellent, where is he, do you have a location?"

The man looked confused, embarrassed. "Well, yes, that's the strange thing."

"Strange? Where is he, what do you mean?"

"Here."

"What do you mean here? In Vinnitsa?"

"I mean here, Sir, in this headquarters."

The enormity of his statement struck us all at once. If the traitor was here, in this headquarters compound, it was entirely possible that it could be a high-ranking officer, or at least a senior officer of some kind to have the means to access secret information and to have the freedom of action to hide a transmitter and quietly transmit in the middle of Army Group South's Headquarters. Once again, politics was a threat to our hunt for the traitor. Supposing it was a General officer, even a Feldmarschal? God help us all.

"Right, assemble your men, Hoffman, we'll look around and see if we can't catch this person."

I looked at him doubtfully. "It could be difficult with the Fuhrer here and all of these senior officers."

"In that case if any of them object the Fuhrer can simply order them to cooperate. We're wasting time, we need to get moving if we're to have any chance of catching the bastard."

I ran out, alarming the Leibstandarte sentries, and told the men to form up. We split into two parties. I went with Wiedel and two of the troopers. Mundt took the other three and went with von Betternich. We went from door to door of the accommodation block, checking bedrooms, dining rooms, offices and storerooms. We drew a blank and began to search outside the main buildings, the stores, ammunition dumps, kitchens and motor vehicle workshops. We were emerging from a spare parts store when I heard a shout from near the perimeter fence. It was Mundt.

We ran over to him.

"Someone went through the fence, look!"

There was a narrow gap, low to the ground, just large enough to enable one person to pass through. Bauer crouched down squeezing through and the rest of us followed, except for von Betternich who stood inside the fence with an unfathomable look on his face, his walking cane clutched in one hand. I had this uncomfortable feeling that he was he was already several steps ahead of us? If so, what those steps were was anyone's guess. I focussed my attention on the job in hand. Whoever had passed through had left a simple trail, footmarks in the soft, damp forest floor. Bauer kept the lead, I followed him and the rest were close behind me. We made good time and soon we were coming up on our quarry, we could hear him making heavy going through the forest. Suddenly his heavy footsteps stopped, he'd gone to ground and I suspected that he had twisted an ankle. We slowed down and cocked our machine pistols.

"Remember, we want him alive," Wiedel said quietly.

I nodded and passed it on to the men. We pushed carefully forward but there was no sign of him, then some sixth sense made me look behind. He had just got to his feet and was standing unsteadily, bringing up a huge pistol, I recognised it instantly, a Mauser.

The Mauser C96 was a semi-automatic pistol, originally produced by our own arms manufacturer Mauser from 1896. Several countries had manufactured unlicensed copies and Russia was no exception. It was instantly identifiable by the integral box magazine in front of the trigger, the long barrel, the wooden shoulder stock that could double as a holster or carrying case, and a grip shaped like the handle of a broom, so that some people nicknamed it 'the broomstick'.

I heard Wiedel shouting, "Don't shoot, we want him alive," then one of the men fired a long, low burst that took him in the legs and he collapsed to the ground. I ran up and kicked the Mauser out of his hands, then looked at him closely. He was a partisan, possibly Ukrainian, but more probably Russian. His cap was adorned with a red star and when I went through his clothes he had a packet of documents in his pocket together with a map.

"Who are you?" Wiedel shouted at him, lifting him up by the shoulders. "Who is your contact inside our headquarters?"

Although in obvious pain, he managed to hawk and spit at the Gestapo man. Wiedel smashed his hand across the man's face, threw him to the ground and put his boot on one of the wounds on his legs. The Russians may have possessed legendary courage in the face of pain but I think we all winced as the animal scream came out of his throat.

"Who are you, who is your contact? Quickly, tell me man and I'll get treatment for your legs!"

He shook his head, his bearded face screwed up in agony.

Wiedel took out his pistol and screwed it into his mouth, causing him to gag and choke.

"For the last time, your name!"

The man's eyes were watering with the pain of the boot on his leg and the gun in his mouth. He started to mumble and Wiedel took out the pistol.

"Colonel Mikhail Romanenko, NKVD on assignment to the partisans, that is all I will tell you."

The NKVD, the People's Commissariat for Internal

Affairs, we'd scored a high-ranking prisoner. Wiedel pressed him further, asking him the name of his contact and putting his boot on the wound again when he refused to answer, but the man passed out with the pain. I heard the sound of footsteps coming from the HQ, when they appeared through the trees it was von Betternich limping along but in front of him was Reichsleiter Martin Bormann. I could hardly contain my surprise. We stood to attention and Bormann spoke first to Wiedel.

"Explain!"

Wiedel told him how we had chased him and shot him in the legs, he told him the name that the man had given us. Bormann took out his pistol, a Luger, and knelt down beside the Russian.

"Who is your contact inside this headquarters? Answer me!"

He pushed the barrel of his pistol against the man's head. "It's no use pretending to be unconscious. If you wish to live, answer me. I will count to five!"

He started counting, one, two, three, suddenly the man's eyes flicked open, he saw Bormann kneeling over him with the pistol and his eyes flared suddenly, it was as if he recognised him, but that was ridiculous. Four, five, 'crack', the sound of the shot whipped around the forest. The Russian fell over, dead with a Luger bullet in his brain. I was so shocked. The second, or third, most powerful man in the Third Reich had just executed a prisoner before our eyes.

"Search him thoroughly and then leave his body for the wolves," Bormann said contemptuously. Then he began walking back alone to Headquarters. Von Betternich had a neutral look on his face. Once more I had the impression that he knew long in advance what was to happen.

"Wiedel, come, we must accompany the Reichsleiter. Hoffman, search him and leave him as ordered. When you're done you'd better make a sweep of the area to make sure there are no other partisans near here."

They walked away and we still stood, frozen with incredulity.

"That was interesting, Sir," Mundt said.

I nodded. "An understatement Willy, something is happening here that we do not understand."

"Did anyone else think that the Russian partisan knew Reichleiter Bormann?" Wesserman asked.

I fixed him with a hard stare. "Schutze Wesserman, don't even think anything like that unless you wish to become a guest of the Gestapo."

He shook his head. "Understood, Sir. But I still don't understand it all."

"Keep it that way, Gerd, you'll find it's by far the safest way."

We returned to the headquarters and an orderly found us beds for the night. In the morning, von Betternich told us that we were returning to Kharkov that day. Our business was at an end.

I wasn't sure if he'd achieved what he wanted or not, I didn't even ask. Between the reported army officers plotting to kill the Fuhrer, Martin Bormann's involvement with von Betternich, which meant the head of the SS, Heinrich Himmler as well as the identity of the traitor giving our secrets to the Russians, there was a nightmare of possibilities. Like an infinite maze that I had absolutely no wish to penetrate. Then of course there were the Russians. There was no question now that we would shortly join battle with them inside the Kursk salient, probably within days. As we drew nearer to Kharkov the signs were everywhere, companies of heavy and medium armour parked alongside the road just inside the trees for camouflage, crews working frantically to bring them to readiness. Infantry everywhere, Panzer Grenadiers, artillery parks under huge camouflage nets, stacks of ammunition crates awaiting transport to their units, it was as if the Fuhrer's message last night had spread like wildfire to the somnambulant armies. The drums of the Gods of War were beating. Soon their armoured legions would be unleashed to bring down a torrent of fire and hell on the enemy.

CHAPTER SEVEN

'The Russian Colossus has been underestimated by us. Whenever a dozen divisions are destroyed the Russians replace them with another dozen'.

Chief of Staff Franz Halder von Armin

After the excitement of seeing the army top brass and even the Fuhrer face to face, the grimy railway yard at Podvirky was a severe dose of reality. It was dark when we got back and I went to report to Muller, there was no sign of von Meusebach. I told him about seeing the Fuhrer. He only had one question.

"Did he have any news about Zitadelle?"

"They're meeting at the Wolfschanze on the first of July, Hitler is giving them the date then. It should only be days away, Sir."

"I hope so, this waiting is getting us all down as is this miserable village of Podvirky. Anything would be better than this."

"Are there any orders for my platoon?" I asked him.

He considered for a few moments. "We've got the anti-partisan patrols covered, so you may as well get some sleep. The CO is in the city at present, he's entertaining some friends in a hotel there."

He must have seen my look. "I know, I know, I'm sure he'll be back shortly."

"But Sir, we're about to mount a major attack, shouldn't he be here?"

He shrugged helplessly, as if to say 'it's out of my hands'. "Report to me in the morning, Hoffman, I'll have a better idea then of what needs to be done."

I saluted and left.

I strolled around the darkened village. The stench of coal dust, oil and excrement was pervasive. Few soldiers moved around, it was as if the whole place was holding its breath waiting. Waiting for the next Russian air attack, waiting for the partisans to carry out one of their lightning raids, storming in and causing massive destruction and death, only to disappear as quickly into the vast steppes. Waiting for one man, the master of all Western Europe, to give them the final order that would fling them into the salient and into the maw of the Russian guns.

It made me think of the legendary English 'Charge

of the Light Brigade', that doomed cavalry charge in the Crimea. In October 1854 Lord Cardigan led 673 cavalrymen straight into the valley between the Fedyukhin Heights and the Causeway Heights, named the 'Valley of Death' by the poet Tennyson. The opposing Russian forces comprised twenty battalions of infantry supported by over fifty artillery pieces. These forces were deployed on both sides and at the opposite end of the valley. Astonishingly, despite intense fire from three sides that devastated the charging cavalry, the Light Brigade was able to reach the Russians at the end of the valley and force them back from their guns, but they suffered massive casualties and were forced to retreat with more than half the brigade lost. Was Kursk to be our own doomed charge, racing to do battle with the descendants of those Russians in the Crimea, with a similar expectation of utter defeat? I was gazing directly at four Tiger tanks, the Panzer VI, massively armoured and mounting the huge, 88mm gun that could dominate the modern battlefield. It would not be another Crimea, we were too heavily armed and equipped to suffer such a rout, but winning was another matter. We were all suffering from low morale, the last few months had brought us all to the point of despair, if we couldn't shake it off we would be handing the Russians victory almost before a shot had been fired.

In the morning a messenger came to tell me to report to von Meusebach. He was as elegantly turned out as usual, although his face looked rather more haggard than I'd remembered, perhaps he was suffering from too much good food, heavy drinking and too many willing women during his frequent stays in the Kharkov hotel. He studied me with bleary eyes.

"So you met the Fuhrer in Vinnitsa?"

I told him I'd been in the same room, which was not quite the same thing and that he would be making his announcement shortly. He grunted. "About time, we all want to give Ivan a beating and go back to the Reich with a chest full of medals, don't we, Hoffman?"

Was that what he intended? For most of us all we wanted was for the war to be over so that we could go home. I remembered his behaviour at the skirmish outside Belgorod. Perhaps someone should inform him that to give Ivan a good beating you first had to face him and swap blows. But that someone would not be me!

"Yes, Sir."

"Good man. I've got another job for you, report to General Hoth in Kharkov, he has asked for an experienced reconnaissance platoon, so I immediately thought of you." He gave me a twisted smile. It was almost a sneer. "While you're there, I've left a briefcase in a hotel room, the Hotel October, you can collect it for me. Room 324, they're expecting someone to collect it, be careful, the contents are top secret."

The Hotel October was where Nadia had been staying,

as far as I knew she was still there. It would be a chance for me to see her, even if it was a brief visit, it would be better than nothing.

An hour later we were clanking along the track that led to Kharkov in our Hanomag 251 half-track.

"Any ideas what this reconnaissance business is, Sir?" Mundt asked me.

I shook my head. "It won't be anything good, Willy. Other than that I've no idea. We'd better go and collect this briefcase first, we may not get a chance once we've seen Hoth, he may send us straight out."

We pulled up outside the hotel.

"Give me about twenty minutes, I need make a brief visit while I'm here, Willy."

He smiled. "Give her my regards."

Kharkov was coming alive, as if the word had spread already that we would soon be moving, the street was bustling with people and vehicles, most of them military. Soon they would all be heading east towards Kursk. I went inside and the desk clerk gave me the key for room 324, I ran up the stairs and put the key in the door. Before I could open it someone snatched it open and I was staring at Nadia. Her face wore a smile that faded into surprise when she saw me and everything clicked into place. So this was where von Meusebach had been spending his nights away in Kharkov. Not that I had any reason to object to Nadia sleeping with who she wished, but him, that flabby, oily lawyer who was doing his best to turn a fighting regiment into a laughing stock.

"I've come to collect your boyfriend's briefcase."

Her face fell at my icy tone.

"Jurgen, it's not what you think, really, but you weren't here."

I knew that I was acting stupidly, but if it had been anyone else I wouldn't have been so angry.

"Would you give me the briefcase, I don't have time to talk, I need to get to Headquarters."

She passed me a brown leather case. Her eyes were on me, soulful and sad.

"Would you come and see me when you get back?"

I realised that I was acting like a love struck schoolboy cheated out of his date by the playground bully.

"I'll do my best."

She smiled when she saw that I had softened a little. "Until then, Jurgen."

Mundt was surprised when I climbed into the vehicle. "You were quick, is everything ok?"

"It could be better, Willy." Damnit, of all people, fucking von Meusebach, it was like a knife in the guts. "Let's go and see what the good General wants of us."

Generaloberst Hermann Hoth, commander of the Ninth Army, was in a mobile command centre festooned with radio aerials on the outskirts of the city, touring the troops that were about to join battle with the Soviets. I waited outside while officers came and went, messengers ran in and out and occasionally I could hear his voice shouting orders to his staff. Eventually an officer came and beckoned me in. There were four steps leading up to the command cabin at the rear of the truck. Inside was chaos, radio operators, staff officers and harassed orderlies taking notes and making marks on a map on the wall. Hoth was at the other end of the cabin, abruptly, he turned and saw me waiting.

Hermann Hoth was fifty-eight, a Colonel-General in the Wehrmacht with a courageous record in the Great War, during which he was awarded the Iron Cross First and Second Class. After leading his troops to victory in France he'd become one of the most successful Panzer commanders on the Eastern Front. He commanded the Fourth Panzer Army and was regarded as one of the linchpins of the forthcoming offensive. The Fourth Panzer Army under his command was the largest tank formation ever assembled. He beckoned me forward.

"So you're the SS officer who brought back those two Soviet engineers from inside the salient?"

I nodded. "Yes, Sir."

I felt him sizing me up with his sharp, ice blue eyes. He was a fit, trim and muscular man despite his age, his steel grey hair was cut close to the scalp and he looked to be a man who should not be underestimated. His past victories served to underline that fact and I had no doubt that Russians had put his celebrated war record under a strong microscope.

"I need to know what my tankers will be going into, Obersturmfuhrer Hoffman." I noticed him struggling with the unfamiliar SS rank. "Take a look at this map."

He led me over to the large map on the wall, the salient stood out like a cancerous growth, an evil physical entity that pierced our front like a bulge in a worn rubber tyre. He pointed to the city at the rear of the bulge, roughly midway from north to south.

"As you know, this is our main objective, we attack from both sides in the classic encirclement tactic, the troops caught inside will be cut off from supplies and reinforcements and we finish them off at our leisure. Apart from destroying the Soviet armies inside the salient, it is vital that we take the city of Kursk because of its strategic importance."

He moved his hand down. "This is our first main objective, the village of Prokhorovka, there is a small railway station there, not much else. We will be supporting II SS Panzer Corps, which I believe includes your own division, Das Reich."

I nodded. "That is correct, yes, Sir."

"I need to know what the Ivans have waiting for us, Hoffman. You've done well supplying us with those two Soviet engineer officers, but that was some time ago and I have to know what they have prepared in the meantime.

You know we'll be going in within days, that means that anything you can find our about the Soviet defences will be worth its weight in gold, the Soviets won't have time to change things around even if they realise that we have uncovered the layout of their defences. So that's your mission, get in there using the routes that you've had success with in the past and find out what lies between here and Prokhorovka. With any luck they won't even know you were ever there. Good luck, Hoffman, report back to me inside of forty-eight hours. We haven't much time left, you know."

"How should we travel into the salient, General?"

He spread his hands. "You're an officer of the SS, man. I've been told that you people are big on using your initiative."

He smiled to take the sarcasm out of his words, but I couldn't help but rise to the bait.

"Then you have been correctly informed, Sir. I'll report back within forty-eight hours."

"Good. Take whatever resources you need, you have my full authority. If anyone gets in your way, tell them I'll have them arrested! I want that intelligence, Hoffman, whatever it takes!"

I looked away as someone called urgently for his attention. I was forgotten. I saluted and left, the men were less than impressed when I got back to our half-track.

"They must be crazy," Voss said bitterly. "How the hell

can we get in and out of the salient again without being caught by the Russians? They're not complete idiots, they'll be waiting for us to try something like this, especially after the last time."

"Horses," Mundt said emphatically.

There was a chorus of groans.

"No, look. It worked last time. It's the last thing they'd expect. If we go in and out at night and they hear us, we know they'll assume it's only their own Cossacks. Why not horses?"

"It's a fair point. Besides, on foot we'd never cover enough ground and there's no way we can use the half-track, the Scharfuhrer is right. Bauer, you know where the stable is, take us there now and we'll see if we can get them to cooperate again."

He started the engine and we clattered through the city streets, turned into the lane and stopped outside the stables. The NCO in charge, Wegener, looked out as we arrived.

"What is it this time?" he asked suspiciously.

"Horses, Wegener. We need to borrow some of your mounts for a couple of days."

Another soldier came out of the stable block, an infantry colonel. We saluted and waited for him to acknowledge. He looked at us with a haughty expression.

"What are you men doing here? These horses are for the use of army officers, not any old ragtag SS platoon looking to have some Saturday night fun."

"I'm sorry, Sir, but I have to borrow some of them, don't worry, we'll look after them."

He was a pompous ass, immaculate in his riding breeches, polished boots and pressed uniform. I should have told him straight away that this was military business, but like our own CO von Meusebach, he was the kind of officer that irritated me on sight.

"Absolutely not, I forbid it. Look at you, man, you're not even fit to borrow a bicycle!" He glared at me for a few moments. "What are you waiting for? Get out of here!"

"Yes, Sir. I'm sorry, but I'm acting under General Hoth's orders, he said I am to arrest anyone who obstructs this mission." I turned to my platoon. "Men, put this officer under arrest and take him to Fourth Panzer Army headquarters."

They stepped forward and took him by the arms. The officer paled. "Hoth? I see, very well, you'd better take what you need."

I waited a few moments for effect and then nodded at the men. "Let him go."

The officer straightened his uniform and strode off. Wegener watched him go with a broad smile. "A good thing you brought that stuffed shirt down a peg, he thinks he's God's gift to the Wehrmacht."

"What does he do?" I asked him.

"He's the catering supplies officer for the Fifty-Seventh Infantry. A total prat, all his men hate him, even the other officers."

He looked over the platoon. "So you all want horses, do you?"

I nodded. "General Hoth's orders. It's an in and out reconnaissance mission, we need fast, reliable mounts."

"Very well. Come in and you can choose the best of the bunch, if you're going behind the lines you don't want a horse that can't keep up with the Cossacks."

I looked at the horses standing in the stables, some were nuzzling at feed in iron troughs set into the stable walls. They were the familiar Panjes, the Russian horses whose endurance was epic, bred for the extremes of heat and cold and rough terrain of the Tsarist Empire and latterly the Soviet Union. I admired a beautiful chestnut mare, shaggy haired like the others but slightly larger and she looked sleeker, even proud. He saw me looking.

"Yes, she's a beauty, that Colonel you spoke to regards her as his personal mount, so it'll stick in his throat if someone else uses her."

"I'll take her then."

We selected nine horses. Mundt was puzzled, "There are only eight of us, why nine horses?"

"I've got an idea, I think we may be able to recruit someone to help us get in and out, Willy."

He looked sceptical. "You mean Irina? No way, she'd

sell us out to the Russians if we gave her half a chance."

"I've got to try, if she says no there's nothing lost, but if we can bring her along it could make the difference between success or failure."

Bauer started the engine and I directed him to Irina's house. A group of local people watched us draw up with surly expressions. When I knocked she answered the door immediately.

"What do you want?"

"Irina, I'm sorry, but I need your help."

"Go away, Jurgen, I made it clear last time that I'm finished helping you Germans."

"We're not all as bad, you know. Just because there are some wicked people in the military doesn't mean that the rest of us are the same. And think about the Soviets, if we're forced out of the Ukraine they'll be back. You know that Stalin has declared everyone that remained behind a traitor? You know what they do to traitors?"

She nodded. "I know. I also know what your troops did to my parents."

"Irina, that was a rogue outfit, you know that most of us are not like that. You also know that if the Soviets come back, most of them are like that. How many Ukrainians have they killed? Hundred of thousands, millions, think of the Kulaks starving and freezing to death in Siberia, it will all happen again. This coming battle could make all the difference, I'm asking you to put your anger aside for now. Afterwards, if we Germans win, at least you can ask the local administration to enquire into your parents death, the Soviets would put you in the Gulag just for asking."

"And if the Soviets win?" she said bitterly. "What then?"

"In that case, we are all dead," I said tiredly. I walked back to the half-track, I'd done my best.

"Jurgen, wait."

I looked around.

"Give me ten minutes and I will come with you."

Bauer drove us back to the stables and we began to make the horses ready for the crossing that evening. I sent him back with von Meusebach's briefcase and a message telling him that we were acting under Hoth's orders, orders that included a blanket arrest warrant for anyone refusing support. He also carried a chit to draw rations and ammunition for all of us. While we waited for him to return, we exercised the horses and tried to familiarise ourselves with them. Irina chose a small blue-roan gelding. Perhaps there was an unconscious message there for me, perhaps not. Wegener made sure that we had the best of everything, every strap, every buckle, every stirrup was checked and checked again, there were no convenient stables where we were going that would happily fix anything that broke. Bauer came back in the Hanomag, we took out boxes of food and ammunition and transferred them to our packs.

"How did von Meusebach take it?" I asked him.

Bauer grinned. "He refused at first, but when he got Hoth's HQ on the field phone and they told him that the General's threat of arrest was real, he couldn't have been more helpful. Mind you, there's something about him, he's definitely got it in for you, Sir."

"Stefan, every day here could be our last, I'll worry about the CO when the time comes. Let's concentrate on getting this job done first."

Wegener let us park the Hanomag in the stable yard and we mounted the horses and rode out in a long line, heads turned as people heard us riding through the city, expecting to see a Soviet Cossack unit about to attack. There was considerable relief when they saw our German uniforms and distinctive steel helmets. In fact, we did have regular cavalry in certain theatres, including a few Cossacks on the Eastern Front. Beginning in the summer of 1942, as a part of our policy of employing ex-Soviet personnel, prisoners of war and deserters, a number of independent Cossack cavalry squadrons and troops were formed under the First Panzer Army in southern Russia. Under German commanders, these units successfully performed long-range reconnaissance and staged raids behind enemy lines in the steppes beyond the lower Don and in the northern Caucasus. Subsequently, the 1st Cossack Division had just been formed in May.

We reached a fork in the road and I asked Irina which way she suggested. She was still cool, helping us against her better judgment. All I'd persuaded her of was that as bad as we were, the Russians were much worse, it didn't make me feel especially proud.

"Where are you heading for?"

"Prokhorovka."

She flinched. "That's open country, it's not an easy place to get to undetected. Lots of open steppes with little chance of concealment, just a few low hills, that's about it. Very well, we'll take the left fork here, there is a place I know about six kilometres away that is a good crossing point."

"Is it another railway tunnel?"

"No."

We carried on in silence. I could live with that, if she got us into the salient undetected. And out again, of course. It took us an hour to reach the point she was aiming for, a massively overgrown balka, so overgrown in fact that even in daylight it would have been almost impossible to see it even when you were staring straight at it. It was now almost dark and we couldn't see it at all. Irina found it because of a ruined stonewall that marked the entrance.

"We will need to lead our horses through on foot," she said. "The undergrowth is too thick otherwise, besides, it is shallow in parts and the Russians may spot us. The balka stretches for almost two kilometres, when we reach the end we will be well inside the Soviet lines."

I detailed Bauer to take the point. He walked quietly up

the ravine, pushing the tangled vines and branches to one side to make headway, his horse was sent to the rear for Wesserman, our back marker. Then we pushed through the darkness of the Ukrainian balka, stumbling, whispering muttered curses as we continually lost our footing on roots and branches that made the going very difficult. The horses seemed to have some sixth sense about the obstacles and daintily high stepped over the worst of them. It took an hour to cover the two kilometres to the end and by the time we stumbled out we were exhausted. I gave them five minutes to rest, but we had a lot of ground to cover to arrive at our destination and be under cover before daylight.

We rode in single file. Irina was back in the lead, taking us along an ancient route probably used by smugglers and criminals for many centuries. We led our horses along more balkas, rode cautiously through the ancient woods that had probably been here for a thousand years. She seemed to have an instinct for where the Soviet armies had made their encampments and more importantly, where they had not.

"It's not too difficult," she said once when I asked her about it. "These routes are almost inaccessible except on foot or horseback, why would the Russian armies come this way?"

Except for the infantry and the Cossacks, I could have replied. But the Soviets tended to use combined arms organisations called 'Fronts' that comprised armour, artillery, infantry and even aircraft, so perhaps she was correct that they would avoid this kind of area. Unless of course a wandering Cossack patrol happened along, we'd have to deal with that if it happened. It was still dark when we reached the outskirts of a small village marked on my map as Belenikhino.

"There's a series of low hills outside the village and a disused and overgrown quarry where we can shelter the horses. If you climb out of the quarry on foot to the hill above you will be able to see the whole area around Prokhorovka. We will have to keep very quiet, there will probably be troops quartered in the village."

I nodded and told her to lead us to the quarry. We reached there while it was still dark and we had to wait until the first lightening of the sky announced the coming dawn. The quarry had almost completely returned to nature, there were no buildings or anything man-made in evidence, only a deep white gash in the ground that soared to a cliff above us. We were in a deep bowl choked with small trees that were ample to give us cover for the horses and ourselves. We dismounted and allowed them to feed and water in a nearby stream, but we left the saddles on, the possibility of having to make a hasty exit was very real.

Gradually the sky lightened and yet everything was silent. I heard the distant buzz of an aircraft, then another, it faded into silence. For a moment I wondered if we were in the right place when suddenly the Soviet tanks began to start their engines to warm them up for the start of the day. I left Beidenberg in charge and climbed to the top of the hill with Mundt and Irina. The sight that greeted us was extraordinary. Within two kilometres was what looked like at least an entire Soviet army complete with almost a city of tents. Armour stretched into the distance, line after line of T34 tanks, like iron centipedes that wound as far to the east as the eye could see. I heard Mundt mutter, "Mother of God, there are millions of them," as he unconsciously crossed himself, I remembered that Willy was a Catholic. Artillery parks were scattered across the steppe, tens of thousands of soldiers were stirring and beginning to form up for the coming day.

"Willy, what's your estimate of the armour?"

He shook his head. "They're out of sight on the steppe, I wouldn't like to hazard a guess."

"Try."

"Maybe five hundred in this sector alone, mostly T34s. If I was to extrapolate that across the whole of the salient, I'm guessing five thousands tanks, perhaps even more."

"So we're going to be outnumbered?"

"It's not just the armour, look at the artillery parks, they must have thousands of guns. Infantry, I'm guessing over a million, maybe two million across the whole of the salient. And minefields, my God, I remember the campaign in 1941, the Russians are the past masters at minefields, they've almost certainly planted everything they've got."

I wrote everything we'd seen in my notebook. It wasn't anything new, I'd reported before on the massive Soviet build-up that I had seen, but this time we were on the eve of the attack. The task we were faced with was daunting, but not insurmountable. Provided of course that we attacked taking into account the enemy that faced us. So far all I had seen was a blind disinclination to believe anything that may be unfavourable to conventional military wisdom, maybe it was the Fuhrer's military wisdom. All I could do was report what I saw and how I interpreted the Russian deployments, the rest was in the hands of our military masters.

"Scharfuhrer, I think we've seen enough already, we'll keep a watch up here for the rest of the day, as soon as it gets dark we'll make our way back."

"I'll take first watch if you wish, Sir."

"Good, I'll make sure you're relieved in two hours."

I climbed carefully back down to the quarry and told them what I had seen. We settled down to wait out the day sensing that a dark gloom had descended over us. The reason was obvious, we were about to go into a battle in which we would need to use every ounce of intelligence, planning and military skill to achieve victory. Even then, at best it may only be a Pyrrhic victory. I recalled my history, after defeating the Romans at the battle of Asculum, King Pyrrhus had lost so many of his troops that he said, 'One more such victory would utterly undo me'. The Russians could lose armour and troops at a rate of three or four times what our own armies suffered and avoid defeat by making certain that we couldn't win.

Irina was concerned at the black mood that had descended on our group. "Don't you think you can beat the Russians, Jurgen?"

"No, not at all. Of course we can beat them, but most battles are decided by on who makes the least mistakes and they have such vast resources that we can't afford to make any. Our soldiers, armour and equipment is the finest in Europe, but we cannot afford to lose too many of them, what we need are commanders, leaders and generals who fight skilfully, not throw their divisions into battles they cannot win and then refuse to withdraw them to fight another day when things are not going well."

"Isn't that what your leader, Adolf Hitler is reputed to do? Throw whole armies away uselessly on battles that are already lost."

I smiled. "You didn't hear that from me."

I sensed that she was thawing, I could hardly blame her for feeling such bitterness towards Germany but I had personally done nothing except try to help her. When we got back to Kharkov I decided I'd try to break down the barriers and restore something of a relationship. We spent the rest of the day dozing, keeping under the cover of the trees. When it started to get dark we began to pack our gear ready to return. Bauer slid down to join us, he was the to keep watch at the top of the hill.

"Anything new, Stefan?"

"I'm not sure, Sir. There is a squadron of Cossacks roaming around, they're not anywhere near us, I hope they've disappeared somewhere else."

"Very well, let's go."

We mounted up and rode away, this time Beidenberg took the lead a hundred metres in front of us. We retraced our route in and managed to get to the balka that would take us across the lines. Beidenberg came back on foot, leading his horse. He signalled us urgently to dismount.

"They've blocked the ravine with a tank, a sodding great T34 parked right across it."

"I suppose it was inevitable," Mundt said. "They're putting much of their armour in defilade ready for our attack, the balka was too good for them to ignore."

"That's all very well, but we need to get past it. Irina, do you have any suggestions?"

"I'm sorry, I've no idea at all. The only possibility, and it's a maybe, is that we could cross open ground and get back into the balka just before the front line."

"It's a hell of a risk, they've got troops every where patrolling this close to the German lines."

"We haven't got any choice," Mundt said. "It's either that or we're stuck here for the duration, Sir."

I weighed up the odds. Whichever way we handled it,

the risks were severe.

"Very well, we'll do it. I suggest we retrace our steps for half a kilometre and we'll give that tank a wide berth."

We turned the horses around and went back over the dark ground until Irina said that we could push through some natural cover that would skirt the tank. It was a group of small trees, low mounds that were scarcely large enough to be classed as hills and between them the darkness of the shallow valleys that would keep us away from Russian eyes. I was tired, so very tired. I hadn't slept very much in days. I may have fallen into a waking sleep, where the mind goes on autopilot, but I suddenly felt uneasy. We were still mounted, walking the horses so as not to make too much noise or risk them tripping on unseen cracks and holes in the ground. The familiar jingle of the harness was soothing and gentle in the background, I realised that someone was talking and was about to warn them to be quiet when I recognised the language. It was Russian.

I strained my eyes to see and listened hard, as well as my platoon ahead and behind me, there was another line of horse moving in the same direction, perhaps three metres to my left. It was incredible, we'd run into a squadron of Cossacks and neither of us had noticed the other, we were just troops mounted on horseback. Mundt was behind me, I slowed my horse until he caught up and then pointed to the left, putting my finger on my lips for absolute quiet. His eyes went wide as he realised the danger. There were about ten of them, I put up ten fingers and showed him and he inclined his head in agreement. We edged slightly further away from them and I whispered to him, "Can you get everyone to make sure they're ready, when we get near the lines we'll give them a burst from the MP38s and then make a run for it."

He eased his horse back to our line and went up and down the right side, away from the Cossacks, making them aware of the danger. I could dimly see them gripping their machine pistols, I already had mine held ready. It was the best we could do, we rode on, each step taking us nearer to the front line. I thought we were going to make it, we were less than half a kilometre away and the Cossacks started to wheel away to their left, away from us. Then one of them turned and called out a question in Russian. He repeated it when he got no answer, then moved his horse nearer. He called out for a third time, then the night was ripped apart to the sound of automatic fire as Bauer opened up on him, hurling him from his saddle. The muzzle flashes lit up the night and we could momentarily see the Cossacks against the sky. The rest of us opened fire, a deafening tornado of gunfire that tore into the Russian riders, some were hit and went sprawling on the ground, two or three survived and rode of rapidly into the darkness.

"That's it, we need to hurry before they come back with reinforcements!"

I spurred my horse into a gallop and surged forward, the

others were recovering from the shock and encouraging their horses on. We all galloped forward, a mad dash that swept us past a pair of startled Soviet sentries, one of my people fired a quick burst that made them jump back into cover, then we were through, crossing the last four hundred metres of open steppe until we circled around a ruined stone wall.

"Wer ist da?" The familiar sound of German, 'who is there'?

"We're German, a reconnaissance party, don't shoot!" I shouted. "Everyone, get off your horses and identify yourselves to the sentries!"

We were surrounded by sentries who were suspicious and pointing their machine pistols at us. In the darkness I made out a tank, one of our older Panzer IVs, the commander was in the turret manning the mounted MG34. Slowly, we got off the horses and I went over to show my documents.

"If you can contact General Hoth's headquarters he will vouch for us."

The Oberleutant in the turret said, "Don't worry, my friend, I'll be doing that right now. In the meantime, keep your hands where we can see them!"

It took him ten long minutes to make contact using the radio in his tank patched through to Hoth's communications centre, but eventually he told us we could lower our hands, we were home. An hour later we reached Hoth's mobile command truck, the General was awake and waiting for us. I made our report and we were dismissed.

We rode slowly back to the stables in Kharkov and roused Wegener out of bed to deal with the horses. Bauer and Beidenberg came over to speak to me.

"What did they General think, Sir, will they act on what we saw? Maybe they could send in the Luftwaffe to hammer the Russian tanks, like we did in 1941."

"I'm not sure what he thought, my friends. And this is not 1941. The Soviets have hundreds of fighters that are as good as anything we can put up in the air. If we send in slow moving bombers or tank destroyers, like the Stukas retro fitted with a 37mm anti-tank cannon under each wing, they'll just send up several squadrons of fighters to shoot them down."

"We've got our own fighters, haven't we, Messerschmitt 109s and Focke-Wulf 190s?"

"We have, yes, but not enough, Bauer. We're short of everything, aircraft, fuel, armour, spare parts, everything."

"Does that mean we're beaten before we even start, Sir?" asked Beidenberg.

I'd gone too far, allowing my own misgivings to affect the morale of my unit. I smiled to take the edge off my pessimism. "It doesn't mean that at all. Remember, we're the best army in Europe, if not the world. No one can beat us when we make up our minds to fight hard. We'll smash them all the way back to Moscow, there is no way the Red Army can stand against us!"

They nodded gratefully and we looked across to the next street as a loud roaring noise and clanking of tracks announced a line of tanks manoeuvring towards the front. We counted them, there were perhaps twenty but they were all Panzer IIIs, which we'd all understood were obsolete, too lightly armoured and mounting a gun that was not powerful enough to fight the T34s. Like so many of our resources, we were so short that we were throwing everything into the battle, even these outgunned Panzers. Bauer caught my eye.

"So is that what we're going to use to smash those T34s we saw all the way back to Moscow?"

CHAPTER EIGHT

'The Red Army and the whole Soviet people must fight for every inch of Soviet soil, fight to the last drop of blood for our towns and villages...onward, to victory!'

Stalin

It was still dark, the morning of the fifth of July 1943. The mass of armour waiting all around us was astonishing, more than any of us had ever seen in four years of war. Hundreds of tanks of all descriptions, from the humble Panzer IIIs that had entered service in the 1930s to the newest Tigers, the Panzer VI with its enormous 88mm main gun and the newer Panzer Vs that so many hopes were pinned on. Along our front artillery were deployed, the crews manning their guns with stacks of ammunition and the gun tractors ready to limber up and follow the advance as it progressed into the salient. We had dozens of STuGIIIs, the Self Propelled Assault Guns built on the Panzer IV chassis that had proved to be more effective than most when repelling and attacking Soviet Armour. At intervals in the line were the fearsome new Panzerjager Tigers, nicknamed the Elefants. With their massive 200mm armour and 88mm gun, they were expected to perform well and clear the T34s from our path, although they carried no auxiliary machine gun and were almost without protection from close infantry attack. We also had many Panzer IIIs and Panzer IVs, too outdated and lightly armoured to tangle with the heavier Soviet armour, but still effective against more lightly armoured Soviet mechanised forces.

We waited in our Hanomag SD251 half-track, one of hundreds of Panzer-Grenadier companies lined up to provide support and covering fire to the Panzers that were so vulnerable to infantry armed with anti-tank weapons. We were towing a Pak 36 anti-tank gun, an obsolete weapon that had earned the nickname the 'doorknocker' because against the frontal armour of the T34 it was all it could achieve, to give it a sharp knock without penetrating. The geniuses in Germany had produced a shaped charge called a Stielgranate, it meant that the Pak 36 could penetrate any armour, but only at a range of less than three hundred metres. Unfortunately, the shell needed to be loaded from the muzzle rather than the breech behind the shield, which made the job of the loader highly dangerous on the battlefield when storms of bullets and shell fragments flew in every direction.

I had mixed feelings about the intelligence I'd brought back from our reconnaissance mission to Prokhorovka. General Hoth and his staff had listened attentively as I read our observations from my notebook.

"A good job, Obersturmfuhrer, my thanks. We will take everything you have said into consideration," he said warmly, turning away in dismissal. I felt that he hadn't listened to a word I'd said.

"General, none of what I've told you is imagined, it's all real, they're well dug in behind layers of defences, minefields and hundred of anti-tank weapons and artillery, quite apart from the tanks."

He'd whirled back around, reddening in anger. "So what would you have me do? The Fuhrer has dictated that we will attack at dawn on the fifth of July. Do you suggest I refuse an order? Perhaps you'd like to give him your opinion?"

He stood glowering at me and I realised that he was trapped, just like the rest of us, a prisoner of his oath to Adolf Hitler and his duty as an army officer to follow orders. I stood rigidly at attention, after a few moments he slackened.

"I believe your report in every detail, Hoffman and we will do our best to allow for the difficulties you outline, more than that I cannot do. Now, I suggest you re-join your unit and prepare as best you can for the coming battle."

Now we were assembled in the darkness ready to begin the attack and there were still so many imponderables. The Lucy spy ring a huge question mark, had our security department, the Gestapo and the SD, really managed to track down and destroy the traitor, or had they managed to give Stalin our plans so that we would be going into a gigantic armoured trap? I hadn't seen von Betternich or Wiedel since we'd got back and the date of the attack was announced. Had they arrested some poor devil and incarcerated them deep in some dark cellar, where they were busily torturing them, ripping out fingernails to try and extract information?

I didn't speculate any more, the guns opened fire, a shattering cacophony of noise that battered at my senses. At five o'clock hundreds of guns opened fire at a single signal, the darkness turned to bright light as a multitude of flashes announced the opening salvo, but it was not our salvo. My worst fears were realised as the Soviets launched a pre-emptive artillery barrage that had us all diving for cover. Staff officers ran frantically up and down the line re-organising our guns and within a short time they were ready for our own opening salvo. Tanks and assault guns joined in, firing repeatedly and inside the salient lit up with explosions. The barrage was planned to last for an hour, first counter-battery fire and then the immense, shattering barrages that were designed to destroy the enemy inside their bunkers and fortifications. The Russians shifted their aim to counter-battery fire and we began to move forward, away from the guns that offered such tempting targets to the enemy. The rain was pouring down in torrents, making it almost impossible to see where we were going, even our half-tracks slipped on the gradients as they struggled to grip the treacherous mud.

Finally we broke out of the worst of the soft ground and began to make progress over the steppe. Our first objective was a hill in the distance and through the rain we could see our Tigers charging across the steppes, the mine-clearing teams worked frantically to keep up with them and when they detected a mine they lay alongside it to mark its position, there was no time to do more. Bauer gripped the wheel tightly as we bumped and jolted along, Mundt manned the forward MG34 and Wesserman the rear. From time to time Soviet infantry popped up with anti-tank rifles and we headed straight for them while Mundt and Wesserman fired streams of bullets that sent them tumbling back into their holes in the ground. We stopped briefly to check that one Soviet gunner was dead but we'd only managed to wound him badly in the stomach. It was a fatal wound, there was only one thing left to do, Mundt pointed the gun down and sent a short burst into him that smashed the remaining life out of him. Perhaps many people would consider it inhumane, but if I ever received such an agonising and fatal wound I hoped that my enemy would deliver a similar coup-de-grace. I picked up his rifle and put it in the half-track to take back with us for later inspection, it was a PTRD-41, ProtivoTankovoye Ruzhyo Degtyaryova, an anti-tank rifle produced and used from early 1941 by the Soviets. It was a single-shot weapon firing a 14.5mm round, although unable to penetrate the frontal armour of our heavy Panzers, it could penetrate the thinner sides of earlier models as well as our more thinly armoured self-propelled assault guns and of course our half-tracks.

I gave the order and Bauer started forward again, racing to catch up with the Panzers. They were making good time and we had to go at full speed to catch up. We were approaching the start of the slope and already the Soviets were pouring fire down on us. Just in time one of our assault guns spotted a Russian KV-1 heavy tank, dug in at the side of the slope, only the movement of its turret alerted our gunners who fired three 88mm rounds in quick succession from the STuGIIIs that destroyed their target. We lurched up the slope and into a gale of fire, machine gunners, riflemen and light anti-tank weapons were all deployed against us. Against the intense fire the mine clearing teams had no chance and we had to just keep going, but we were lucky on that occasion and no mines were encountered. Then we broached the top of the hill just as a company of T34s was rolling forwards to meet our attack. We attempted to keep the infantry in check while the armour slogged it out, gun to gun, for possession of the hill.

On that occasion our Tigers totally outclassed the Russians, they poured tight, accurate disciplined fire on the Russians and we lost one Tiger that simply exploded to a direct hit, to eight T34s destroyed. Five of them were completely destroyed by multiple hits, the other three were damaged and immobilised, we saw the crews bailing out and diving for cover but machine guns from Panzers and half-tracks swept the immediate area around them and most were cut down in the open.

More T34s appeared in the distance heading towards us and the turrets of the Panzers swung around to begin engaging. I shouted for Mundt.

"Willy, deploy the PAK 36, we need to cover the Panzers."

He nodded, put Voss on the machine gun and took three of the men to uncouple and prepare the gun. The rest of my Panzer Grenadiers jumped out and started to check the trenches and foxholes that littered the hilltop. A bullet whistled past my head, I shouted "Sniper," just as the men jumped for cover, and several shots were fired in the direction that the bullet had come from. Mundt's team worked feverishly to deploy the anti-tank gun, braving the flying metal that flew everywhere and the sniper that was hidden somewhere in front of us. One of the crew, Schutze Vogel, threw up his arms and collapsed to the ground as the crack of the sniper's rifle announced another kill. We searched the terrain but the man was well hidden and it was impossible to discover his stand. All that could be done was to lay down a curtain of fire in his general direction and hope to keep his head down until we could deal with him. Voss and Wesserman poured machine gun fire towards him while Mundt set up the gun. Finally they were loaded and able to take shelter behind the shield. Immediately they sighted on a T34 that was less than two hundred metres to our front, I heard Willy shout 'fire!' and the weapon sent the missile hurtling towards the Russian. It hit the side of the tank, a direct hit on one of the fuel drums that the Soviets carried on the deck of the T34 and the whole armoured vehicle exploded in a sheet of flames and smoke.

We were faced with the dilemma of reloading from the front while there was a sniper loose. I shouted to the machine gunners to keep up the rate of fire and Mundt bravely rushed out to load the projectile. He slammed it in the muzzle and turned to run back just as a bullet cracked out from the unseen sniper and whistled past the position he'd just vacated, it hit the armoured shield of the gun and ricocheted off to hit the side of his steel helmet. He flinched but ran behind the shelter of the gun, chased by a second bullet that the sniper snapped off to try and finish him. I shouted orders at the men.

"We need to deal with that sniper, he'll kill the next man that goes out to load the gun. Bauer, drive the half-track forward and we'll try and flush him out. Keep clear of the PAK, they need to keep shooting at the T34s. Machine gunners, watch for him and keep your heads down!"

Bauer roared across the hilltop, it was desperate. We had to get near enough to the sniper to see him, yet keep our distance from the marauding T34s. One saw and fired off a shot that narrowly missed the body of our Hanomag, but Mundt had seen the danger and he sent another shot from the PAK 36 that caused the Russian to catch fire, black smoke belched across the battlefield coming straight towards us and protected us from the vision of the sniper. We reached his approximate position and the two gunners poured bullets in his direction while the rest of us jumped out and circled around warily to look for him. We couldn't see far inside the black smoke, which meant that neither could he. At first there was nothing, just endless grass and tangled foliage.

Then another bullet cracked out, not aimed at us but we distinctly saw the slight disturbance in the grass as the bullet left his rifle. Vellermann was the nearest, he ran up to the spot where we'd seen the bullet come from and emptied a clip from his MP38 into the ground. The barrel of a rifle tilted and pointed straight up, almost a gesture of surrender. I walked over to look into the sniper's stand, he was sprawled at the bottom of a shallow hole, still clutching his rifle but it has twisted to point up at the odd angle as he died. I nodded at Vellermann, "Good work," then we raced back to the half-track.

We drove the short distance back to the PAK 36, Mundt and his crew were busily engaging the Soviet armour, it was easier to keep loading the 'Stielgranaten' now that the sniper had been dealt with. There was little for us to do, we kept watch for Soviet infantry with anti-tank weapons but they seemed to have been dealt with by our Panzer Grenadiers, taking them on foxhole by foxhole. Soon the last of the Soviet armour had disappeared, it was time to move. We hitched up the gun and started after the Panzers. Almost instantly we stopped again, a Soviet infantryman had popped out of a foxhole fifty metres in front of us. He hadn't seen us and was fixated on one of our new Panzer Vs that has stopped only two hundred metres away to attend to a breakdown.

The crew didn't see him, they had opened the engine hatch, smoke poured out and they were scrambling to repair the problem. It was another PTRD-41, he was loading the cumbersome weapon and I had time to run towards him, I heard some of my men coming behind me. Just before we reached him his head turned and he spotted us, several heavily armed SS troopers rushing towards him. He looked down at his gun for a moment, obviously thinking about taking the shot, then put up his hands. We came up to him and one of the men jumped into his foxhole and searched it for weapons, but apart from the anti-tank rifle he was unarmed, probably he had been part of a crew that had run off when our attack started. We were able to talk to him in broken Russian and German, but his actual dialect was a mystery to us, he certainly wasn't ethnic Russian, possibly he was from Uzbekistan or one of the outlying satellite states.

"Which unit are you from?" I said to him harshly.

He spoke in a garbled language. The only sense I could make out was that he was part of the Voronezh Front, which we already knew was the combined arms unit that faced us. It was impossible to get any further with him, I considered tying him up and waiting for one of our support teams to take him into captivity, we had to press on quickly to catch up with our Fourth Panzer Army, but suddenly an armoured car came towards us, an eight-wheeled SD 232 drew up. The hatch opened and von Meusebach's head popped out.

"What's going on, Hoffman?" he shouted down to me.

I was so taken aback that I couldn't answer for a few seconds. I'd thought he was in the centre of our Regiment, controlling his companies and platoons and directing them during the battle. Instead he had obviously just come up from the rear. He realised why I was so surprised and hastened to explain.

"We had a slight electrical problem, that's why I'm

delayed. What are you doing with that prisoner?"

I told him I was about to tie his arms and legs and leave him for the rear units to collect when they came through.

"I can't have Russian prisoners running loose in the rear, Obersturmfuhrer. I'll take him back to our HQ for interrogation, you may carry on."

"Yes, Sir."

I pointed to the armoured car and pushed the Russian in its direction. One of the crew opened a lower hatch and took the prisoner inside. Without looking at the CO I climbed into our half-track and gave Bauer the order to drive away. Mundt was next to me, manning the MG34. He looked at me meaningfully.

"Shut up, Willy."

"I didn't say anything, Obersturmfuhrer."

Several minutes later, he spoke again. "We need a leader, not a yellow bastard like him!"

"I know, Willy, I know." I was tired of all of it, the politics, the posturing, soldiers that seemed to do everything except what they were paid to do, to fight. We drove to the edge of the hilltop and looked down on the steppe that unfolded in front of us. It was almost like watching a war game at the staff college, laid out on a table. Except that this was no game. Hundreds of tanks from both sides wheeled and manoeuvred, tens of thousands of infantry, the fortifications were visible, tank traps and ditches, barbed wire, some of the Soviet armour was hull down, dug into defensive positions where they could shoot at our own armour in enfilade.

The first of our own Panzers had started down the hillside and some of the half-tracks were already following.

"Bauer, you know what to do."

He accelerated away down the slope, driving at full speed to make us a harder target. Already we could see our own objectives, the Soviet anti-tank crews that were deployed to start shooting at the Panzers. I didn't need to give the order, Bauer turned towards the nearest enemy strongpoint just as the rest of our half-tracks were doing all over the forward edge of the battlefield, the noise was incredible. Explosions, sharp cracks of shells, machine gun fire and the roar of the tank engines. Everywhere there was smoke and chaos. The crew of the Soviet anti-tank gun saw us and shifted aim. They had a 45 mm anti-tank gun, their M1942 backed up with a Maxim heavy 7.62mm machine gun in support, the distinctive wheeled design with the metal shield to protect the crew.

The Maxim opened up on us and Mundt and Wesserman fired back short, accurate bursts that caused the Soviets to dive for cover, except the crew of the anti-tank gun, who ignored the machine gun fire to crouch behind their gun and continued loading. We were a hundred and fifty metres away from them when they suddenly fired the first shell, I felt a brief moment of terror as the shell rocked towards us, I could even see the black disc of its outline just before it hit. I knew we were finished, there was an appalling crash, I must have closed my eyes, I opened them again and we were still alive. Behind me there was a huge jagged hole in the bodywork and another the other side. Voss laughed nervously.

"Silly bastards loaded with armour-piercing, it went straight through."

Bauer had stopped, I looked up and the enemy were rapidly reloading, I knew that this time it would be high explosive. They wouldn't make the same mistake twice.

I shouted, "Bauer, get moving before they can reload!"

He drove forward at top speed, lurching towards the enemy gun. Our MG34s kept up a high rate of fire, making the Russians keep their heads down. Two of the machine gun crew were already down, sprawled on the ground and the gun had stopped firing, the danger to us was the anti-tank gun. One hit from a high explosive round would finish us, Bauer understood the danger and bore down on it, we were only metres away when they looked up and saw our charging half-track. They immediately fired but it was not an aimed shot, the shell whistled over our heads and disappeared. Seconds later we hit them with a mighty crash, the gun was thrown over and the crew leapt to avoid the meeting of half-track and artillery, the buckled and bent steel threatened to overwhelm them.

We leapt out of the vehicle with machine pistols blazing, one of the Russians was trying to bring the Maxim into use, another was ramming a new drum magazine into his PPSh. Our only chance was to kill them before they killed us and we fired and kept firing until they lay dead, a crumpled heap of brown uniforms. It was time to move on, I shouted orders and we left the bodies and broken steel and pressed on to the next enemy position. We worked with the other platoons, clearing enemy defensive positions, marking and clearing mines and taking out enemy armour whenever the opportunity presented itself. By nightfall we had advanced several kilometres and had to stop and wait for dawn, advancing in darkness would have been a certain recipe for disaster. We clustered around in a wide circle, like wagons in the old Western movies. We were in the lee of a tank park, having dozens of heavily armoured Panzers between us and the enemy was comforting. Bauer brewed coffee and Beidenberg unpacked cold rations for us to eat. Mundt leaned over to me and said in a loud whisper, "Have you seen von Meusebach lately?"

I knew exactly what he meant. I was lost for words, torn between my duty to the CO and my contempt for the man.

"No, Willy, you know perfectly well he hasn't been around since he took that Russian prisoner back. Muller has been running around in a half-track trying to keep control of the Regiment, but unfortunately he hasn't a radio in his vehicle so he can't keep in communication with HQ."

He grunted. "We could have done with the armoured car, a couple of our half-tracks were lost. He should have been there to look after them," he stared at me. "Look, Sir, we need a CO, there's no room on this front for cowards."

"Indeed there isn't, we've taken care of that problem!"

We all whirled around. For the first time I saw a Gestapo officer on the battlefield. Wiedel, von Betternich's assistant, together with Muller.

Wiedel grinned, unusual for him or any Gestapo man. "May I introduce your new commanding officer, Obersturmbannfuhrer Muller!"

"What happened to von Meusebach?" I asked, not believing that he could have been killed in action when he was so careful to stay away from the fighting.

"He has returned to Berlin," Muller replied. "There has been a lot of disquiet at Division about his lack of enthusiasm to get to grips with the enemy, Obergruppenfuhrer Hausser gave him the choice of returning to a desk at RSHA or leading tomorrow's first battle. From the front." He looked around to make sure that we understood the significance of his words. "Von Meusebach decided that his health was preventing him from giving of his best to the Deutschland Regiment and this afternoon he began to pack his things to get the train back to Germany, where he can get medical attention and perhaps return to the front at a later date. In the meantime

I am back in charge."

"Congratulations, Sir," I said, meaning it.

"Thank you, Hoffman. We're due to carry on in the morning. I assure you I will be leading the Regiment. The armoured car that von Meusebach used will be returned tonight and I will be using it to manage the Regiment."

He walked away and Wiedel hung back.

"I trust that you had something to do with this, Wiedel."

He shrugged. "Sometimes we have to intervene in areas where we would be least expected to get involved. In this case, someone reported that your CO was a coward who was causing difficulties to the Deutschland Regiment, von Betternich passed it up the line to SD Berlin and they contacted Himmler's adjutant who issued the ultimatum. None of us was surprised that von Meusebach opted to pack."

I thought he was re-joining Muller, but he hung back.

"What? What is it?" I asked him.

"How have you found things on the first day, any real problems?"

"Apart from the Red Army, do you mean?"

"I mean anything to suggest that they were better informed about our movements than they should have been."

I thought about the artillery barrage, timed to start an hour before our own barrage, nothing could have been calculated better to cause us the maximum difficulties. I told him about it.

"Yes, we heard about that from the front commanders. Anything else?"

"They were dug in on our exact line of advance, yes, they certainly knew a lot more than they should have done. Was it Lucy?"

He nodded. "We're almost certain, there were too many coincidences. The artillery barrage you referred to, the way their defences seemed to anticipate our lines of advance, it seems that the mysterious Lucy is something of a thorn in our sides. Very well, we'll keep looking. If we need any help from your platoon, I'll radio Muller."

"In that case I'll have to hope that his equipment is not working."

He grinned. "Still bitter, Hoffman. Remember, there was nothing any of us could do to save one life, no matter what you think. We cannot override the authority of Reichsfuhrer Himmler. But if we can unmask this Lucy traitor, we can save thousands of lives of your comrades, perhaps even stave off defeat."

I looked at him quickly. The Gestapo had arrested and executed people for saying less than that. But it was no slip of the tongue.

"Yes, I see you're surprised. I've been reviewing the intelligence from our over flights of the salient. The battle today was just the first of many you will need to win to take your objective. Do you know that the Soviet defences go to a depth of seventy-five kilometres?"

I was shocked, I'd seen the extent of some of their preparations but hadn't realised that they were even bigger than I'd seen, much bigger. "Are you saying we've got to do the same again all the way through to Kursk and beyond?"

He nodded. "We've counted eight full lines of defence so far, there may be more. They've anticipated every step we've taken and are going to take. We need to find this Lucy and fast. I'll call you if we get any developments."

He walked away and I sat thinking about what he'd said. I couldn't tell the men, it would wipe out their morale if they knew the scale of what we faced.

In the morning we continued with the attack. We fought on for three more days. As Wiedel had predicted each day was like the last, we had to put maximum effort into taking every metre of ground, the Soviets clung on tenaciously, refusing to retreat until they were almost wiped out to the last man. Now that we were deep inside the Soviet defences, they were able to use their anti-tank guns to devastating effect on the weaker side armour of our Panzers and the losses were mounting, losses that we couldn't replace. The Panzer Vs that the Fuhrer had held up the attack for so long for proved almost useless, they were constantly out of action with engine fires and mechanical and electrical failures. On the evening of the fourth day, we were called to a Regimental Officers' briefing. Muller presided as CO once more, Glasser, his adjutant fastened a map to the wall of a ruined barn that we were using as a briefing room. The CO pointed to a village many kilometres to the southwest of Kursk.

"Men, this is Prokhorovka. It is our objective for tomorrow, General Hoth has decided that this is where we will place our maximum effort. Every tank within his command will be used to press home this next attack, about six hundred in all."

We stood there stunned. When the battle started we, the Fourth Army, comprised more than twice that number, almost fifteen hundred tanks. We'd lost more than a half of our armour for the pitiful few kilometres we'd advanced so far and already this operation smelled like an all or nothing last-ditch attempt. It wasn't an admission of failure, but it certainly suggested that defeat may well be not too far away.

In the morning the wind came up and blew dust everywhere, visibility was reduced to a few hundred metres. We began the advance, as usual following the Panzers, giving them protection from the Soviet anti-tank infantry and other defences that lay across their path. Our mine clearers had been in action during the night and the lines of advance were marked with small flags. The Panzers travelled at speed and began firing as soon as the Russian targets came into view but the battlefield soon descended into chaos. The smoke from the explosions and the burning tanks, frequently the fuel caught fire and sent even denser cloud of black smoke into the air mixed with the dust storm to form an impenetrable fog.

"How's your vision?" I asked Bauer, we'd narrowly avoided running into a ravine and I was anxious that we would wreck our vehicle by hitting some other unexpected obstacle.

"I can manage for now, but at least it stops the Red Army from being able to see us," he said happily. "It's like a destroyer smoke screen, Sir."

"It's stopping us from seeing them too, Bauer. If we can't see them we can't destroy them."

I had no wish to leave whole divisions of Russians in our rear, ready to cripple out supply lines and enable them to come at us from two sides at once, but all we could do was keep following the Panzers. We pressed on and I estimated that we were less than a kilometre from Prokhorovka. A tank rolled out of the smoke and dust and rolled past us, I could hardly believe it, the compact, angular shape of a Russian T34 with its red star emblazoned on the turret. I shouted urgently to Bauer.

"Stefan, there are T34s all around us, get us behind some cover so that we can stop and unlimber the gun!"

He found a narrow balka in the ground and drove the half-track in so that most of the body was inside the shoulders of the entrance of ravine. There was no time to think, we had to get the gun into action.

"Uncouple the gun, make sure we have some cover and

load with armour piercing, we've got ourselves tangled in the middle of Soviet armour."

They started to drag the gun back out of the balka and set it behind a low bank of earth that would give us some protection. While we watched the smoke cleared briefly and we could see what looked like a scene from hell, tanks from both armies wheeling and fighting, guns blazing, smoke and flames pouring out of stricken vehicles, crews leaping out of burning tanks, their uniforms on fire and their comrades trying to beat them out.

"Ready!" Mundt shouted.

I watched carefully, there was one Soviet tank, a KV-1, not as nimble as the T34.

"Tank, eleven o'clock, fire when you're ready, Willy!"

He spotted the target and his gunners rapidly worked the gun around to lay it on the target. The was an enormous 'boom' as he fired and seconds after we saw the shell strike the Russian, but it had hit the heavy frontal armour and failed to destroy it. Wesserman rushed around to fit another shell into the muzzle and dashed back behind cover as Mundt fired again, this time it hit the side of the turret and exploded, flames began to lick out of the tank, then the whole vehicle exploded in a furious eruption of fiery metal fragments. They were already reloading and I searched for more targets amidst the chaotic fury of the battle.

We fought through the day in that position, the armies

seemed to be stalemated. At one time the battle seemed to abate, just after midday, and we caught a pair of Soviet anti-tank gunners unawares. They'd set up in a nearby foxhole without noticing we were already hiding in the balka, Bauer was a good shot, he had his Kar 98 clipped inside the half-track and he picked it up, took aim and shot both the Russians. We rushed out to check them, one was dead, the other fatally wounded. Their unit insignia were the 5th Guards Tank Army.

"That's an elite unit," Mundt said thoughtfully. "They only give them the 'Guards' designation when they've proved themselves in battle. This is going to be one hell of a fight."

"It already is," Voss protested. "It can't get any worse than this."

None of us dared to reply. In the afternoon the Luftwaffe came over to take on the Soviet tanks, Stukas with twin 37mm anti-tank cannons and took their toll of the enemy armour, Heinkel 111 bombers flew sortie after sortie, smashing the Red Army legions where they lay, in theory making our job easier. The Red Air Force came up in swarms and there was a constant battle between the fighters for supremacy over the battlefield, a mad, Wagnerian fury that lit up the sky with smoke, flame and noise. We pushed on, metre by metre, pushing back the Soviets, nearer and nearer to Prokhorovka. It was clearly in sight, Muller kept rushing from platoon to platoon, company to company, "We need to give our Panzers more support they're almost there. Just one more push and we'll roll over the Soviets and take Prokhorovka!"

We never did take that flyspeck of a Soviet village. The following morning we were still attacking, tanks and artillery, Stukas and Heinkel bombers pounding the Russian positions, but it seemed that every time we destroyed a company, a regiment, a whole army, another one stepped forward to take its place. Our tank force was dwindling. The rate of fire we were able to sustain was dropping, hour by hour. A gap opened up in front of us where a Soviet position had been destroyed in the last bombing raid, we had a chance to dash forward and take it before they sent in more troops. Mundt looked across to me, waiting for the order.

"Shouldn't we go now, Sir? We've got a gap we can exploit, if we leave it any longer the Soviets will come back in force and make our job that much harder."

I shook my head. "Look around, Willy. We're losing it, how many of our Panzers have you seen mounting attacks lately?"

"It's true, things have been a bit quiet. I assumed they were regrouping for a new attack."

"I'm not so sure, the battlefield is littered with wrecked armour and not all of it is Russian. How the hell can we sustain those kinds of losses?"

He scratched his head. "If what you're saying is correct,

Sir, it's all over. We can't just sit here, either we go forward or back. And if we're not going forward, that's it, we're finished."

"I may be wrong, my friend, but I think we should wait before we stick our necks out."

Up and down the line things had gone quiet. I imagined that if the commanders did the maths, in terms of our losses for each kilometre of ground taken, they would find they were unsustainable. Reaching Prokhorovka was only a partial objective, once we'd taken it we would still need to push through the formidable defences that stood between here and Kursk. It didn't add up. We waited hour after hour, but the battlefield was static. Night fell and movement stopped almost entirely. The following day we started pulling back, out of the salient and nearer to Kharkov. We all knew that the next danger we had to face was the inevitable Soviet counterattack.

"We'll almost certainly need to strengthen the defences in Kharkov itself and give ourselves space and time to regroup before they attack," Muller said confidently when he came around to check preparations for our withdrawal. "They'll need a long time to recover from the pounding we just gave them."

I wondered how long we'd need to recover from the pounding we'd just received from the Soviets, but it wasn't the kind of question that would be well received by a senior officer.

CHAPTER NINE

'Those who want to live, let them fight, and those who do not want to fight in this world of eternal struggle do not deserve to live'.

Adolf Hitler

It was the beginning of August and we'd been back in our new regimental headquarters for three weeks, an old school on the outskirts of Kharkov, a welcome change from the miserable hovels of Podvirky. After the battle for the salient we were exhausted, but at least we could take comfort from the fact that the Soviets were undoubtedly feeling it more than we were. When we'd left the battlefield the landscape was a litter of bodies and broken armour, most of it Russian, although we'd lost a dangerous number of our own Panzers. Muller had managed to recruit forty

Hiwis to help us create defences against the Russian attack that was expected in the autumn. They were still dragging sandbags around the old school yard when the salvo arrived. We dived for cover as the first shells bracketed our positions, Mundt and Bauer were next to me in a newly dug slit trench.

"Jesus Christ, they didn't take long," Bauer said, wide eyed at the colossal weight of shells that were landing all around us.

In an incredibly short time the enemy had brought up their big guns, hundreds of them.

"They must have been ready for us, Stefan. I have the distinct impression that for a long time we've been playing the Russians' game. You know what good chess players they are rumoured to be."

"They should stick to chess, Sir," Mundt said bitterly. "This is getting damned hot."

If anything, he understated the case. The school behind us, our supposed new quarters was completely destroyed as shell after shell struck home and reduced it to rubble. Even while they were still firing the Soviet light bombers came in, a flight of Ilyushin IL-4s, twin-engine aircraft that unloaded thousands of kilos of bombs on us and other targets, some of them just churned up the rubble of the destroyed school.

"Where's the Luftwaffe?" Voss shouted bitterly, he'd run over to jump into our slit trench after his sandbagged machine gun emplacement was destroyed in a bomb blast.

"I think half of them are destroyed on the ground inside the salient," Mundt said bitterly, "alongside half of our Panzer force."

The barrage of bombs and shells lasted most of the day, our own guns desperately used counter battery fire in a vain attempt to dilute the Russian artillery, but they were only partially successful. More flights of IL-4s came over, our anti-aircraft fire was ready for them this time and dozens of our four-barrelled Flakvierlings opened up on them, together with every other gun that was able to shoot. We brought down five out of a flight of fourteen, but the others ignored the ground fire and relentlessly went on to drop their bomb loads. Belatedly, a pair of Focke-Wulf 190s cam roaring in to do battle, chasing after the bombers and downing another three.

"A pity the bastards didn't do that before they dropped their bombs," Voss said, continuing his rant about the Luftwaffe.

I said nothing. The Red Air Force had become more and more effective, at least along this front. Whereas a few months ago, our Messerschmidt's and Focke-Wulfs could roam the battlefield freely, they were now more frequently engaged by Soviet fighters who were taking a huge toll of our irreplaceable pilots and aircraft. Their aircraft had improved, as had their pilots, to deadly effect. And like on the ground, they had more and more of them, a seemingly inexhaustible supply. By evening the bombing and shelling had largely ended from both sides and we spent an uneasy night waiting for it to begin again. By dawn it was quiet everywhere, as if the armies were gathering strength. We were enjoying a quiet moment, drinking coffee, when a messenger came in. I was to report to Gestapo Headquarters. The only transport we had was the half-track, its body dotted with scars and holes from stray fragments but largely undamaged, but I decided to leave it and walk. It was only two kilometres and I wanted to get out of the cramped conditions for a short time and stretch my legs. I left Beidenberg in charge of the platoon and took Mundt and Bauer with me, they'd become more than just soldiers in my platoon, they were companions too, despite the difference in rank, after all, this was the SS.

We had barely gone half a kilometre, strolling along a rubble-strewn street when a shot rang out and clanged on Bauer's helmet and we dived undercover, I was relieved to see that he was uninjured.

"Did anyone see where it came from?" Mundt asked, scanning the surrounding wrecked buildings anxiously.

"Probably quite a distance, Willy. If he'd been nearer, the bullet would have penetrated his helmet."

"So what do we do, Sir? Just leave him there to shoot the next German soldier that comes past?"

"You're right, we need to find him and finish him. Let's move out in the direction of the shot and see if we can't flush him out."

We moved cautiously from building to building, I'd estimated that he was hidden in a ruined office block about four hundred metres away. We crawled until we were only fifty metres away. It was time to get him to show himself.

"Stefan, go back to that low wall we came around, be behind it and show your helmet. If he puts his head up we should reach him with the MP38s from here."

He nodded and crawled away.

"Are you ready, Willy?"

"Yes, Sir, a pity we haven't got a rifle, though, we could have made certain."

I smiled. "We're the SS, Scharfuhrer, it's our job to make do."

"That's all we ever do these days. Maybe for once they'll give us the equipment and men to finish the job."

It was not like Willy to moan so much. The battle in the salient had gone badly, very badly. We'd inflicted heavy losses on the Russians, but there were just so many of them. The whole of the war in Russia had become a war of attrition, of killing and destroying as many of the enemy as possible while they inflicted the same heavy punishment on us. A foolish strategy, I reflected, one that could only benefit the Russians. I wasn't sure if we had a choice, if the opportunity to conduct the war in a different way existed, but if it didn't, why had we ever come here in the first place? It was a question that only the politicians could answer.

"Bauer should be about ready," Willy said, jerking me out of my thoughts.

I cocked my MP38 and waited where I could see the wrecked building, it had once had several floors but was now nothing but rubble. I surveyed every metre of the jumbled pile of rock, nothing. Then I looked again, there, in the far corner there was an old steel filing cabinet that had tumbled down, one of the drawers had fallen out. Inside the open door space I had seen a tiny movement. Was it the sniper? Then Willy shouted, "Stefan is lifting his helmet, look out!"

It all happened so quickly. I saw a rifle barrel extend from the wreckage, inside the metal cabinet. As he fired a tiny puff of smoke ejected from the barrel and the crack of a rifle shot echoing around us, I leapt up. I could see him, framed by the steel, his startled face behind the gun. I aimed quickly and squeezed the trigger, sending the whole clip into the narrow space, Willy saw where I was firing and adjusted his aim to pour his own fire into the same place. The face disappeared and we rushed forward, slamming in new clips as we ran. We simultaneously cocked our weapons and rounded the broken metal, ready to fire instantly but we needn't have worried, he was dead, torn apart in a storm of gunfire. We turned as there was a clatter of boots, but it was only Bauer.

"Did you get him, Sir?"

"He won't be shooting at any of our men again, Bauer."

Mundt picked up his rifle, a Moisin Nagant and smashed it repeatedly against the stonework, putting it out of use. Then we headed back to the street to make our cautious way into the city.

We had to walk past the Hotel October to reach Gestapo Headquarters, as we neared it I could see a crowd of people on the pavement looking up at a lamppost, a body swung there.

"It looks as if the Einsatzgruppe has been hanging partisans again," Mundt said nonchalantly, as if such horrors were part of normal life. I nodded automatically as I was more concerned to keep alert for snipers, even this close to the centre of the city the risks were very high. I heard Bauer say, "Christ, she must have been a pretty one," and something made look around at the body they were trying to cut down.

Her face was horribly distorted, in death it had gone a ghostly white, all of the features distorted, but I still recognised her. Nadia Vlasov, the girl we'd brought back on that mad horseback ride through the salient, the girl who I had hoped to be with again before she had entertained von Meusebach in her hotel room. As was usual for these executions she had a cardboard sign hung around her neck, but it was in Russian script, not German. So the partisans had finally got to her, presumably in punishment for her father's betrayal of Stalin. Mundt recognised her too. "I'm sorry, Obersturmfuhrer, that was a bastard thing to do."

"It's a bastard of a war. Poor kid, she didn't deserve that just for what her father did."

We stood and watched them cut her down, then she was taken away for burial with the other thousands of casualties that were the victims of the shelling and bombing, the snipers and the Einsatzgruppe. We walked on to Gestapo HQ and I went in alone to find von Betternich. He was in his office, sat behind his desk staring into space.

He looked up as I went in and saluted. "Ah, Hoffman, I was just thinking about the latest military disaster."

"Does that mean that the battle for the salient is officially over? There won't be any reinforcements to try again?"

He looked baffled. "The salient? Of course not, don't you know that the Fuhrer has already issued orders for more of our armoured divisions to be transferred to Italy?"

"Italy? I thought we could contain them on Sicily, what about the Italian army?"

He shook his head. "It is only a matter of weeks before the Allies reach Messina and begin to cross to the mainland. I'm afraid the war is taking a turn for the worse, Obersturmfuhrer, you can certainly forget about trying to retake the Kursk salient."

"So it was all for nothing, all of the losses, the deaths, the sacrifice?"

He spread his hands. "My dear fellow, that is war, is it not? There are winners and there are losers. To the victors the spoils, is that not what they say?"

"What do you want me for, Sir?" I snapped out. "I'm far too busy to run around playing these games."

His expression hardened. "I'm sorry you don't find it to your liking, Hoffman. Most people find that wars are not entirely to their liking. Especially when they are on the losing side."

"Are you now saying that we are losing?"

His expression softened. "I didn't say that. What do you think?"

"What do you want me for this time?"

He smiled at my refusal to answer his question. "We need to make an arrest, at least one."

"Does that mean you've found the Lucy traitor?"

"I'm afraid not, no. The person we want is General Schmidt of the Second Panzer Army. Perhaps you and your men would accompany me. I have a Kubelwagen outside, we can use that."

I was so astonished I didn't even think to ask him what the General had done. I assumed he must have been passing secrets to the Russians, although it could have just been theft. He got up and limped down the stairs, the men fell in behind me. We climbed into the Kubi and drove out to the headquarters of the Second Army. Von Betternich showed his pass and we were ushered into Schmidt's office.

"Yes, what can I do for you?" The General who looked up was lean and tough looking. His sharp eyes took in me, and my troopers standing behind the SD man.

"Have you men come to volunteer for the Panzers, God knows we could use some new men?"

"General Schmidt," von Betternich announced in formal tones. "You are under arrest for treasonable activities, you must come with us!"

His jaw dropped. "Treason, are you mad? This is nonsense, I'll contact OKH immediately and tell them to sort it all out, this is just a stupid mistake!"

"The order was issued by the Supreme Leader of OKH, I'm afraid there is no mistake."

He looked worried now, uncertain, but not afraid. "What the hell do they think that I've done?"

The SD Man took out a document. "It says on the warrant that on the 17th of June you said in front of witnesses that in your opinion, and I quote, 'This mad man Adolf Hitler is leading us to disaster, he's leading us from one defeat to another'.

"Yes, so? What I said is absolutely true," he said incredulously. "We all know it, Stalingrad, the Kursk salient was another disaster. The Allies have landed in Sicily. Need I go on?"

"You need not, no. What you have just repeated is indeed treason. Hoffman, get your men to take him away!"

The adjutant and staff stood watching with expressions

of horror as we marched their CO out to our waiting vehicle. The adjutant had already been on the radio to OKH to confirm the order and he had to stand back and watch the charade take place. I felt sick as I led the brave, front line officer out of his office, but I had no choice or they'd arrest me too. I knew we couldn't go on like it, arresting our valuable and knowledgeable senior officers and allowing one man with little or no military experience to make decisions that would plunge whole armies into disaster. We drove back to the city centre in silence. General Schmidt seemed to have gone into a state of mental paralysis. He knew it was an error from which he'd never recover and he'd be lucky just to stay alive. We deposited him in the cell and left the building, but von Betternich called me back. "I want you back here tonight, Hoffman, we may have a lead on our Lucy spy, be here for seven o'clock. With luck we might have the bastard in custody before morning."

I saluted and walked away, still sick to the stomach to see that Panzer general put into a cell when he was so desperately needed. We marched carefully back out of the city, wary this time of snipers but this time there were no random shots fired at us. Beidenberg had the men repairing the fortifications, Hiwis were busy helping dig trenches and carry more sandbags to the gun emplacements.

"Any problems?" I asked him. "Apart from the obvious, of course."

He smiled. "All quiet at the moment, Sir, but I think the Russians must surely be massing not too far away to attack the city."

I nodded. "I think you're right, this damned place has been like a bone in their throats almost since the start of Barbarossa, they'll certainly be working out how quickly they can take it back off us. Your defences will be sorely needed before too long."

I left him and went to the Regimental HQ nearby, Muller was outside with Glasser, the adjutant.

"What was that business this morning?" the CO asked me.

"General Schmidt, they arrested him for treason, Sir."

He momentarily closed his eyes. "Dear God, if they take all of our best commanders we'll have no one left to lead us. It's almost as bad as the Stalin purges."

"Are there any signs of another Russian attack, Sir?"

He shook his head. "We haven't noticed unusual armour and troop movements, but we know they'll come shortly. It's a pity we lost so much of our own armour trying to take Kursk."

I asked him were there any estimates of our losses yet. He looked around carefully, to make sure no one was listening. It was such a common gesture in the new Germany of Adolf Hitler that I barely noticed it.

"Unofficially, they put our losses at around a thousand Panzers across the whole of Army Group South and Army

Group Centre. They're not all totally destroyed, of course, but the ones that are just damaged are out of action until we can repair them. We have about six hundred Panzers left, if we scrape up everything including some of the more obsolete stuff."

It was a day for bad news. "Can we hold them with those numbers, Sir?"

He gave me a look that was very eloquent. "You need to make up your own mind about that, I'd rather not guess."

Glasser was looking worried in case his CO said something that would incriminate him. I looked at them both. "I think we've made up our minds already."

They both nodded.

The Soviet Air Force appeared to be as exhausted as we were, there were few signs of enemy aircraft in the sky and we began to relax until a flight of four Soviet fighters stormed over the lines, spraying cannon and machine gun fire in their path. We dived for cover in the newly dug slit trenches, holding our breath for the bombs that the small Russian fighter bombers carried, but these were Yak 1s, a single-seat fighter designed more for aerial superiority and escort duties for bombers and low level attack aircraft like the Ilyushin IL-2 Sturmovik. The fortifications protected us from the worst of the storm of fire and while the Flakvierlings sent torrents of fire skyward to bring down the raiders, we kept our heads down and waited for it to be over. As they flew away our anti-aircraft fire hit one of them but the other three flew out of range and out of sight.

"Bloody Luftwaffe again," Voss moaned, "what the hell are they thinking of? Has anyone seen any kind of air combat patrol today?" We all shook our heads. "Damn right, they're all lying in bed."

"I think many of them are lying dead on the battle field of the Kursk salient, Karl-Heinz. Some of them may have been transferred to Italy, of course."

"Can't the Italians protect their own country?" he snapped. "I thought they were supposed to be Allies. They're bloody useless."

"Karl-Heinz is right, you know," Beidenberg said, surprising all of us, he rarely said anything while we were discussing the progress of the war. "They collapsed at Stalingrad where they were supposed to be holding the line and they collapsed in North Africa. They're hopeless soldiers. They'll lose the whole of Italy if we don't prop them up."

I felt sorry for the Italians. Before I came out to Russia to join the Deutschland Regiment, I'd trained with several of them at officer training school in Lichterfelde. They tried to explain Italian politics to me. The problem was the Mussolini's fascists were very much in the minority, unlike those who admired Hitler in Germany who were very much in the majority, especially after he enjoyed his early triumphs in Alsace-Lorraine, the Danzig Corridor,

Austria and Czechoslovakia. After we conquered France he could do no wrong, unlike Mussolini who was viewed with the utmost suspicion in Italy. They maintained that it wasn't that the Italians couldn't fight, just that most didn't want to. I felt bound to defend them, I remembered them as young men who loved life, who enjoyed wine, women and opera in equal measure.

"As I recall, Rommel was defeated in North Africa," I said quietly. "And wasn't General von Paul defeated at Stalingrad too? It's not just the Italians that are losing."

They were silent at the enormity of what I'd just said. It was only the truth, but the implications for all of us were shocking. The attack seemed to be over and we went back to work, but it was work that seemed increasingly without reason, without purpose, without hope.

I took my trusty NCO, Willy Mundt together with Stefan Bauer into the city to report to the Gestapo. The senior SD officer von Betternich was waiting for us together with Gerd Wiedel, his Gestapo counterpart. Wiedel had a map of the city pinned to the wall, he pointed to a location on the northern outskirts.

"We've pinpointed a radio transmission coming out of here two nights in succession. We deliberately kept away from him to make him feel as if he was safe to use that location. Tonight, with any luck, we'll have him."

"Is it Lucy?" I asked him.

"We think so, but his transmissions are encoded, we

can't be sure until have him in our hands. If we can take him it will change everything. The radio van is ready as soon as he starts transmitting and we've made the Kubi available for you."

Von Betternich was smiling to himself as Wiedel spoke, evidently he didn't share his colleague's enthusiasm. I went back outside to bring the Kubi around to the front. We scrounged coffee from the Gestapo canteen and sat around waiting. Even the Gestapo couldn't do better than the foul-tasting ersatz coffee and as I looked around at the broken, rubble-strewn surroundings that no one had bothered to tidy for several weeks, at the peeling paintwork and cracked masonry of the Gestapo headquarters building, I couldn't help but wonder what kind of masters of Europe we Germans had become. More and more it seemed as if we were masters of a huge, lice-ridden rubbish tip, except that the lice carried machine guns and often rode in tanks.

"There was an article in Volkischer Beobachter last week," Bauer said abruptly, apparently just making conversation. Mundt and I looked at him expectantly. "They're still asking for applicants to apply for farms in the German occupied part of the Soviet Union. The General Government, what used to be Poland, is still short of people too, they say there are lots of empty farms just waiting for Germans to come forward and claim them."

"Did they say what happened to the former owners of the farms, Stefan?"

"No, they didn't mention that, Sir."

He was half smiling, the story was of course true, those articles were always appearing, but the way the war was going made the occupancy of a farm in the former regions of Poland and the Ukraine more like suicide with every week that went by. He was smiling broadly. It was one of those word games we often played, recounting the latest idiocy from Dr Goebbels's Propaganda Ministry with a straight face in the hopes of catching your audience with a laugh.

"Stefan, I've thought about another article in the Beobachter."

"Yes, Sir, what's that?"

"It's about an SS Schutze playing word games outside of Gestapo HQ."

He looked around quickly and his face fell. "I'd forgotten that."

Mundt and I both laughed then, the joke had fallen on his head like a bolt of lightning.

"He's broadcasting, we need to leave now," Wiedel said as he rushed out into the courtyard. Von Betternich came limping after him and Wiedel helped him into the funkwagen and then joined us in the Kubi. We roared out of the courtyard and made our way at speed across the city.

"We want him alive," Wiedel said as Mundt and I checked and cocked our MP38s.

I nodded. "Don't worry, we'll only shoot if he starts shooting at us."

The truck stopped just before an intersection.

"This time we'll go forward on foot, Hoffman, if he sees the vehicles he'll make a run for it."

I nodded. We left Bauer with the Kubi and walked carefully forward, I saw the door of the truck open and von Betternich climbed out and followed at a distance. We rounded the corner and Wiedel pointed out the target building.

"Willy, take Bauer and go around the back, I'll go in the front with Herr Wiedel."

The Scharfuhrer nodded and walked quietly along the street and disappeared down a lane that led to the rear of the building. Wiedel led the way to the front of the building and tested the front door quietly. It was locked.

"Can you smash it open, Hoffman?"

I nodded, handed him my machine pistol to hold and stepped back three paces. Then charged the door with my shoulder, it splintered and opened inwards. I grabbed my weapon from Wiedel as I rushed through the entrance. The sound of a Morse Code transmission in progress was coming from an upstairs room. I charged up the stairs with Wiedel close behind, there was a second flight of stairs and we went up to the top floor, the beeping of the Morse Code was loud, then it stopped. I went into the room where I estimated it had been coming from.

There was a dressing table and a brass bedstead. On the dressing table was a potable radio set that was packed in a canvas case, opened to allow the set to be used. At the side was the Morse key, a wire came out of the side of the radio and stretched upwards, I looked up and there was a trapdoor into the ceiling above the dressing table that led into the roof space.

"Whoever he is, he's obviously gone up there," I said to Wiedel. "I'll go after him, I would suggest you check the rest of the house in case there is another way out."

I climbed onto the dresser and swung myself up through the trapdoor. The wire aerial disappeared through an opened inspection cover in the roof, I ran across the tops of the roof beams to reach it when it suddenly slammed shut. I pushed hard but whoever had closed it had bolted it, it was a dead end. I went back through the hatch, climbed down again, and ran out to the stairway. Wiedel was on the next landing down. I shook my head.

"He was up there, but he's bolted his escape route shut, we need to go outside to find him!"

We ran back down the stairs and out of the front door. There was no sign of him, he had to come down the outside somewhere, but where?

"Wiedel, you go to the left, I'll go to the right."

He nodded and ran off to the side of the house, I went the other way but still there was nothing. Mundt and Bauer came towards me, how could he have slipped through our net? Then I saw a small building tucked into the corner of the garden wall, covered in green ivy that almost completely hid it from view. The door was shut so I went carefully towards it, kicked it in and rushed in with my machine pistol ready. A German officer was sitting on an old wooden stool. He looked up as I crashed through the door.

"There was no need to smash the door, my friend, it wasn't locked."

"Who the hell are you?" I asked him, keeping my weapon pointed at him.

He sighed. "Captain Helmersdorf, Abwehr, Army Intelligence. What the hell are you doing here?"

I was taken aback, it was almost as if I was the quarry and not him. I told him who I was and what we were doing here.

"There seems to be a misunderstanding," he said. "You have interrupted an Abwehr operation, I suggest you leave."

"And I suggest you explain yourself to the Gestapo," Wiedel's voice interrupted as he walked into the tiny room.

The Abwehr man stared at him. "The Gestapo has no jurisdiction over the Abwehr."

"In matters of treachery we have absolute jurisdiction, as you know. Hoffman, arrest him, we'll take him back with us and question him more!"

"I insist that I contact Army Headquarters to clear this

up," Helmersdorf said firmly.

Wiedel walked up to him and punched him hard in the face. "Traitors don't insist on anything, you piece of shit. Shut up or the next one will be a kick in the balls. You should save your energy for later, I'm sure you'll have lots to tell us."

I felt slightly ashamed at seeing the Gestapo man hit the officer, but I turned a blind eye. Meddling in Gestapo business was never a good idea and besides, if he really was the traitor, he deserved whatever he got. I sent Mundt and Bauer to fetch the spy's radio equipment. Von Betternich limped up to us, eyeing the Abwehr man.

"So this is the Lucy traitor, is it?"

"We think so, Sir."

"I am on a mission for Army Intelligence, you fools," he snarled. He winced as Wiedel went to hit him again but the SD man put up a hand to stop him.

"Which mission is that?"

"We had a report of unauthorised transmissions coming from this area and I came to investigate," Helmersdorf said. "I was looking in that garden workshop when your men came crashing in, they made so much noise that if there was a spy here he's long gone."

"That's bullshit," Wiedel said. "Are you saying that you came here on your own?"

"Sometimes it is better to be subtle, not something the Gestapo had much of a reputation for," he sneered.

Wiedel raised his hand but von Betternich stopped him again and gave the Abwehr officer a hard stare. "I warn you, whatever you may think of the Gestapo, their methods of extracting information are very effective. We'll discuss this further when we get back, take him away."

Mundt and Bauer took an arm each and escorted him to the Kubelwagen. Von Betternich looked at me. "What do you think?"

"I think it's him, Sir. He was almost certainly hiding from us. Besides, there's no one else around. It has to be him."

He nodded. "I'm sure you're right, we'll soon find out either way. Wiedel, while you're questioning him I'll make some discreet enquiries at Army Headquarters and see if they have anything to say about him."

We rode back into the city centre in silence, unsure as to whether we'd uncovered a traitor or fallen foul of an ongoing Abwehr investigation. As we got near the centre it was obvious that something was wrong, lights were coming on, vehicles and armour were starting to move and men running through the streets. We were stopped at a crossroads by the Feldgendarmerie checkpoint. Wiedel asked the sergeant what was up.

"It's the Soviets, Sir, they're attacking the city. They've got two or three fucking Soviet armies descending and coming straight at us!"

CHAPTER TEN

'One must not judge everyone in the world by his qualities as a soldier: otherwise we should have no civilization'

Erwin Rommel

We reached the Gestapo Office and left the two security officers with their Abwehr captive, then we made our way back to Regimental HQ and I reported to Muller.

"Obersturmfuhrer, the signs are that we're in for something of a shit storm. Our intelligence reports that the Voronezh and Steppe Fronts are coming out of the Kursk Bulge and heading for Kharkov. Von Manstein and von Kluge have just got back from the Wolfschanze, our orders are to hold the city at all costs!"

"How long have got before they hit us?"

"I've no idea, Hoffman. Perhaps two weeks, that's the

word from HQ."

I left him reflecting how the fortunes of war had changed so suddenly, only recently we were attacking the Kursk salient with a view to putting the impetus back into our Eastern Front offensive. Now we were just talking about hanging on at all costs. That evening I was able to get away and I only had one destination in mind. Irina. I knocked on her door and she opened it "Yes? What do you want?"

"Irina, in spite of everything, I want you to come and have dinner with me."

She stood for a moment, indecisive. She'd been about to say no, I realised that, but a glint came into her eyes. "Yes, alright. I'll get my jacket."

She came out of the house with a thin cotton jacket, the evening was warm and balmy, at least the weather hadn't turned on us, it seemed that everything else had. We found one of the few remaining restaurants still open. This one was tiny, little more than the front room of a private house. She'd hardly spoken to me but after the first course was served and the waiter opened a bottle of local wine, I asked her what was on her mind.

"You know why I came to help you last time, you persuaded me that it was important that you Germans win the war."

I nodded. "Isn't that still true?"

"It would be, if it was possible, but Jurgen, you know it

isn't going to happen."

I thought about her reply. It was true that we'd suffered some reversals on the Eastern Front, but we hadn't lost yet, I mentioned that to her. She smiled.

"Do you think we don't listen to the news? We know that the Allies have taken North Africa, they've taken Sicily and they'll soon be on the Italian mainland. Leningrad is holding out, Stalingrad was a terrible defeat and the last battle in the Kursk salient was hardly a victory. The Germans are losing."

I didn't agree with her, not entirely. We weren't winning, certainly, but we weren't completely losing either, we had massive forces at our disposal.

"I still think we will win eventually, Irina," I told her earnestly, although as I said it I knew that it was a wildly optimistic statement. We needed to find a counter to the vast and overwhelming numbers that the Soviets could bring to the battlefield and so far, we hadn't found the solution. We desperately needed the secret weapons the Fuhrer kept promising. When would they come?

"I want you to get me to Germany, Jurgen. When the Russians take Kharkov, you know I'll be shot as a spy, don't you?"

"Irina, they haven't taken Kharkov yet, you're quite safe."

She sneered slightly. "You need to wake up, Jurgen, they retook the city before and they're massing their forces outside the city to take it again. I have to leave before they come back."

"You're thinking of Nadia Vlasov, the girl the partisans killed?"

"There have been many such hangings of supposed traitors, so yes, I'm terrified. But Nadia Vlasov wasn't killed by partisans."

"But, I saw her hanging there, with a sign on her chest, it had to be partisans!"

She smiled. "That is what it was supposed to look like, but some local people saw it happen, they work inside the hotel. The Germans suspected her of passing information to the Russians, so they murdered her and made it look like a partisan reprisal. It was propaganda, pure and simple, but I suppose if your people hadn't got her, the Russians would have, sooner or later. I have to get out, Jurgen. Please will you help me?"

I was only half listening to her. Our people had killed Nadia Vlasov. It made no sense, unless it was part of some devious plot by the Gestapo or even more likely, the Sicherheitsdienst. And that meant only one person, the most senior SD officer in Kharkov. SD Obersturmbannfuhrer Walter von Betternich, who had shown himself to be totally capable of arranging a murder if would further his own ends, or the ends of the Third Reich, which was not necessarily the same thing. I realised that Irina was still talking to me.

"Sorry, what was that?"

"Damnit, Jurgen, listen to me! I have to get out of here, can you help me?"

I heard myself telling her that I would find a way to get her back to Germany, but I was still reeling at the thought that von Betternich may have been behind the public hanging of Nadia Vlasov. I knew there would have to be a confrontation with him sooner or later, but one that I would have to prepare for thoroughly, he was a formidable opponent. Would I kill him? It was a tempting thought, he certainly deserved to die, but in the vicious slaughter of the Russian war, perhaps most us were not without blame. I pushed the problems to one side. I needed to concentrate on Irina.

"Yes, I'll do what I can. If I can possibly find a good reason to get you on a train returning to the Reich you could leave with the correct documentation, I can always say that you are my fiancée. When you get to the Reich, you can find yourself accommodation and work, it won't be difficult, everyone is desperate for workers these days."

She smiled. "Your fiancée? That would be wonderful. When are we to be married?"

I nearly choked on my wine. "I only meant..."

"I know what you meant, don't worry. I thought of going to Berlin."

"Berlin? You cannot be serious. It's being bombed to rubble. You need to find somewhere quiet, away from the worst of the bombing. Dresden would be worth considering, it's a beautiful old city and you'd love it. Very medieval, it's somehow managed to stay untouched by the war."

"In that case I shall set up home in Dresden."

We finished our meal and the band started to play, I took her out onto the dance floor and we held each other tightly, clinging to a little warmth, a little love and hopefully a little more later. I wasn't to be disappointed.

"Jurgen, when you take me home tonight, I don't want to be alone."

"Nor do I, Irina."

When we got to her house we couldn't wait to get to the bedroom, there was a thick rug in front of the empty hearth and we tore off our clothes and literally savaged each other's bodies. It was a lust born of animal need. A lust that understood that tonight, like every other night on the Eastern Front, could be our last. We stroked and caressed our partner's bodies as if they were a mighty treasure, a golden prize in the lottery of life and one that may only be won once in a lifetime. Afterwards, we lit cigarettes and lay together comfortably on the rug, smoking in silence. Eventually, I had to get up and get dressed.

"So duty has to call again, does it?" she smiled.

"I'm afraid so. Someone has to keep the railway line to Germany safe."

Her face fell, I realised at once that I shouldn't have

brought the war back to this rare moment. I kissed her goodbye and slipped out.

When I got back to my unit, they were already up and racing to reinforce the defences. I found Muller and asked him what was up.

"The Red Army, that's what's up," he snarled grimly. "Intelligence said that it would be at least two weeks before they were ready to move, the Russians were much too weak after Kursk. Last night, the First Tank Army and the Fifth Guards Tank Army attacked in force. Belgorod has fallen, while adjoining and supporting Soviet forces have widened the gap, they're converging on Kharkov, Hoffman, I suggest you prepare your men. I'm expecting the city to come under attack later today!"

I found the men and passed on the grim news, but the regimental grapevine had already informed them. We were ordered to move forward to a prepared defensive line five kilometres outside the city and we began to load the half-track with the supplies we would need. A few Panzers rumbled past us heading east to guard the defences, but they were awfully few.

"That was a real work of genius, moving our armour to Italy," Voss moaned. "We'll need more than this pitiful bunch to hold back the Reds."

"They're all we've got, Voss, we'll just have to manage," I said curtly. "Besides, it was an order of the Fuhrer that they were transferred to the Western theatre."

"That's what I meant," he said slyly.

I let it go, he had a point, it was poor bastards like him and the rest of us that would bear the brunt of the failure to come to grips with the Soviet hordes, not OKW, OKH or Reichsfuhrer Himmler. We were about to leave when the air raid siren sounded.

"Out, out, take cover!"

We scrambled out of the half-track and jumped into the slit trench. The Soviets were using IL-2 Sturmoviks with a top cover of Yak-1s, not that the escort fighters were needed. Just like our armour, the aircraft losses of the Kursk salient had been crippling and the Luftwaffe were still struggling to catch up. The Soviets seemed to have no such difficulties. They came in huge air fleets while our aircraft were nowhere to be seen. While the Yaks circled overhead the Sturmoviks came in one after the other, dropping their bombs and waiting for their following aircraft to complete their bombing runs, then coming in for a second pass to shatter our position with cannon and machine gun fire. When they'd finished they had the sky to themselves and the Yaks came down on us and shot up the camp. We had two Flakvierlings, the four-barrelled anti-aircraft guns that fired constantly at the enemy, hurling curtains of shells upwards and bringing down two Sturmoviks in flames, one of the Yaks was also hit and fled east trailing smoke from our gunfire, but when they had gone the damage was incalculable. Our half-track was destroyed, as were most of the vehicles in our unit, including the CO's armoured reconnaissance car. Smoke and fire was everywhere, much of our stores had been destroyed and the medics were already laying out bodies on the ground where they had taken a direct hit to several of the sandbagged shelters and two of the slit trenches. One of the Flak guns had been destroyed too, smashed into ruin by multiple hits from a cannon. Ten minutes before we'd been an understrength regiment, now, we had barely enough equipment and personnel for a company. Muller came around to check on us, his face was chalk white.

"We lost so many, Hoffman. All gone, men, equipment, everything. How the hell we're going to stop the Soviets now I don't know. Glasser's dead too."

Glasser, the Regimental adjutant.

"I'm sorry, Sir, we all liked him. We'll manage, somehow."

"Will we, Hoffman, will we? I hope so, you'd better proceed independently to the defensive positions, we're desperately short of men now and they'll be glad of any they can get. Make sure you take anti-tank weapons."

"They were in the half-track, Sir."

He went away, shaking his head.

The men were looking bitterly at the remains of the half-track. "When do we get a replacement?" Mundt asked. The others were watching carefully, waiting on my reply.

"I suspect there won't be a replacement, Scharfuhrer. We'll have to walk, like Napoleon's Grand Army did before us. Let's get moving, we need to man the defences before the Russian armies arrive. Mundt, see if you can find some anti-tank launchers, we lost all of ours."

They started to gather equipment and twenty minutes later we marched out of the camp, heading for the city defences. Mundt had found several spare launchers from platoons who would no longer need them and they'd loaded everything onto a two-wheeled cart that they were pulling behind us. We were indeed reduced to a re-enactment of the Grand Army of Napoleon, compelled to travel on foot with a handcart for our supplies. When we reached the defences we were assigned a position on a low hill and we started to dig a slit trench. We were only just in time as in the distance we all heard the rumbling and squealing of tank tracks. I stood up to inspect our defences. We had a STuGIII assault gun to either side of us. A platoon was dug in on a nearby rise with a 3.7cm PAK, and to the front of us were our few remaining Panzers, one Tiger that was dug into a defensive position, clearly it was unable to manoeuvre and was being used as a defensive gun. There were half a dozen Panzer IVs, and two of the new Panzer Vs that presumably had been repaired. I knew that all had broken down during the battle for Kursk.

"It's not much, is it, Sir?" Mundt said. He'd come up to look with me.

I shrugged. "I wish I could say it's enough, Willy, but no, it's not much. We lost so much at Kursk, the Russians don't seem to have been affected all. We need time, time to recover, to get more men and more tanks to hit back."

We stood looking at the scratch defences that had been hurriedly thrown together.

"It's a bit of a merry-go-round, isn't it?" he said suddenly. "Backwards and forwards all the time, will we ever have enough to beat them with?"

"Perhaps the new secret weapons, Willy."

He looked pessimistic. "I hear the Fuhrer believes in black magic. Perhaps that's what he means by secret weapons. Do you believe in all that stuff?"

I couldn't help but laugh. "You mean fairy stories, bolts of fire from the heavens, that kind of thing? I think if we're reduced to believing in that kind of crap we're really done for."

"I hear that Himmler believes in it too, Sir," he persisted.

"In that case he should grow up and find us some more Panzers and aircraft, Willy. That's what we need to hold back the Russians, not witches' spells."

"But..."

"Shut up, Willy," I laughed. "Before I get Himmler to turn you into a frog. Now, how are we going to handle these T34s when they come at us?"

He put his attention back to the ground in front of us. "Defence in depth, we need to hit them hard when they come up, then pull back to the next defensive position. Hopefully, we'll stop them before they reach the city."

"I agree. I'll have a word with Muller, he's probably thinking along the same lines, and ask him to arrange for his Hiwis to start preparing our next defensive position. In the meantime, supposing we arrange a forward position to ambush our Russian visitors? There's a balka down there that goes all the way forward to that gap between the two ridges, they'll have to come through there. If we set up a few of our anti-tank launchers we could take out some of their armour and then retreat back down the balka."

He followed the lines of terrain where I was pointing and nodded.

"It could work, yes, it would certainly knock out some of their armour before it gets here. It'll be very risky, though, if they're carrying tank riders, they'll be all over us."

"We'd better take the MG34 forward with us, then. I'll see if Muller can spare another machine gun, then we can keep this position manned, we could do with the extra firepower."

I went over to Muller's position and told him what we had planned. "Yes, we'll be pulling back to the next positions if we can't hold them here. Are you sure you want to take the chance with that forward ambush?"

"I'm sure, yes, Sir. We need every advantage we can get."

"Very well, I'll detail two men to bring over another machine gun. We've got two of the new MG42s, you can have one of those, they have a higher rate of fire than the 34." I thanked him and went back to our unit.

We started to load up our equipment. I took Mundt, Bauer and Wesserman with me. Beidenberg stayed behind to man the position with three other men and Muller's promised machine gun crew turned up with their MG42 and deployed it ready for use. Laden with anti-tank Panzerfausts, machine pistols and ammunition belts, as well as the MG34, we started down the hill and into the balka. We stumbled along for half a kilometre until we came to a point where there was a natural low bulwark of stone and mud that we could use as a shield.

"Bauer, set up the machine gun but keep out of sight unless we see any infantry. Wesserman, Scharfuhrer Mundt and I will operate the Panzerfausts, if we see any tank riders, Wesserman, leave the Panzerfausts and start loading for Stefan. Any questions?"

"If they pull back in a hurry, it'll be a bastard lugging that machine gun," Mundt said.

"You're right, if we run for it, leave everything, just take the personal weapons."

We hurriedly deployed. More Panzers were coming up from the Fourth Army and it looked as if we'd have a strong force to hold back the Russians, but of course it was relative. They'd surprised our intelligence people by mounting any kind of a counter-offensive at all so quickly after Kursk, so God only knew what kind of surprise they had in store for us now. We didn't have long to wait, they started with an artillery barrage, a great rumble in the distance that became a whistling noise in the air and then the ground trembled as the first of the shells landed. We dived to the ground and waited for it to end.

The barrage lasted for two hours, all we could do was huddle in the balka, trying to dig ourselves deeper and deeper to keep out of the flying steel and shattering explosions that threatened to destroy our main defensive position half a kilometre back. Several shells fell short and dropped around us, we had to keep our heads well down to avoid the shards of steel that scoured the battlefield. Then it stopped as suddenly as it had started, but now there was a new sound, the rumble of tank engines, the squeaking and screeching of their tracks. There was no need to say anything, we climbed to the parapet of the ravine that sheltered us and five hundred metres away were the enemy. I estimated about eighty T34s and half a dozen of the heavy KV-1s, most had troops riding on them. Our own guns opened fire. The Tiger's 88mm gun bellowed and was joined by the big assault guns of the STuGIIIs. The rest of our armour followed and immediately we scored hits on the Russians. Three of their tanks slewed to a halt, soldiers flung from them like chaff on the wind. The rest of them kept coming, ominously, firing their main guns as they rolled forward. They were firing armour-piercing rounds now, trying to blunt the edge of our armour and our Panzers and assault guns engaged in a duel of increasing intensity as they drew nearer. The Tiger took several hits but seemed to shrug them off, the T34s were faring much worse, the shells from our heavy tanks were starting to thin out their ranks. I pitied the Russian infantry riding on top of the tanks, subjected to the hail of steel that whistled around them and slashed through their ranks. It seemed peculiarly cruel to subject the frail bodies of these brave men to the kind of gunfire that was designed to destroy tanks, an unequal contest between the highest of military destructive arts and the frailties of the human flesh. But the T34s shrugged off the gunfire and came on.

"Time to prepare the Panzerfausts!" I shouted. "Bauer, bring up that machine gun, by the time their tanks are in range, we'll need to start hitting the infantry."

We lined up on the lip of the ravine, three of us with a Panzerfaust each. Bauer had the MG34 ready, a belt loaded and boxes of ammunition next to him. Wesserman was ready too, I noted that he had looped several belts of MG34 ammunition around his body, ready to load for Bauer and to keep up with him if they had to change positions in a hurry, as so often happened when the enemy were able to flank your position. Or of course in the case of a counterattack, which was not a likely scenario on this battlefield. The main guns of our Panzers and assault guns knocked out more T34s, but still they got nearer, then they were within range. I sighted the nearest tank and pulled the trigger, seeing my missile launch and fly true towards the Russian. It exploded on the side, a good hit that smashed the track and stopped the vehicle moving any further, but it wasn't finished, they were still firing their main gun which at this range threatened even the colossal armour of the Tiger tank. Mundt saw the danger and fired at the turret, scoring a hit that stopped the firing, Wesserman shot at another T34 and then a KV-1 saw the danger and lumbered towards us. Tank rider infantry were racing towards our position now, intent on crushing our forward post, but Bauer opened up with the MG34 and mowed several of them down before the rest dropped into cover. The KV-1 was still coming and we launched more Panzerfaust missiles against it, seeing them strike the heavy armour again and again without effect. Mundt managed a hit on one of the track linkages that stopped it dead, but the main gun swung towards us to swat the annoying nest of opposition that threatened their advance. As shells landed around us, we fired missile after missile against the turret, eventually seeing smoke rise as we hit something vital, then the tank simply blew up, taking with it twenty or thirty infantrymen who were crouched nearby. Three T34s started to edge towards us, it was time to move.

"Drop everything, let's go!" I shouted.

We hurtled back along the balka. A machine gun had started to fire at the Russians. The crew of the MG42 set up alongside Beidenberg had seen the danger and were giving us covering fire from the pursuing Russian infantry. Some of the Soviets managed to jump down into the balka and start after us and several shots came over out heads until we rounded a bend in the ravine and were out of their sight.

"How many of them do you reckon?" I asked Mundt.

"About four or five, not too many, Sir."

"Maybe we should hit them when they come around that bend, Willy, otherwise we'll be sitting ducks, we can't fight them at long range with out MP38s."

He nodded. "Good plan, Sir. Bauer, Wesserman, stop, we're going back to the bend in the ravine to wait for the Russians."

We raced back and crouched down. In the distance we heard the excited shouts of the Russians, the pounding of their boots and then they were in front of us, five Soviet infantrymen. Each of us was lying prone on the ground to minimise our target profile but the enemy were clearly visible, easy targets and we knocked them all down in a series of short bursts, at a range of no more than fifteen metres the MP38 was unbeatable and they stood no chance. Three of them had Moisin-Nagants that could have shot us at a range that rendered our machine pistols virtually useless.

"That's it, they're all down, let's go!"

I jumped to my feet and made sure they were all up with me and we ran for our next defensive position. The Panzers and assault guns continued their deadly duel with the Soviet armour, but it was clear that there were too many for us and after a few minutes I ordered the position evacuated and a fall back to the next defensive position. As we started to run I saw other platoons of Panzer Grenadiers heading the same way, then our armour started to back away, keeping their heavy frontal armour towards the enemy.

We fought from the next position, constantly whittling down the enemy forces and pulling back, but when the pace of the battle finally died down and the Soviets stopped attacking, we were dangerously near Kharkov. Muller came around and gave orders for us to fall back to the city and establish the last line of defences there. We set off at a fast march and crossed into the relative safety of our own lines of armour and guns.

"What do we do now?" Wesserman asked. "Are we going to just wait and keep retreating every time those bastards attack? Why aren't we hitting back?"

He was tired and angry. We were all tired and angry. It seemed that no matter what we did the Soviets had the answer for us, they had repelled our attack on the salient and were now smashing back at us almost without drawing breath. Our own forces were worn out, exhausted, low on men and morale, low on armour and aircraft, low on petrol and ammunition. I shook my head.

"I don't know, Gerd, I'm sorry. If I was to guess I'd say that we'll be retreating from Kharkov fairly soon, if the Soviets keep attacking in the kind of numbers they seem to be able to muster."

I thought of Irina then, I'd promised to get her out of the city and on a train back to Germany. I had to get her out tonight. Tomorrow the Soviet hordes could attack in such massive numbers that we'd be driven out of the city in the first attack.

"Scharfuhrer I need to go and see Muller, take over the platoon. I may have business in the city, if I'm given permission to go I'll be gone for a couple of hours, no more."

"Give her my love, Sir," he grinned.

I raced to find Muller and told him what I needed to do.

"You may as well go, Hoffman," he said tiredly. "It doesn't make much difference now. Call into Divisional Headquarters and see if they have any dispatches for us."

He wrote out a movement order for me, as I watched him I was shocked at his appearance. He had always been neat and smart, the perfect senior officer. Now he was ragged and dishevelled, unshaven, streaked with soot and grease, his shoulders hunched over in resignation.

"Do we have any idea of where we may be going next, Sir?"

He shook his head. "Only that it will be towards the west, Hoffman. We've started this retreat and God only knows where it will end. We're fighting for our very survival."

"But, Sir, we've got massive forces in place, we can beat back the Russians!"

He smiled sadly. "I appreciate your enthusiasm, but I'm not sure if it is well-founded. We need men, Hoffman, equipment, tanks and guns. What do they send us? The fucking Gestapo."

I'd never heard him swear before either, I saluted and left, Muller's demeanour suggested that the future for us was not likely to be the golden future we had been promised.

I managed to avoid the snipers on my way into the city. Two of them took shots at me but I was moving from cover to cover. I found Irina and told her to put a few things in a bag.

"Are the Russians coming then, Jurgen?" she asked me, surprised at the sudden urgency.

"Irina, they could be here within days, you need to move now before most of the city tries to get out!"

We got to the station and I produced a document I'd had drawn up earlier, stating that Irina Rakevsky was formally betrothed to Obersturmfuhrer Jurgen Hoffman and was travelling to the Reich on his behalf to prepare for the wedding. Despite the prevalence in Russia for recruiting women to fight on the front lines and fly fighter aircraft and bombers, as well as man the Soviet armaments factories, in the Reich the Fuhrer, Adolf Hitler, still place family life above all. A woman's place was in the home and there was nothing unusual about the arrangement I'd made with Irina, who after all was a citizen now of the Greater German Reich as well as betrothed to an officer of the SS. I managed to get her a ticket to change at Leipzig en route to Dresden. I gave her the address of an uncle of mine who lived in the centre of the city.

"Contact him, I've included a letter of introduction, he'll give you all the help you need. When I get back I will contact him for your address. Good luck."

Her eyes were damp and shining. "Jurgen, my darling, I wish you were coming with me."

I grinned. "Maybe you'd soon get fed up with me, I'm just a German soldier after all. Make a life for yourself. Dresden is such a nice, safe city. I'll look you up when I am able, now go."

We kissed passionately, then she broke away to climb on the train, most of the doors were closed and the guard was signalling frantically it was time to go. She waved out of the window. I waved back and went out of the station.

At the sandbagged Feldgendarmerie post outside I showed my papers to the sergeant. He looked at them carefully and then offered me some advice.

"Obersturmfuhrer, a word of warning, we've had a lot of partisan attacks around here lately, they seem to be targeting the area of the main station. I'd watch your step as you leave, if I were you."

I thanked him but before I had walked ten steps a familiar figure stepped out in front of me.

"Hoffman, how interesting to find you here. Did Miss Rakevsky get off alright?"

I fixed him with a hard gaze. "She did, yes, Sir, so you can forget about her. Tell me, why did you have Nadia Vlasov executed?"

He stepped back slightly at the force of my question. "Who said that I did that?"

"Never mind who said it, why did you do it?"

Over his shoulder I could see an opened window, a dark space inside an empty office building. I remembered the sergeant's advice and kept an eye on it as I was talking to von Betternich.

"You have to understand, it's politics, Hoffman. The fortunes of war, if you like."

He grinned. I saw a barrel poke out of the window, it had to be a barrel, yet it was a perfectly round disc, which meant it was pointing in my direction. At least, in von Betternich's direction, he was giving me protection from it with his body. I opened my mouth to shout a warning, then I though of Nadia, of Heide too, the Jewish nurse he had sent to a camp. My mind went into a kind of fugue, should I warn him, should I not? Did he deserve to die for what he had done? It was as if everything happened in slow motion, I swore I could see the sniper, the gun barrel moved a little as he straightened his aim. This evil Svengali would be finished forever, out of my life and unable to threaten the lives of those around me. He had to die, I hesitated a fraction more, then I leapt forward and threw him to the ground as the bullet hissed pass us, digging chips out of the cobbles and disappearing to bury itself into a thick wooden fence. The Feldgendarmerie nearby had heard the shot and rush out to hunt down the sniper. I picked up the SD officer and helped him to regain his balance with his walking cane.

"Thank you, Hoffman. I wonder that you bothered, you could have let me die, why didn't you?"

I shook my head, "I don't know, just forget it."

"But I won't forget it, my friend. I owe you a favour, remember, favours are like money in the bank in the German Reich."

"Just stay away from me then!"

He smiled broadly and sighed. "Ah, the one favour I cannot grant. But for the time being, I will manage without your valuable services. Until we meet again, Hoffman."

I nodded, but I couldn't bring myself to acknowledge him. Had I done a very stupid thing, saving his life? Or would it have cost me my own soul to let him die? I imagine that only a priest could answer that kind of question, but I had little time for priests. I had a war to fight and they would have their work cut out anyway with the broken and bleeding souls that war always generated in unlimited quantities. Von Betternich and people like him, Hitler, Himmler, they could find their own particular road to hell, mine was already mapped out. I thought of Bormann and that odd shooting in the Vinnitsa wood. The most probable explanation was that he had killed the partisan to stop the man revealing Bormann's involvement with supplying the Russians with information, perhaps the Reichsleiter was already treading his own particular path to hell.

In the distance, I could hear shouts of alarm as people were running. The Feldgendarmerie sergeant ran back to us.

"Soviet armour, they're moving on the city, they could be here any moment!"

The wind changed suddenly and the clank and squeak of tracked armoured fighting vehicles was distinctly audible. The Russians were returning to reclaim what was theirs, what we'd taken from them and we had little with which to counter their armoured might. At least I'd got Irina away in time and I'd managed to keep my conscience clear with both her and von Betternich.

It was time to return to my unit and continue fighting the unending battle, the conflict that left the steppes covered in spilled blood and broken iron, all that remained of the ambitions of glory that had brought the fallen to this war, never to return home.

THE END